Praise for

A Quest for Heroes:
Official Movie Novelization

"*Mythica: A Quest for Heroes* is a classic adventure with all the elements that make readers love fantasy. Nielsen's excellent writing makes the story leap off the page and brings the characters to life in ways that can only be done in a book."

—Paul Genesse, bestselling author of the *Iron Dragon Series*

"Fans of the film will be delighted, and anyone looking for a brisk tale filled with unexpected magic, relatable characters, and tension-filled action will love it too. . . . *Mythica: A Quest for Heroes* has all the elements of a classic fantasy adventure and Nielsen's writing gives the story incredible depth and excitement. Highly Recommended."

—Michael Darling, author of *Got Luck*

"Kevin Nielsen's Mythica: A Quest for Heroes novelization is an epic fantasy thrill ride with a dash of poignant humanity.... Bringing together the best elements from dungeon crawling and epic fantasy, Mythica is not to be missed."

—David J. West, author of *Whispers Out of the Dust* and *Cold Slither*

Other Books by Kevin L. Nielsen

Sharani Series

Sands

Storms

Skies

"Twins"

Successive Harmony Series

Resurgent Shadows

MYTHICA

A QUEST FOR HEROES

OFFICIAL MOVIE NOVELIZATION

WRITTEN BY KEVIN L NIELSEN

Future House Publishing

Mythica: A Quest for Heroes: Official Movie Novelization

Future House Publishing

ISBN: 978-1-944452-55-1

Cover design by Jeff Harvey
Developmental and substantive editing by Emma Hoggan
Copy editing by Claire Nielsen and Stephanie Cullen
Proofreading by Brooke Sorensen
Interior design by Emma Hoggan

To Derek Morgan, a Redthorn in word, deed, and honor.

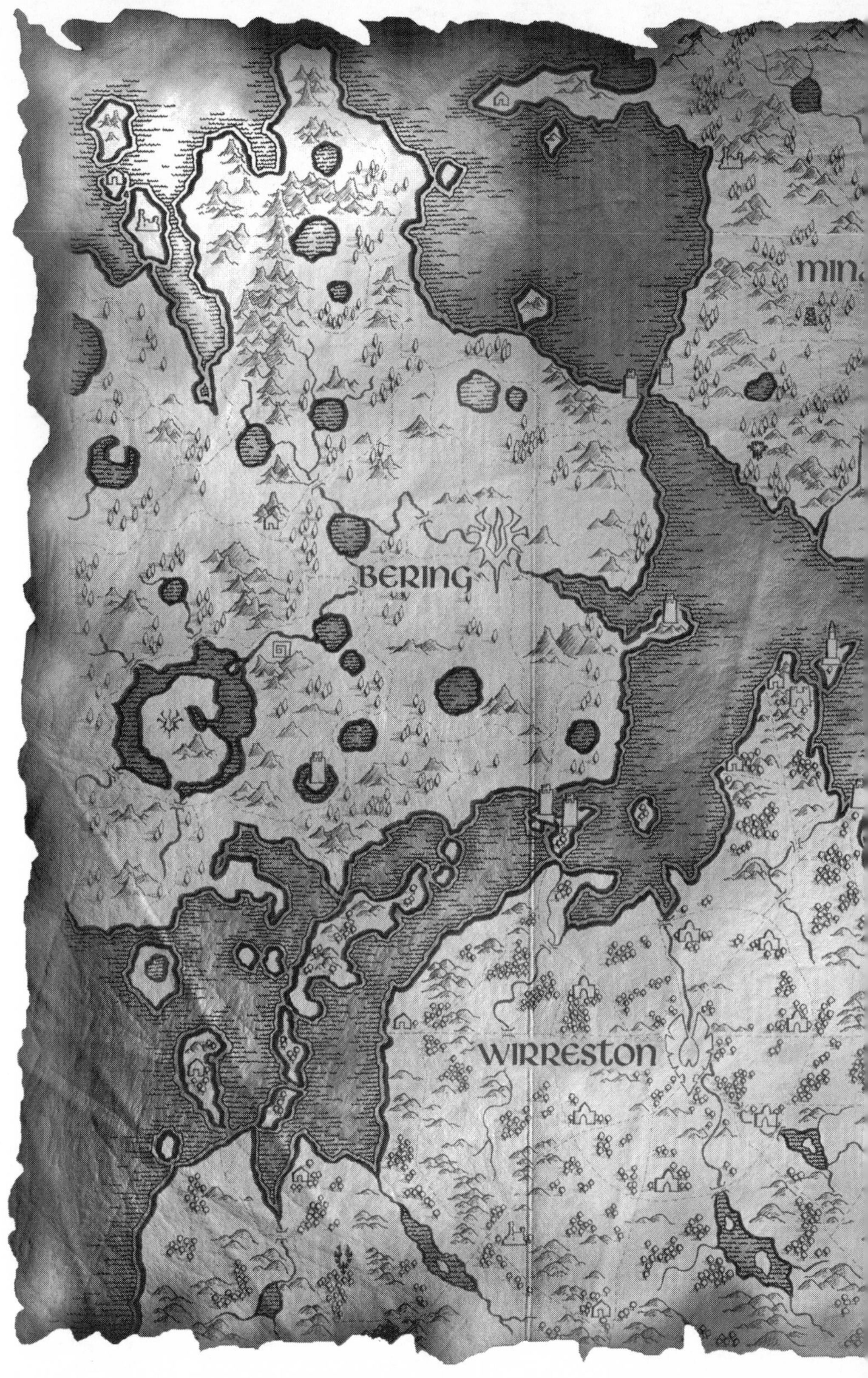
BERING
WIRRESTON

MERREN
ILKENAU

FOREWORD

One of my favorite memories from Mythica was actually from our first day of shooting. I remember it well because it was the day I died. Not my character, Thane. No sir. I, Adam Johnson, died.

Okay, so I didn't technically die, but I'm pretty sure I flatlined. I'll explain. We were shooting way up in the mountains, around 8,000 feet above sea level, and I had just flown in from California, so I wasn't used to the altitude. I could barely breathe as it was, and then they took it one step further and strapped me into what we later figured was probably around one hundred pounds of period wardrobe—chainmail, sword, shield, the works.

We started shooting for the day. First up were two scenes that had us running from ogres and Hellhounds. You know the drill. It was simple enough, except, of course, I was wearing that hundred pounds of wardrobe. We had to shoot them over and over until Anne Black, our director, decided that we had been tortured enough. By the time we finally finished those scenes, I was about ready to keel over.

We immediately shot the next scene, which had

us running into an open field. Nicola (Teela) and I were supposed to run in and drop to the ground to catch our breath before Melanie (Marek) came in. She was supposed to limp about halfway through the field before seeing a dragon and turning to run the other way, conveniently towards the ogres and the Hellhounds we talked about in the last scene. Melanie, instead of hobbling through the scene like she was supposed to, took off at a full-on sprint. It was my job to outrun her. Colorful expressions kept popping into my mind to gently convey my frustration. Once I reached her, I threw her over my shoulder, and ran back to the opposite treeline. Keep in mind, I was still half dead from the last scene. As I ran for dear life, Melanie's cape flopped over my eyes. Perfect. I had no idea where I was running. Was I about to smack into the camera? A tree? Off a cliff? Was I already out of earshot, and had they already quietly called "cut?" (That happened many times. They must have thought I was just being methodical. It's funny, because afterwards I WAS thinking of ways I could methodically kill them all.) I didn't want to stop TOO soon, because we'd have to shoot the scene all over again. I ran until I almost blew a heart valve. I remember thinking Wow, they're going to get my death on film. That's really cool. Maybe I'll get on TMZ. Maybe they'll mention me at the Oscars. I wonder if they can get Adele to do the tribute song again. I bet they have great food at those Oscar parties. Is Emma Stone still with Andrew Garfield? I think Kate Beckinsale is single again. I wonder if they'll have sliders?

Anyway, I stopped before anything tragic happened.

That was day one of shooting, way up in those beautiful mountains, asking myself the age-old question: What was I thinking?

This turned out to be just a taste of what would turn out to be a royal feast of bringing this epic saga to life.

Shooting Mythica was a dream come true. When I first auditioned for the role of Thane, I never would have thought I'd be in the position I am today. You always hope for the best, but you never know in this business. At the very least, I thought I might get to wear some cool costumes, and maybe hone my acting craft a little. Instead, we found a home with a truly enthusiastic audience that has really fallen in love with these characters. As a cast, we've put real blood, sweat, and tears into these characters, and to see our audience grow to love them the way you have is the greatest gift we could have asked for. I'm so thankful to the fans we've had from the very beginning and, of course, those we've met along the way.

I'd like thank the directors, Anne Black, A. Todd Smith, and John Lyde, for their guidance and for making me look as cool and tough as possible. I'm also indebted to the creators and producers of Mythica, Kynan Griffin, Jason Faller, and Jennifer Griffin, for trusting a goofball like me to take on such a serious character as Thane. I'd also like to thank them for putting together a cast of such wonderful people. We have enjoyed working together so much, and have bonded through these films to become lifelong friends.

On that note, I hope you enjoy this novelization of Mythica by this very talented writer. Enjoy the journey all over again.

—Adam Johnson

Prologue

Caeryn raced through the halls, heart pounding. Her flight was fueled by the sounds of metal striking metal, screams of pain and anger, and the empty, hollow absence that followed. Each new scream echoed off the thick stone walls and brought a fresh spike of fear through Caeryn's veins, one which only intensified as the echoes faded away into empty silence.

Alarm bells tolled loud, clarion notes that mingled with the sounds of battle and then cut off abruptly. Raids were not uncommon, though the bells weren't calling them to defend the walls. No, the notes sounded out a warning to flee. Despair blossomed in the pit of Caeryn's stomach and threatened to claw up her throat, restricting her air as she ran.

Her long, white robes whisked against the stone floor in strange counterpoint to the screams. Ahead of her, the temple elder shuffled with surprising speed toward the ancient center of the building. He had simply told her to follow him when the alarm bells first sounded. Long years in service to her mistress, Ana-Sett, had taught her obedience, at least, and so she'd followed despite her terror. She told herself the Goddess would protect her, though fear coursed through her with enough force to almost make her question that belief. Almost. She prayed Teela would be safe as well.

"Where are we going?" Caeryn called. Her words sounded loud to her own ears, and her voice shook despite her best efforts to still it.

The temple elder turned down a side tunnel without responding and rushed through an ancient archway into the inner sanctum. Beads of sweat stood out on his brow and his breath came out as ragged, hoarse gasps.

Unlike the rest of the temple, which was magnificently carved and adorned with soaring columns of stone, the inner sanctum consisted of the remnants of a natural cavern, the blocks of its walls coming together in broken, jagged cracks. Caeryn noticed it in a detached sort of way, though she would have normally been overwhelmed by the sheer honor of it. The terror of the moment, the unadulterated fear, cut through the sanctified experience. The inner sanctum contained only the most holy and precious artifacts of their dying order, those too hallowed for a simple priestess such as herself to see or touch. Were they here to retrieve something? Was the attack really bad enough to fear that someone might reach this most holy of holy places? A spark of indignation broke through the fear at the thought of this holy ground being desecrated by unclean, violent men. Caeryn swallowed hard, struggling to suppress the frightened voice within her own mind, and turned her attention back to her companion.

The temple elder strode to the far side of the room with three quick, determined steps. Several boulders formed a shelf of sorts there. Worn smooth by age, the reddish-brown rock seemed an altogether quiet thing against the backdrop of the battle. The elder stopped before the shelf, standing almost directly within a shaft of broken light bleeding down from where the boulders met unevenly in the ceiling above. A statuette of the Goddess, Ana-Sett, rested atop a woven cloth of gold and tan on the stone shelf. Next to it sat a scroll bound loosely in twine. Caeryn felt a momentary flare of curiosity, but a scream of pain echoed down the passage behind her and snuffed it out completely.

The elder lifted the statuette with care and passed it back to Caeryn, who took it with one quavering hand and clutched it close, taking comfort in the presence of even an effigy of her Goddess. The statuette, barely a foot tall, was surprisingly light for how solid it looked.

More screams, this time coupled with war cries and guttural bellows, echoed from the passage behind them. Caeryn recognized the porcine sounds with a shudder that worked its way up from her calves and settled at the nape of her neck.

Orcs! What are they doing here, this far to the north? Why are they attacking the temple?

Caeryn swallowed hard and forced herself to pay attention to the temple elder.

The elder pressed on determinedly, moving the scroll aside and then pulling free the cloth to reveal a small bundle wedged into a crevice in the rocks. He reached in and pulled it out with a decidedly ginger touch, though his movements were deliberate and careful. Some sort of cloth-wrapped talisman, perhaps? Caeryn kept her eyes fixed on it as the elder turned to her.

"Here, my child." His voice held the calmness of the sea after a storm, an immovable rock in a gale.

He tugged the cloth free. A dark, purplish-black stone lay in his palm. It was unlike anything Caeryn had ever seen before. Little purple-red sparks floated out from it, dancing in the air like spores from some strange fungus, though the stone itself remained cool. It glowed with an inner amethyst light that pulsed like the beating of a heart blackened by sickness yet still laboring onward.

"Take this to the paladin at Sung Hill," the temple elder said, covering the stone with the cloth once more and pressing it into Caeryn's free hand.

"I am too old to make the journey."

Caeryn felt a chill run through her as her hands wrapped around the little bundle. She silently muttered a prayer to the Goddess, trusting in her faith to lend her strength. Ana-Sett had never failed her before. She wouldn't begin now.

Outside, the screams grew louder, announcing the approaching battle. Caeryn glanced over her shoulder down the passageway, then back to the temple elder. His countenance was calm and resolute now, but his grip on her hands was firm, stronger than a man of his age had any right to possess.

"Run," he said in an eerily calm voice. "Do not lose the stone. Of all tasks given our order since its founding, none is more important than that which I now lay upon you."

Caeryn took a measure of comfort in the steadiness of the words, if not their meaning, and nodded. *No task more important in the history of their order?*

The temple elder's grip tightened painfully on her hands. "Run!" This time, his voice held the hardened burr of stone.

Caeryn grit her teeth and ran back down the passage toward the screams, clutching the cloth-wrapped stone to her chest and praying the Goddess would protect her. She raced out of the inner sanctum and into the temple proper, holding the little bundle in one hand and her robes, together with the statuette of the Goddess, in the other.

She felt guilty leaving the elder behind, but it was a single bitter note amidst the cold, dark, chaotic jumble of emotions floundering within her. She allowed her gaze to sweep from side to side as she ran down the passage, hoping and praying to the Goddess that her sister was still safe and that she'd be able to find her.

"Teela!" Caeryn dashed down a main passageway wrought of carved stone and massive columnar pillars. The passage was dark, lit only by a few scattered oil biers around the room, forcing Caeryn to mind her step as she frantically searched for her sister.

The orcs had come for the stone, whatever it was, that much was clear. The temple elder wouldn't have gone through such lengths to secure its safety if it wasn't in danger. She'd been entrusted with its care, though, by a temple elder of her Goddess, Ana-Sett. The Goddess would not let her fail. Temple workers and lesser priestesses ran the other direction, terror making their passage swift.

"Teela!"

Caeryn prayed to the Goddess that nothing had happened to her younger sister. Teela had come to the order only after Caeryn herself had joined the ranks of Ana-Sett's priestesses. If anything happened to her, it would be Caeryn's fault. She would never forgive herself if that—

Teela appeared out of the gloom as the light of a nearby lantern flared in the night breeze. The flame cast sparks into the air, illuminating her fine red hair and casting her proud features into sudden, sharp relief. She, too, was garbed in the white robes of their order, though Teela, as was her way, carried her steel-clad staff in her right hand.

Caeryn felt a flood of relief wash over her and blunt the fear for a fleeting instant. Teela was safe. They could do this together. Caeryn reached out and grabbed Teela's hand and together, they raced through the temple, heading for a way out into the night and toward the teeth of battle.

The temple elder—he had stopped thinking of himself as anything but that decades before—stood in the pillar of light in front of the little shelf from which he had removed the Darkspore. He raised his arms in supplication to his Goddess, aged limbs protesting the motion, and prayed she would watch over Caeryn in her flight away from this place. The orcs had come for it, though he suspected a deeper motivation, another force moving behind them and pushing them along. Orcs were, by their very nature, a simpleminded, need-driven race. They didn't have the complexity of thought to orchestrate an attack of this magnitude. When the wizard had left the stone with them nearly two decades past, he'd warned them dark forces would come for it eventually. The elder hadn't thought it would happen in his lifetime, but he'd been proven wrong before. This, perhaps, would be his final lesson to learn. Regardless of what lay behind the attack, neither the orcs nor their benefactor would get the stone, not while he or any of his order were around to stand in their way.

In the middle of his prayer he heard the sounds of booted and armored feet pour into the room behind him. He suspected he knew what he was going to see even before he turned to greet the invaders. He felt no fear, though he knew he should. Decades serving his Goddess had already steeled him for the day he would greet her in person.

A bald man with smoldering orange eyes, a Golgotian mystic warrior, stalked toward him. Orcs in battle armor spread out around him. They reeked of blood, sweat, and other odors too foul to describe. The temple elder felt outrage thundering in his ears at the desecration of his holy sanctum, but the Golgotian didn't give him a moment to even breathe, much less protest the indignity.

"Where is the stone?" the Golgotian demanded, stopping only a foot away from him.

The glow of the warrior's eyes seemed brighter up close, the effect enhanced by the dark scars and deep wrinkles which surrounded them and looked far darker by contrast.

"You will never find it." The temple elder met the orange, glowing eyes and found that while he had no fear of death for himself, anxiety graced his thoughts of Caeryn and her mission.

Run, Caeryn!

The Golgotian's glowing eyes intensified and the temple elder felt a momentary curiosity flit through him for an instant before the mystic warrior raised his right hand. Pain lanced through the temple elder's body and a white-blue light poured from him, clouding his vision. Panic gripped him as his knees lost their strength and he found himself sinking to the ground. Images passed through his mind and, with a surge of horror, he realized the mystic warrior was seeing them too. The statuette of Ana-Sett, Caeryn, the Darkspore, then Caeryn again as she fled into the temple halls. They all passed through both his own and the Golgotian's mind.

No!

He struggled to breathe, though his lungs wouldn't work. His body was becoming weak, too weak to do anything but succumb to the darkness spreading across his visage. Part of his mind called out to the Goddess, begging for her embrace even as he fell. White-blue light, his essence, his very soul, poured from him and into the mystic warrior's clawlike hand. The temple elder continued to fall, eyes slipping closed as he returned to his Goddess's embrace.

Caeryn fled down the temple passages, feeling, more than seeing, Teela whip her head around to check for pursuers. Caeryn didn't stop or look back, instead leading the way through several smaller passages to a lesser-used exit out into the temple yard. Even as she ran, she struggled to come to grips with the enormity of the task given her. How was she going to get through the yard and to the paladin through the chaos of what was sure to be a pitched battle? The nearest settlement, Merren, the capital city of Deira, was leagues away through untamed wilderness. Even with Vitalia's presence within the once-independent kingdom, that path lay fraught with untold dangers.

They burst from the temple and into the pale semi-darkness of a fast-approaching dawn besought by flame, death, and nightmare. Thought vanished.

Smoke billowed and filled the air, making each breath Caeryn took painful and belabored. Indistinct blurs in the rough, blocky shapes of people passed through the haze. Screams of pain, terror, anger, and lust mingled in Caeryn's mind and formed a wedge of agony that pierced her to the core. The smells of blood, death, and fear assaulted her senses and left them over-extended and hyper-acute. She tasted bile, but swallowed it down.

Thought returned, though it came in scattered dollops of intermingled crystalline clarity and shattering confusion. She knew roughly where they'd come out of the temple and where they needed to go, so she took the lead in a mad dash across the temple yard, Teela only a few steps behind.

A group of terrified women wearing white appeared out of the haze, screaming and dodging. Caeryn darted around them and narrowly avoided the orcs who pursued them. She ached to help the women, to do *something,* but hers was a greater task, a duty which precluded all others, according to the temple elder. She tried not to think about the fate she knew awaited him.

Breathing heavily and fighting back helpless tears, Caeryn ran onward, doing her best to avoid both her own people and the orcs. Fear lent her both speed and a desperate, hope-filled agility.

A rocky hill appeared before them in the mist—

dawn's first light casting thin rays over its edge—and, for a moment, Caeryn felt a rush of hope and relief almost as great as when she'd found Teela only moments before. The ridgeline marked where the road split out and worked back toward Merren. She'd expected it to be guarded, or at least blocked in some manner, but it appeared to be clear. One corner of her lips twitched into a hapless grin. They were almost out. They could make it. They . . .

She pulled to stop, Teela staggering a few steps further before skidding to a halt as well. A massive, hulking ogre pulled itself up over the top of the cliff, blocking out the light.

The ogre dropped to the sand on the other side—Caeryn's side—with enough force to send a tremble running through the ground that reached Caeryn a dozen paces away. The twenty-foot-tall behemoth saw them and leered.

"Pretty."

The ogre's voice dripped with a lechery so pure that Caeryn felt violated. She grabbed Teela's arm and pulled her in another direction.

Caeryn's heart raced, pumping blood through her body at a rate which was only beaten by her racing mind. The main road *had* been blocked. The only other way out lay to the north in the direction of Vitalia proper. She steered their flight in the appropriate direction.

People milled about them, though Caeryn largely ignored them, only taking the time necessary to ensure Teela was still with her and the strange purple stone the temple elder had given her was still safely within her grip. The ogre's thunderous footfalls sounded behind them, thudding into the ground like the cacophonous echo of a battering ram against steel-clad gates.

They darted into a small side canyon, following the crowd trying to flee the battle. Caeryn turned right in the direction of the road to Vitalia, only to find herself up against a rocky cliff wall. Panic flooded through her. She must have gotten turned around in all the confusion. She took several small steps, turning with each of them so she could try and find her bearings. She had no idea where she was. Licking her lips, she spun back the way they had come, Teela at her side.

The ogre stepped into the mouth of the small canyon, filling it completely.

Caeryn sucked in a lungful of air in one sharp, frightened breath and glanced at her sister. Teela stood just in front of her with her steel-clad staff clutched in a white-knuckled grip. Caeryn felt her own grip tighten on the statuette she still held in one hand. Her other hand closed around the cloth-wrapped stone.

The ogre leered at them both again, blackened

teeth almost as terrifying as the rest of the beast, and then lumbered forward with a speed that belied its bulk. Teela cried out as one massive fist caught her a glancing blow and sent her tumbling to the ground. She landed several feet away and rolled onto her back, clearly dazed, her staff clattering away from her. Caeryn's eyes darted toward her sister, but the ogre continued forward, closing on Caeryn with fixed determination.

Caeryn took a step back, meeting the ogre's gaze, and found within herself a resolve as hard and firm as the temple elder's had been. It was there, burning like a bonfire within her chest next to the faith she held in her divine guide, the Goddess Ana-Sett. As the ogre stepped forward, Caeryn spied Teela through the gap in its legs. Her sister struggled to raise herself from the ground.

"Run, Teela!" Caeryn shouted, keeping her gaze locked onto the ogre's own dark, soulless eyes. "The Goddess will not let me die. Find help."

Teela stood on unsteady feet as the ogre bore down on Caeryn. "No, I won't leave you!"

Caeryn looked away from the ogre for the space of a single heartbeat, locking eyes with her sister. Caeryn attempted to pass the faith she had in the Goddess, all her love for her sister and their order she could muster, and the silent command to flee through that momentary glance. Then she blinked and looked back up at the ogre as it reached out one massive hand toward her, thick fingers almost as big around as her arm. Not even a trace of fear passed through her.

"Go!" Caeryn shouted.

Teela ran.

CHAPTER 1

Marek didn't need to use her crutch in the small confines of the narrow room, though she kept it close just in case. Having been born with a twisted foot, the crutch was a constant companion no matter where she was. Her bare feet passed over the hard-packed dirt floor and thumped against it in a steady, half-sliding rhythm as she limped about the room gathering ingredients for her spell. As a slave, the cost of the components already in her hands alone would have been the single biggest obstacle to her using magic. That and the stupid Vitalion laws outlawing its practice in any form on penalty of death, that is. That said, being a slave in an apothecary allowed her ready access to just about anything she could ever need, provided she didn't mind liberating it from the shop's supplies, which she didn't. Master Vagamal owed her that much, at least.

Marek glanced at the small cauldron bubbling on top of the messy table, the contents steeping amidst an array of dried plants, apparatus, and other ingredients she'd already used and set aside or which were awaiting use. She passed wide of the swinging carcasses and plants hanging from the ceiling which were drying or curing and awaiting use at some later date, and moved to the other side of the room.

A fire crackled in the dim reaches of the chamber, sending a scent of ash and smoke to mingle with the acrid smell of the various crucibles being heated over candles on the table, wafting pale fumes into the air. Marek picked up a small earthenware bottle and a handful of dried herbs, which she dropped onto a mortar stone before setting the bottle aside and using the pestle to grind the herbs into a chunky powder. That done, she hurried across the room to grab another bowl.

"We shouldn't be doing this," Egan's voice said from behind her, tremulous and weak.

Marek looked back at Master Vagamal's young apprentice after gathering a few more ingredients from a counter behind her. Her ebony hair bounced from where it poked out beneath the cloth which kept it only partially contained and hid the slave tattoo on the back of her neck. Egan stood next to the table, shifting nervously from foot to foot and glancing about the room as if expecting to get caught at any moment. She'd convinced him to help her with the spell, though she was beginning to doubt his resolve. The boy's curiosity would only take him so far, she decided.

"Nonsense," Marek replied, giving him her best winsome smile. Egan gave her a half-hearted one in return.

She turned back to the table and gathered up a few herbs and her bowl, silently wishing Egan didn't need as much encouragement as he normally required. She was the slave, after all, and lame at that. Someday the Gods would take Master Vagamal and Egan would inherit the entire shop, as was customary in crafts such as these. What did *he* have to be nervous about? If Master Vagamal caught them, he'd get assigned to wash out pots or clean out the shop by himself. At the least, she'd get a beating. At worst, the apothecary could turn her over to the Vitalions for using magic and she'd get hanged. She looked up and noticed Egan watching her.

She knew Egan fancied her. He liked her slender frame and overlooked the persistent brown stains around her nails, which bespoke a constancy of dirt there that Marek could never quite remove. He wasn't a bad sort, not really. At least, not for someone two years her junior. In all honesty, Egan and her magic were the only things that made this prison of a life even remotely tolerable. As a slave, everything in her life was about one thing. Obedience. As someone with a physical deformity which limited her movement, it was figuring out how to do that without getting beaten, not being able to do it the "regular" way. Magic didn't care about any of that. Her magic was the one thing which made her feel truly free, her one true, unadulterated passion and skill.

She turned away from the table almost at once and gathered a few more ingredients, counting them off in her head before tossing them into a small bowl with the other herbs she'd already crushed. Looking up at Egan, Marek pushed the bowl into his startled hands. Egan took it and looked back at her blankly, blond hair splayed over his eyes.

Marek sighed internally and pantomimed working a pestle in the bowl, pointedly looking from her hands to the bowl in Egan's, eyes wide. Could he do *anything* without having to be told first?

The boy started and then began hastily pounding at the herbs in the bowl, muttering an apology under his breath, which puffed out before him in a little cloud of white mist in testament to the cold.

"Gentle." Marek stood poised near the edge of the table and leaned her small frame forward to give Egan a serious look, "or we'll go 'poof.'" The last word was more of a sound effect than a word, turning it from a true chastisement to a gentle tease. She was serious, but Egan didn't need any more reason to be nervous right now.

Egan shook his head, but his hands slowed in their work and Marek couldn't help but chuckle softly. If nothing else, she could always count on Egan to be earnest, even at the worst of times.

Ignoring him for the moment, Marek turned back to the main cauldron, which lay simmering and bubbling, on the table between them. The contents of the spell frothed and hissed within. Marek picked up a small vial of yellow powder and a wooden spoon, sprinkling it into the mixture as she stirred. Her hands were steady, though excitement raced through her veins. According to the spell Gojun Pye, Merren's clandestine spellcaster, had given her, the spell was almost ready. It just needed a few more moments and a couple more ingredients to be perfect.

She cleared her throat and picked up a glass jar of a darker yellow powder. Egan put down what he was working on and picked up the bowl of crushed herbs with one hand and the original bowl of ingredients with the other. His hands shook as he brought them over the cauldron, the crockery clinking together and making a sound like glass trembling in a window frame during a storm.

"Stop shaking." Marek barked out the command in a voice that brooked no argument. Still, Egan's hands didn't still.

"I can't."

"Pour."

Egan swallowed, though Marek only noticed in a peripheral sense. Her eyes remained fixated on the spell before her, watching the components melding together as Egan poured them in. She was glad her own hands were pressed flat against the table or else her excitement would have made them as shaky as Egan's.

"Nothing's happening," Egan said, his voice as shaky as his hands. "We should stop."

"Ah," Marek said, looking up and locking eyes with the younger boy. "On my word, pour the rest in."

Egan held her gaze for half a moment, then looked back down at the bowls in his hands. He started to pour them in and Marek felt a flush of exasperation. Hadn't she *just* told him to wait on her word? She held up a hand and made a noise in her throat that was halfway between a grunt and a hiccup. She didn't know if it was the hand or the noise, but Egan hesitated. Marek waited a few more seconds, watching the bubbles in the stew-like liquid below her with myopic focus, anticipating the exact moment the spell described. She picked up a pair of powder vials.

"Now, Egan."

They poured together. The contents of the cauldron hissed and bubbled as the herbs and powder mingled with the thick liquid. Almost immediately, tendrils of white smoke as thin and vaporous as the mist that pooled around each of Marek's breaths leapt up and shot toward Egan. Marek stepped back, hand raised in a mixture of surprise and confusion as the tendrils of smoky vapor shot through Egan's nose. Egan, for his part, shuddered and made sounds of mingled terror and shock, like a mouse being trodden upon. Marek didn't begrudge him that. Her skin prickled with nervous anxiety and anticipation. The smoke exited his nose and mingled with other tendrils dancing in the air over the cauldron.

Marek's eyes followed each of the little trails of smoke, her focus darting from one to the other as they coalesced together and then undulated apart, like the tentacles of some sea leviathan from the stories old men told when they'd had one too many drinks. Gojun, the wizard, had said this was a vision spell, though Marek didn't know what was supposed to happen beyond that, not with any real specificity anyway.

A pool of smoke suspended in the air lithely pulsed and formed the image of a snake. The spell hissed and frothed in the cauldron and the snake itself reared as if to bite Marek where she stood. Marek jerked back, eyes wide with shock, though she hungered to lean forward instead and study the magic before her.

The snake pulsed and then collapsed in on itself, drawing the other tendrils of smoke toward it in a sudden rush of air which drew it down toward the small cauldron containing the potion itself. Flames burst up in an explosion of power as the smoke condensed back into the potion. Marek was flung backward by the sheer force of it. She stumbled on her bad leg as her momentum continued pushing on her, throwing her against the wall. She hit hard enough that her head jerked around and she had to reach out and keep herself from tumbling to the floor. She was half aware of Egan lying prone on the floor, though her main focus followed the column of smoke-vapor which shot upward from the cauldron and seemed to vanish up through the thatched roof.

Marek stared, wide-eyed and with her heart threatening to burst out of her chest, around the room and found herself half gasping and half laughing as the vestigial smoke and mist wafted around the room. Egan stared up at her from the ground, face scrunched up in utter incredulity, then pulled himself up using the table for support. Marek sucked in a breath and felt the smoke burn in her lungs. She started coughing and waved a hand in front of her face in a vain attempt to clear the air. When that proved fruitless, she turned and limped over to the nearest window and pushed it open, sucking in a cool, fresh breath. Light flooded into the room as Marek looked out at the ramshackle hamlet and picked up the faint buzz of voices in conversation.

"I don't know what went wrong," Marek said, breath coming in long, panting gasps which puffed into mist and added to the room's haze. Her eyebrows came together as she considered that statement. "Maybe I need more basilisk blood . . ."

Egan, on his knees and still grasping onto the edge of the table, coughed and shook his head. "No!"

Marek tilted her head and narrowed her eyes at him. *No?* He didn't understand her magic, though he indulged it on occasion. Gojun was the only one who really understood, the only one who didn't treat her like a slave. Marek shifted her weight to head back to the table, confident in her ability to convince Egan that, of course, they needed to try it again and that the only obvious choice was to add more basilisk blood, when a gruff voice shouted out from down the hall.

"What's that smell?"

Fear rushed through Marek with more ice in its grip than the snows which covered the ground outside.

"Take care of this!" she hissed, gesturing toward

the mess on the table.

Egan glanced toward the hallway, then leapt to his feet, face ashen. Marek gathered up her skirts in her hands and rushed toward the other end of the room, her limp slowing her progress and making her step lopsided and painful. Egan began throwing things haphazardly into a basket. He wouldn't get done before the master arrived. Marek rushed over to the basket piled high with clothing to be laundered in the corner and bent to retrieve it, silently cursing her bad leg. Hoisting it onto her shoulder, she rushed toward the doorway leading into the adjacent room. Footsteps sounded in the hallway and Marek pushed forward, intentionally blocking Master Vagamal's view of the room. Behind her, Marek heard items clatter into Egan's basket and she stepped from side to side, making noises as if she were trying to get out of Master Vagamal's way, though she was, in fact, doing the opposite. Despite the seriousness of the situation, Marek felt a small flush of satisfaction at being able to irritate the ornery old man.

"Out of my way, gimp!" Master Vagamal growled, shoving against the basket with enough force to send Marek careening to the floor, spilling the laundry everywhere.

Master Vagamal stood framed in the doorway for a long moment, looking around the room with what most people would have considered a suspicious expression. Marek, however, simply knew it as her master's permanent features. She groaned, leg twinging in pain as she struggled to rise. Master Vagamal promptly kicked the wicker basket at her face.

"You clumsy wench." Marek knocked the basket out of the way before it could hit her, but Master Vagamal took a step forward in his anger, towering over her with murder written across his face. "You're not worth the gruel it costs to feed ya!"

Marek let out a small sound of pain, more a forlorn whimper than a true sound. Her foot throbbed in aching agony and her elbow twinged where it had struck the ground. She knew a bruise would be forming there, but it would mingle so well with the dirt that no one would notice the difference. Not that anyone would care even if they did. Beneath the pain, anger smoldered. Beneath that, a small child who'd survived countless beatings by pretending not to care wept broken tears.

Egan started working again suddenly, making more noise than was necessary as if trying to show that he'd pointedly been ignoring the whole scene.

"Leave that," Master Vagamal snapped, turning his gaze on the boy. "Let the gimp finish it."

Marek felt the smoldering anger swell into a few tendrils of actual flame. She *hated* that word, especially the way he said it. The master's upper teeth protruded from his mouth like a wild boar's tusks, which forced his upper lips to slide twice the distance his bottom lip needed to travel when forming words. The result was to make Master Vagamal sound as if he was half drunk all the time, which, Marek mused, he probably was.

Master Vagamal turned his head to the side as if suddenly remembering something and fumbled inside his thick overcoat. After a moment, he produced a small leather bag and tossed it to Egan, who almost didn't catch it.

"Here," Master Vagamal said in as soft a voice as Marek had ever heard from him, "Take this into town. Get coin from the wizard."

Marek looked up sharply at the mention of the wizard. Egan usually let her make the apothecary deliveries to the wizard in his place, which was fortunate. She needed to see the man herself. The vision spell hadn't gone perfectly, true, but there were other things he could teach her. In truth, part of her hoped he'd just buy her from Master Vagamal and free her from this horrid life. Just thinking about it made her want to simply run away, though she'd be hanged if caught. She was trapped, so she seized any chance she could to get out of this place, even if only for a few hours.

"I want you back before first watch," Master

Vagamal continued, pointing a gnarled finger at Egan. "I don't want any trouble with the guards."

Egan nodded, the gesture curt and immediate, becoming almost a small bow. Master Vagamal sneered as he turned to leave. Marek flinched away as he passed, though he didn't so much as spare her a glance as he left the room. His retreating steps let her know when it was safe to try and get up. She grunted with the effort, but managed to get to her feet without needing to resort to asking Egan to help her. Her pride—what little of it she had left—was already bruised enough.

"I'll go," she said, glancing down the hall and then turning to limp toward the table where Egan had placed the pouch Master Vagamal had given him. She picked it up and then limped toward her crutch, which lay near the door.

"No," Egan said, though he didn't move to stop her. He knew her too well for that, for which Marek was grateful. "Your leg. You won't get back before dark. They'll catch you and—" His voice caught for a moment. "—they'll brand you as a runaway."

Marek looked back at him as she opened the door, letting in the light and a rush of cold air so profound she nearly gasped. She pulled a shawl from a peg near the door and hugged it close, then glanced back at Egan. His pleading, innocent eyes met hers, but again, he did nothing to stop her. For a moment, Marek wondered if he could see into her, see the fierce need to get away from this place and be more than simply a slave, but then dismissed it. He was just a boy still, after all. Before Egan could change his mind and stop her, Marek pushed out into the light and closed the door behind her.

CHAPTER 2

Marek pushed her way past the outskirts of her little hamlet, her crutch making small, round marks in the snow that appeared almost pretty next to the elongated smudges her clubbed foot made alongside it. Her anger faded as the hours passed and she walked the long route from the small hamlet where Master Vagamal's apothecary rested toward Merren, the capital city of the once-kingdom of Deira. It was the long route for Marek at least, which simply meant it took twice as long for her walking with her crutch as it would have anyone else. Vitalion soldiers were out in force, looking intimidating in their gleaming armor and red surclothes, though she was mostly ignored by all who passed.

Egan always spoke of the city as if it were a grand place, worthy of special attention and awe. Marek disagreed. With the unpleasant press of unwashed bodies and the smells of refuse and rotting food doing battle in the air around her, the city became nothing more than the least-bothersome boil on the buttocks of an ogre, with one small exception: Gojun Pye, the wizard. Though the practice of magic itself was, strictly speaking, against Vitalion law, Marek assumed the man had some sort of arrangement with the magistrate or local guards which allowed him to remain unmolested. Without a doubt, the arrangement included the exchange of a fair bit of coin.

She reached the wizard's house within a few short minutes of passing through the narrow market district and pushed inside without bothering to knock. Their relationship had passed far beyond that sort of thing by now.

The interior of the wizard's hut could best be described as the perfect domestic version of a hoarder's cave. Marek ran her hands along the spines of strange books in half a dozen languages resting on one of dozens of large shelves scattered throughout the room. Bottles of every variety, some thickly covered in the dust only borne of an age far beyond Marek's years, lay among them. What little space remained either on the shelves or atop the workspaces was crammed with loose, dark parchment. Marek paused for half a moment to pick up one of the bottles, studying the amber liquid within.

Gojun Pye sat behind the desk on the other side of the room, scribbling on a parchment, content to ignore and be ignored by Marek, which wasn't unusual.

Marek breathed in the musty scent and felt all lingering worries and care slip away into the aether. It had changed so little since her first visit here so many years ago. She'd been making deliveries for the apothecary then too, and had soon seized upon every chance she could get to come see the man. Content to let the wizard write for the moment, Marek limped over to one of the shelves and began poking through it, picking up an odd, shriveled *something* and studying it with a minutia of focus before setting it down and shifting aside a pile of slate writing boards to see what was hidden behind.

"I mastered the vision spell you gave me," Marek said after a moment in a voice she hoped sounded off-hand and carefree. "I think it needed more basilisk blood though."

"And what did the basilisk blood project?" Even without seeing the man's face, the smirk on his face came through in his tone.

Marek busied her hands on the shelves, picking up some small bottles and what looked vaguely like a shell of some sort and then putting them back down again.

"An eagle," she said, unsure how the wizard would react to the truth of the snake and resultant fire. Gojun always warned her to be careful with magic. Marek, if she was truly honest with herself, was rarely, if ever, careful.

"That's fascinating," Gojun replied, tone pensive. Marek glanced over at him and noticed he'd stopped writing and straightened in his chair. "I was certain basilisk blood would result in nothing less than a fireball."

Marek gave a small half shrug and turned back to the shelf with a "hmmm." She should have known he'd see through her lie. Gojun rarely missed anything. Still, he said nothing further and after half a moment she heard the sound of his quill scratching against parchment once more.

Marek bent down to look at another shelf, studying what looked like a spell and a strange, solid brown cylinder while contemplating her next comment for perhaps the thousandth time. She had a purpose here, after all, much more than just to escape the apothecary—which was not an inconsiderable motivation by itself—or to even make the delivery. No, this was the one place she felt like herself. The one place she felt safe. The one place she could come to learn about magic.

"I think I'm ready for some new spells." Marek glanced at Gojun's back, then away again quickly.

"Oh really?" Gojun chuckled, a deep, throaty sound of genuine mirth without a trace of actual spite. So different from anyone else Marek knew. Maybe this *was* the right time. "What kind of spells?"

Marek glanced in the wizard's direction, then bit her lower lip and looked down toward her feet. In all the times she'd come before, she'd avoided this, avoided asking about the one thing which she most desired outside of her own freedom.

"Healing." Marek winced at the sound of it, the soft, pleading undercurrent which lay just north of true desperation. She heard the soft rustle of papers as Gojun put down his quill. She glanced in his direction.

"I'm not a holy man." Gojun tilted his head toward her as he spoke, though he didn't fully turn and meet her gaze. "You need a healer. Magic is not an art of faith, but of understanding." Marek turned her whole body to face him at this, disappointment filling her with leaden weights inside her chest.

Faith.

Faith to be healed? What worth did a slave have, did she have, when her piety amounted to a muttered curse to Rathos, God of War, when she burned herself or after she had received a beating. Her piety could be measured in motes of dust. By that measure, she was unworthy of any holy man's touch.

"However . . ." Gojun continued.

Marek felt a rush of sudden hope return and chip away at the blocks of hardened sorrow.

"I do have something for you. Bring me that

pile of parchment."

Parchment?

Marek looked around, curiosity and confusion masking her melancholy. She'd been so hopeful, so *sure* Gojun could help her. He was the kindest, wisest, most powerful man she knew, even if he was a bit eccentric. Though he was constantly distracted and rarely gave anyone a straight answer, he'd been kinder to her than anyone else she'd ever known. She felt closer to him than anyone, even Egan. She found the pile in question, picked it up, and hurried to where Gojun knelt next to the crackling hearth. The heat from the flames was a welcome relief from the bitter cold of winter which still lingered in the wizard's hut.

"Ah," he said, riffling through the piles until he found the parchment for which he was looking. "There. A displacement spell. Very useful."

Marek took the paper by instinct, automatically starting to glance over it before the second plummeting motion of her disappointed heart hit her. Part of her, however illogical, had wondered if perhaps he'd thought of a way to help her after all.

"Just don't use it on a living object," Gojun said in a distracted tone as he shuffled the rest of the papers back into a loose pile.

"Why not?"

"'Cause they'll most likely cease to be living,"

Gojun answered, and then began casually tossing the remaining spells and papers into the flames.

"What are you doing?" Marek shouted, dropping to her knees in a panic alongside Gojun. She grasped at some of the papers as flames licked at them, but the heat forced her back.

"I'm leaving." Gojun said it in such a matter-of-fact tone that it made Marek stop what she was doing and look up at him, aghast. The firelight cast his smooth, angular face in a mixture of shadows that highlighted his eyes. Marek had always thought Gojun a paradox of a man. His face was surprisingly youthful, except for a grizzled head of hair and the odd age line around the eyes. Those eyes shone with far too much wisdom and knowledge to belong to anyone under the age of fifty. "These things are not safe to be left behind. Nothing is safe here anymore."

Gojun made a vague gesture with one hand and turned away. Marek stared after him, still on her knees next to the fire. One of her hands rested against the hearthstone to lend her support, her fingers ignorant of the heat there in the shock of the moment.

"You're leaving?" she asked, mind numb.

"There's too many eyes," Gojun said. He grabbed a travel pack and started shoving objects into it. The pack itself appeared half-full already. Marek wondered how she'd missed seeing it when she'd come in. "Too much lust for power. I've stayed too long. The Vitalions grow suspicious of an old hermit who knows more than he should and interacts with the world around him far too infrequently to have gleaned that knowledge. Even those I've paid to keep quiet."

Marek grabbed up the remaining papers on the ground in a sweeping gesture and clutched them to her chest with one arm while staggering to her feet. Panic flooded through her with the force of a raging blizzard, just as powerful and just as cold.

"Take me with you!"

Gojun didn't stop packing. Marek couldn't remember him ever acting quite this determined, this single-minded. Usually, he was so distracted, focusing on everything and nothing at once. What had happened to make him change so much now?

"You've got a strong mind, Marek, and a gift for learning."

"You could teach me," Marek said, dropping the papers and limping toward Gojun, hands clenching and unclenching at her sides. "You could buy me and you could teach me."

Gojun turned at this, finally, and regarded her with brooding, intense eyes. In that moment, Marek was reminded of how tall Gojun really was. His eyes searched her appraisingly for a long moment, as if considering her words, then he raised the scroll he'd been holding in his right hand and pointed it at her. When he spoke, his words were slow and deliberate, and his eyes locked onto hers as if he were trying to imprint the words into her memory.

"There's an inn. It's just outside of town." Gojun sucked in a breath, as if he'd been running, then tossed the scroll he'd been holding into his sack. "You ask for Hammerhead. You will find the experience that you lack there and someone will be in need of a conjurer."

Marek stared at him, mouth working for a moment as she struggled to trap the thoughts flitting about within her mind into words.

"I—I can't," she said in a voice so soft it was almost a whisper. She looked away from Gojun, down toward her feet. "I'd be alone, a runaway—hunted down and hanged." There was more than that, deeper and more meaningful reasons, but Marek couldn't bring herself to give them voice. She knew, deep within the pit of her stomach where a block of fear as frozen as the ground outside rested, that without Gojun, without his aide and teaching and guidance, she was nothing more than a simple slave.

"You are a fighter, Marek," Gojun said, meeting her eyes again and speaking in that slow, deliberate tone. "It would be a shame to see that flame go out."

"But I can't—" Marek began, but Gojun cut her off.

"No, Marek." Marek heard the deeper meaning behind the words, even if she didn't fully understand what it was that he intended. "It is getting dark and you must go. And so must I."

Marek felt the numbness spread throughout her body, and she shifted her gaze about distractedly, unable to focus on anything in particular.

"Here," Gojun said, shouldering his pack and then handing her a small pouch of coins. "It's for the hogsroot."

"Please don't go." Marek tried to meet his eyes, to plead with more than just words for him to stay, but her sudden hopelessness made her movements lethargic and her vision slow to rise above the level of the floor. "You're my only friend. The only one who can help me. The only one who cares."

"Good friends aren't so hard to find," Gojun said with a shallow smile that did little to dispel Marek's despair. He put a hand on her shoulder and gave it a gentle squeeze. "Our paths will cross again. Now, haste. It's after first watch. The guards will be looking for slaves breaking curfew."

Marek held his gaze for half a moment, then nodded and turned to leave. Her sluggish thoughts registered the wisdom in Gojun's warning about the watch, even if part of her was in denial that Gojun himself was leaving her to such a fate. She limped away, pace quickening as she crossed the room. Halfway across she paused and looked back over her shoulder, holding her skirt up with one hand and clutching the displacement spell in the other. Gojun watched her with a blank expression, dressed to travel and not showing any sign of relenting. For half a moment, Marek hated him more than anything she'd ever hated before. Her vision stared to blur along the edges. Fighting down tears, Marek spun around, picked up her crutch, and vanished out into the fast-approaching night.

CHAPTER 3

Thane only half looked up as a girl with a crutch stepped out onto the cobbled street. He watched her for a moment through the curtain of his dark hair before deciding she wasn't worth his time. He was, after all, quite busy getting well and thoroughly drunk. He took another swig from the earthenware bottle and allowed his chin to tuck back down against his chest, resting against the cool metal there. Armor was such a nice thing upon which to rest a drunken head, especially when a crowd of idiots had gathered to pay homage to the royalty of fools. Thane half grinned at his own joke and wondered if perhaps he should get drunk more often.

"What's going on?" the girl asked of a passing boy.

"Adventurers," the boy said in a sickeningly awed, almost worshipful tone. "They have dragon eggs."

Adventurers. Idiots more like. The glory and honor of adventure was a dead thing, long since gone to rot. Let the fool boy run off and worship fools. What did he care?

Thane heard the boy and his cohorts scamper off toward the throng of people blackening the street only a short distance away. Their shouts, guffaws, and praise sounded like little more than the wallowing of swine. Fools, the lot of them. The girl—young woman really, but again, what did Thane care about specifics—started running, except this time an odd sound accompanied her stride, a steady thunk, thunk, thunk of wood against stone. Curiosity overcame the drunken stupor in which his mind rested and he raised his chin, hand immediately drifting toward the bottle at his side.

The crutch. He'd almost forgotten noticing it before. Thane almost snorted at his own foolishness. Almost. Years—decades really, but who was counting—of constant fighting in the name of the Vitalion Empire had left him wary of everything, including himself. Even drunk, he'd managed to place his back up against a wall at the intersection of two alleyways with a view of them both. Once a soldier . . .

The girl pulled the hood of her cloak down low over her head as she limp-ran. Thane decided to ignore her and took another swig from his bottle, feeling the amber liquid slip out the corners of his mouth and down his beard. Raucous laughter came from the side alley on his right.

What now?

Thane glanced through his long hair and saw a man dressed in fine silks and an expensive coat flanked by three men who some might call henchmen or lackeys. Thane preferred a more accurate description. Thugs. They were the sort of men who proliferated this part of the Deiran Outlands. They were men who preyed on the fear and weakness of others, men in the Thieves Guild who, though the Vitalion government would deny it wholeheartedly, owned the local magistrate and the Vitalion garrison.

The girl with the crutch ran straight into them and was sent sprawling to the ground.

"Watch where you're going, gimp!" one of the thugs growled.

The girl struggled to rise and her hood fell back, revealing her dark hair and wide, frightened features. Thane thought he could almost smell the fear wafting from her as the four men all laughed and the more well-dressed man—he looked vaguely familiar though Thane couldn't quite place the face—put a booted heel on top of her lame leg. The girl let out a small scream of pain, though she bit it off halfway through. Stupid girl. Better to scream and hope someone would hear and look their way. Not that it would stop this sort of man, but it was better than stubborn pride. Idiocy like that would get you killed.

"Now, what do you think of that?" The well-dressed man leered down at the girl and laughed along with his cohorts. With a sudden motion, the man bent and pulled back the girl's hair. From his angle, Thane couldn't see what was there, but assumed it was a slave tattoo or brand. The girl fought upright again, though the man holding her wrapped one meaty hand around her chin and along one cheek as she struggled. He moved his other hand around her face in a sickening mockery of a caress.

"A slave girl, huh," he crooned, teeth bared like some great feline predator. "But you are not so young. I could sell you as a fifteen-year-old . . . say, sixteen years old in the right light?" He grinned up at his thugs, who laughed. "But that twisted foot. It's not my type, but some men—some men, they pay extra for a girl like you." He licked his lips as the girl struggled in his grip.

She had spirit at least, Thane would give her that. She was a fool, and about as stupid as they come for getting herself into this mess to begin with. First watch had come and gone. Any slaves out afterward were either short on wits or were looking for death. But to get taken by Peregus Malister? The man's comments about paying for girls had sparked Thane's alcohol-addled mind. The man was well known among the dregs of the Thieves Guild, poor girl.

Just then, the girl got a hand free of Peregus's grip and lashed out with all her force. She caught Peregus across the face and dug into flesh, the nails cutting three clear, bloody gashes across his forehead from his right temple to the middle of his brow. Thane would have whistled in admiration if he could have only remembered how. His brain felt a little fuzzy, though part of him was glad he didn't have sense enough to actually complete the whistle. He didn't need to be a part of this. He was off duty. He didn't need the attention of the Thieves Guild right now either. They controlled the garrison and everything in it. They could make his life a hell so hot he'd wish for his own death.

"Take her to the den," Peregus yelled, shifting off her as his thugs stepped forward and seized her around the arms. "Take her!"

"No!" The girl struggled as rough hands pulled her up and hauled her down the narrow alleyway back in the direction from which they'd come.

Peregus spat to the side and then got to his feet. He put a hand to his head, feeling at the blood there, and scowled. A dark look crossed his face and his eyes fell upon the girl struggling in the clutches of his thugs. Thane watched it through a half-marred gaze. Whatever Peregus had been planning for the girl, whatever torment he'd previously held within his dark, twisted mind, had now been replaced by something much, much worse.

"Find out who owns her rights in case somebody wants to claim her," Peregus ordered.

The girl struggled and thrashed against her captors, keeping hold of her crutch despite it all. A valiant fight.

Before he could stop himself, Thane was on his feet, though his movements were far from fluid. His armor rattled against the stone and his shield felt like it weighed more than an entire regiment's worth of rations.

"Hold." Despite his drunken state, Thane felt a little rush of pride that his voice, while not loud, was both steady and firm. It still bore the weight of command, though that mantle had not been his in years.

Peregus and his henchmen stopped, and Peregus turned back with an upraised hand. When he spoke, his voice dripped with the oil all politicians bathed in daily.

"My slave, she ran away, but I caught her." He waved the upraised hand dismissively and turned his back on Thane.

Thane felt a flush of irritation push through his befuddled senses. What was it with people assuming arrogance was the same as authority?

"He's lying—" the girl shouted and may have

continued, but one of the thugs wrapped a gloved hand around her mouth and her screams devolved into wordless, muffled squeals.

"No slaves out past first watch," Thane said. What was he doing? Hadn't he just decided he couldn't afford to interfere? "She'll have to come with me."

"Like I said." Peregus turned back to Thane and made a curt gesture with one hand. The slimy quality in his voice was gone now, replaced by a hard, warning edge, like bared steel. "My slave girl ran away, and I found her." He dug in a pouch at his waist and produced a coin that clinked against its fellows as it was withdrawn. "There's no harm done here." Peregus bit his lower lip and flipped the coin at Thane with a flick of his wrist.

Thane didn't take his eyes off Peregus's face as the coin hit him in the chest and clattered to the ground. Only once the coin had come to rest did Thane glance down at the ground and then back up to Peregus. Why had the fool man gone and done that? Thane's loyalty cost more than that by far.

"That's for your troubles." Peregus smiled broadly and threw both hands into the air as if making merry during a dance.

"What's her name?"

The sound hung in the air between them for a long, pregnant moment. Peregus grinned the slow, wily grin of a fox and raised both his hands again, fingers spread. He chuckled softly and spun slowly on one heel away from Thane.

"Kill him!" Peregus barked, walking away from Thane with purposeful strides.

Peregus's thugs rushed him. The girl, freed from their grasp for half a breath, scrambled to get away, but lost her footing. Peregus had her by the arm in the half second it took Thane to draw his sword and take stock of the approaching thugs.

In the space of a single heartbeat, years of hardened skill and training took hold and the hand gripping the sword whipped forward and sent the blade spinning through the air toward the nearest attacker. The man, a tall, boulder-like fellow with a squashed nose and an ugly face, caught the sword in the throat. He fell to the cobbles with barely a sound.

The other two thugs didn't even pause as their companion died. They rushed forward like lumbering bulls, swords held in meat-cleaver hands.

Thane raised his shield and batted one of them aside with a well-placed blow to the man's jaw. The force of it sent ribbons of pain up his arm. Pivoting, Thane brought his knee up into the man's gut as he fell, using the man's downward momentum to give added force to his upward-thrusting knee. The thug didn't have the luxury of wearing armor, like

Thane, so the blow sunk deep into soft flesh and blew the air out of the thug's lungs in a rush loud enough to punch through the ringing in Thane's ears. The thug crumpled to the ground in a limp heap, clutching at his stomach.

The other thug slammed Thane against the wall with a flurry of powerful punches. Thane hit the wall hard, his shield careening off the stone with a clarion clang, though his armor offered him some protection from any real damage. Still, air rushed from his lungs and Thane gasped for breath. The thug, a massive fellow who smelled like he'd spent the last several months wallowing with pigs in their own filth, drew his blade and charged, sword point digging for flesh.

Thane spun his hand up over the blade as it came in and pulled the thug's arm in close to his own body, thus allowing the man's own momentum to carry him into the wall as Thane pivoted into the motion. Thane helped the thug along with a shove, knocking him to the ground. In one fluid motion, he took the man's own sword and rammed it into its owner's gut.

Thane turned toward the remaining man, lungs heaving and sweat beading on his brow. His long brown hair stuck to his forehead in wet clumps. His head pounded with the thundering of his heart and the muddling effect of drink, though that effect was dulled even further by the thrill of battle running through him. He cursed himself a fool for getting involved, but now that he was in the thick of it, there was no place he'd rather be. Battle was an integral part of him, death his devout lover. Vitalia and the legions be damned. This, this was an honorable fight.

He heard indistinct shouts from behind him and spared a glance in that direction as the remaining thug approached. Thane noticed the girl struggling with Peregus out of the corner of his eye. The girl batted at Peregus with one arm, putting up a valiant fight despite her deformity. She sank her teeth into one of Peregus's arms and the man released her, swearing loudly. He started after her, but even as Thane watched, the girl swung her crutch and struck Peregus a resounding blow across the face, leveling the man. Thane would have grinned, or perhaps even winced, but the remaining thug seized that exact moment of distraction to charge.

Thane stepped into the charge, losing sight of the girl, and took a pair of blows from the man's sword on his shield. Thane's arm cried out at the abuse, though long years of battle and training—along with the more-than-liberal amount of drink still running through him—allowed him to ignore the pain of it.

The man swung again and, this time, Thane

lashed out with his shield as the blow descended, catching the blade and pushing it aside. He'd learned a long time ago that battle itself was rarely won with the strongest blow, or even the quickest. No, battles were usually won either by the smallest of opportunities seized at exactly the right moment, or by the seriously lucky. This time, Thane fell into the former category rather than the latter.

The sword dissuaded from its original course, Thane pivoted inward on his left foot and continued the momentum of his shield. His hand, outside the straps of his shield, remained free to grab the thug by the wrist and pull him in close. Thane's other hand, the one balled into a fist, came down against the thug's thick cheekbones with all the force of a rampaging ogre. Thane's hand exploded with pain, but he didn't relent, allowing his anger to push it aside. The thug staggered back and Thane pushed forward with his shield, pinning the man against the wall and raining blow after blow down on the man's face.

"I will find you!" The shouts came from Peregus, down the alleyway back by the girl, though Thane barely heard them over the ringing in his ears and the meaty smack of his fist against unyielding flesh and bone. He gave the thug one last, devastating blow and let him drop to the cobbles, face a mess of blood, bruises, and broken dignity.

Thane stumbled back from the fallen man, then turned to face Peregus, shield still bound to his left arm. He spat blood, though he couldn't remember when he'd taken the blow which had caused it. Thane's breath came in ragged heaves and his right hand throbbed with pain. He felt it swelling already and knew bruises would cover his knuckles by the next morning. A thin trail of blood trickled down his bottom lip and into his beard. All in all, it had been a most excellent fight.

"You, uh, you don't know who I am, do you?" Peregus spluttered. The man stepped back, putting distance between them. Thane wondered if Peregus knew how ridiculous he looked with the three lines of blood running down his forehead and a swelling bruise blossoming on one cheek from the girl's crutch. He spat more blood onto the cobbles.

"I have a general idea." Thane's voice sounded tired to his own ears, but there was a harsh burr in it, which he recognized as grim determination.

Thane started forward deliberately. He knew his face must have looked hideous, covered in the dirt and grime of his earlier drunken revelry and now streaked with blood, both his own and that of the thugs who now lay in the alley behind him. A small part of him relished the look of terror that crossed Peregus's face. The man drew a small dagger and danced backward quickly, the dagger pointed in

Thane's general direction. Thane almost laughed at the absurdity of it.

"If you cross me, you will pay," Peregus snapped, then, looking sideways, darted down another alley and was soon lost from sight.

Thane snorted and glanced around for the girl. She was gone, of course. Good for her. He hoped she made it home. It'd be a pity if she were caught and hanged for violating curfew after all the trouble she'd put him through. At least he'd gotten a good fight out of it.

Now, where is that bottle?

CHAPTER 4

Marek hobbled along the muddy road, ignorant of her surroundings as her feet squelched in the freezing mud. Pain shot through her with each step and her mind refused to work. It had simply been through too much today to do more than trudge along at the same pace as her feet. First Gojun leaving in such a mad flurry of decisions and oddity, then nearly being forced into an even worse fate by those men in the alleyway, she simply couldn't focus on much else. It was like trying to see through a blizzard. Vague shapes and movement was all she noticed.

The sound of an approaching cart momentarily pulled her from her stupor and she moved to one side of the road, stopping to let it pass. The lack of motion, the end of the steady, repetitive act, allowed her mind to clear even further, though it still felt as if she were walking through mist inside her own mind. She glanced down the road, taking stock of her surroundings, and noticed a Vitalion checkpoint ahead at the edge of the trees. If the cart hadn't come along, she would have blundered right into it.

Panic cut through her mental lethargy and gave her a sudden clarity of thought, like stepping outside into pristine, unbroken snow right after a storm. The cart rolled by, white tarp pulled over the back to keep out the snow. As quick as she could, Marek limped up, lifted the edge of the canvas, and tossed her crutch inside. A moment later, she threw herself in as well, working her way deep into the prickly confines of the surprisingly warm straw, a small smile playing about her lips. Now *this* was how one traveled back to town. Marek closed her eyes in contentment, settling her back deeper into the straw.

Someone sniffed right next to her.

Marek's eyes snapped open and spread to their fullest. She turned her head in the direction of the sound with the speed of a cat investigating a mouse's hole.

A man lay in the straw next to her. He grinned, revealing a perfect set of teeth and lips only slightly marred by a thin mustache and beard. His eyes danced with the upward turn of his smile and his mildly-long brown hair shone yellow in places where straw had laid claim to it. He reached out and placed a finger against her lips, then made a shushing sound and pointed forward toward where the driver sat. Or he could have been pointing toward the checkpoint. Either way it was the same general message. Marek's heart fluttered in her throat as she glanced in that direction, then back down at the young man. She forced her body to relax, though she kept one fist clenched at her side. She'd already been accosted by four strange men today. She wasn't about to let it happen again. She almost flinched when he took hold of her crutch and lifted it up to inspect.

"You thrust this in with some force, m'lady," he whispered with a pert little pursing of his lips.

Marek snatched it away from him and dropped it behind her out of his reach. She wasn't about to let him at the only weapon she possessed.

"The effect," he continued, "was nearly disastrous."

He grinned at her again. Something fluttered in Marek's throat and she swallowed, feeling a warmth spread through her body and threaten to color her cheeks. She was just deciding how to respond when a gruff voice barked a greeting from outside the wagon.

"Ho there," the voice said. "What do you carry?"

The crunch of boots came close. Inside the wagon, the man held a finger to his lips and turned carefully so he was looking in the direction of the driver. Blood pounded in Marek's ears and the fluttering in her throat seemed to grow hands and start to claw at her windpipe. She couldn't tell if it came from the fear of being discovered or the close proximity of the stranger in the cart with her.

"Straw," came the driver's reply.

Marek's breathing quickened with the sound of approaching hooves. The man in the cart met her eyes. She saw his eyes widen as an unmistakable scrape of metal rang out. Marek let out a small, involuntary gasp. The man's hands shot out quicker than Marek thought possible and clamped strong fingers over her mouth, stifling any other sounds before they could even begin. Marek breathed through her nose, sounding almost like a horse to her own ears. The man's eyes roved around the canvas above them, as if searching for something.

Suddenly, he darted back. An instant later a sword sliced through the canvas and sank into the straw where he'd been only a moment before. Marek felt a spike of fear run through her and she squealed, though the sound was muffled, to the point of being almost rodent-like, by the man's strong hands. A heartbeat later, Marek felt herself yanked forward, her body smashing up against the man's in a flurry of straw as he pulled her on top of him. She felt the press of her body against his and heard the sword cut through the canvas where she'd been and then exit the canvas again with a thin rasp. She made another small sound of fear, cursing herself and wondering if, at any second, the blade was going to plunge down again and sink its steely bite into her flesh. The man rolled her off of him, though he kept his hand clamped firmly over her lips.

A moment passed. A horse brayed and the steady clop of hooves against stone came from right alongside the wagon.

"Move along," said a muffled voice. "Move along."

The man's hand loosened on Marek's lips, but didn't lift free as the driver flicked the reins and the wagon started moving again. The man's face was still tight and his eyes roamed about the back of the wagon for a few more moments as if he expected something else to pierce it, but after a short time he relaxed.

Marek's breath came in short, ragged gasps, matched by the man's. It was warm beneath the canvas, with two bodies pressed so closely together amidst the straw, so their breath didn't throw up a cloud of mist. If it had, though, Marek was sure it would have filled the entire space with a thick fog. The man's hand lifted from her mouth and drifted downward, coming to rest on her breast. Before Marek could react, he'd given it a little squeeze.

"Get off me!" Marek sputtered, shoving his hand away with as much force as she could muster.

He rolled away, chuckling softly. His grin took

up half his face, stark, white teeth flashing toward her as he smiled. He raised a hand and made a small gesture as he rolled back toward her.

"A thousand pardons, m'lady. I couldn't help myself." His face took on a serious note, the grin fading, and he reached for her hair, picking a loose piece of straw from it. "A beautiful lady, intimate moment in the straw . . ."

He glanced down her body in a quick darting of the eyes and placed the bit of straw he'd pulled from her hair into his mouth. For some reason, Marek felt herself flush as she glanced down at herself too, her body responding in all sorts of strange ways she had never experienced before. The man peeked out from beneath the canvas and gave a soft sigh.

"But alas, work calls. The magistrate isn't going to cuckold himself, now is he?" He paused and gave her an impish look, mischief alight in both his rougish hair and merry eyes. "Pleasant travels."

He nodded at her and then slid out the back of the wagon in a single graceful movement. Marek lifted her head slightly to watch, then dropped back to the straw, her hands across her stomach. *That man!* He was clearly nothing more than a rogue, an annoying, self-centered fop who preyed on the naïve and unsuspecting. At least his fondlings were far less demeaning than her attackers in the alley had been. And his smile was nice, at least, for a self-important scoundrel, that is. Anyway, he was gone now. She relaxed and her fingers traced the edges of her belt and twisted around one of the ties there.

Empty ties.

She looked down, fingers dancing over the leather cords and beginning to tremble as badly as they had when the sword had flashed down by her head.

"Oh no! The coins!" Master Vagamal's coins. Gojun's payment for the herbs.

Marek rolled over and scrambled to the back of the wagon, flipping the canvas covering up over her head so she could see out unobstructed. The man who'd been in the cart with her dashed across the snow toward the tree line, a number of Vitalion soldiers giving chase.

No!

She sat there in shock as the group disappeared into the trees, not bothering to lower herself back down into the straw. Master Vagamal expected that money. She already knew a beating would be waiting for her for being out after first watch, not to mention the fact that she'd gone out instead of Egan to begin with, but this? This would be a beating far beyond mere punishment. Her mouth went dry. What was she going to do?

A dark shape appeared in front of Marek's face. It only took her a moment to realize it was a Vitalion soldier, but in that moment he'd reached down under the canvas, yanked her out, and tossed her down into the snow.

CHAPTER 5

Full darkness lay over the village as the horse carrying Marek trudged into it, the steady clop of its hooves announcing its arrival even with the muffling blanket of snow which covered much of the street. From where she lay, slung lengthwise across the horse's shoulders and, basically, across the Vitalion soldier's lap, Marek could see the villagers scattering toward their homes with panicked, deliberate haste. Such was the effect the Vitalion soldiers had in this part of the Deiran Outlands, where the only difference between villains and heroes was the color of the clothes they wore. Doors creaked shut all around them and those brave few who remained outside huddled around small fires and tried not to look like they were staring.

The soldier reined in before Master Vagamal's apothecary. Marek felt one of her ribs dig into the horse's saddle and winced, though she retained her silence. The soldier hadn't been unkind to her when he'd forced her owner's name from her, but he hadn't been gentle either. And he smelled like the underside of a rotten log.

"Who's the man here?" the soldier shouted into

the darkness.

The door to the apothecary opened with a creak and Master Vagamal stepped out onto the stoop. In the light cast by a nearby fire, Marek could just make out his face. It showed the proper amount of subservient respect due a Vitalion soldier, though Marek knew it was all an act. She could see the rage dancing behind Vagamal's cold, hard eyes.

"Does this belong to you?" the soldier wrapped one massive hand around the back of Marek's head and forced it down practically into his horse's flank. His other hand pulled none-too-gently on her hair, exposing the marks of slavery tattooed along the back of her neck.

"Yes," Vagamal said. Though Marek couldn't see him, she heard the hesitation in his voice. "I trust this can be forgotten?"

The soldier's hands moved away suddenly and Marek heard the sound of coin above her. The soldier gave her a little shove and she slid off his saddle and sprawled into the snow, unable to keep her feet. She clambered upright, wincing at the pain of half a dozen bruises and the incessant ache of her bad leg. The soldier moved off without looking back at them, bouncing a small pouch of coins on his palm.

Marek sniffed against the cold and glanced after the soldier, then over to Master Vagamal. The old man stared after the soldier with a scowl once again hovering on his lips. If she hurried inside now, he may not even notice her.

Master Vagamal caught her just before she reached the door. One gnarled hand tangled itself in her hair and wrapped around her ear, twisting it painfully. Marek tried to turn her head in the direction he was pulling, but he simply continued to twist.

"You led a Vitalion guard to this house?" Master Vagamal shouted, spraying her with spittle. His free hand clenched her cloak at the shoulder and he shook her roughly. Marek whimpered with the pain of it. "Where's my coin?"

"I'm sorry," Marek said. She sucked in a breath and backed away. "I was robbed."

Vagamal backhanded her across the face. The blow struck just below her cheekbone on her left side, pushing her weight toward her bad leg. Already taxed to its limit by the events of the day, the leg crumpled beneath her and she fell to the ground with a shout. She immediately tucked both her legs up to her chest, years of beatings having taught her to protect the soft parts of her body before all else. Vagamal loomed over her, buck teeth glinting in the light where they stuck out over his lower lip.

"Are you trying to make a fool of me, girl?"

Marek panted, holding her stomach. "You

manage that yourself," she muttered in a soft voice that, nonetheless, carried.

Vagamal promptly kicked her in the stomach. Even with one arm there for protection, the force of the blow sent Marek rolling backward and she cried out in pain. It would be over soon. He'd knock her around, but eventually tire of it all. That's how beatings like this normally went. She looked up at him as he loomed over her again. His hands dropped to the buckle of his belt.

Not again.

"You're finished here, girl," Vagamal growled, rage making his already ugly face twist into that of a demon in human flesh. "I wanted you clean, to keep your price up, but now I'll just take what's mine."

The belt came free of his pants and he bent it double in one hand. This wasn't going to be an ordinary beating. She could see it in his eyes. Hatred gleamed there, and something else this time, something new. She'd seen it before though, earlier that day. It was the look the men in the alley had given her when assessing her capacity to serve in the brothel houses. She tried to scramble back, elbows digging into the snow, but her leg wouldn't move, wouldn't support her weight. The belt slapped down onto her back and shoulder, and she screamed.

"I'll sell whatever's left of you to the whore house."

Blows rained down on her. A lash of the belt hit her in the arm, then across the back, and then down one leg. The belt rose and fell, leaving behind stinging pain and tearing ragged screams from Marek's lips with each blow. Her ears rang with the sound of her own cries and the slap of leather against cloth, then leather against flesh as the cloth was torn through and dug into her skin. It was pain beyond comprehension, pain beyond imagining. The belt fell again, seven times. Nine. Ten. Marek stopped counting after thirteen.

She heard the sounds of doors opening around her, though it was a distant, hollow sound. The other villagers were likely investigating the screams, though Marek didn't even bother hoping one of them would help her. Few would even care. Most would likely watch it all take place, every bit of it, and do nothing other than think their dark thoughts and slink back to their holes like the slimy insects they were.

Vagamal grunted and brought the belt down again, harder now with each blow. Spittle blew from his mouth with each breath. Marek's back arched when the belt struck there, then rocked forward again as another blow caught her in the stomach. Her mouth opened wide as screams flooded out of it. Her mind started to go numb, though she rolled her head back to look up at Vagamal as he pulled his arm back for another swing.

A feeling Marek had never experienced before surged up within her. The pain vanished in an explosion of deep, violent anger which clawed up through her gut and thundered through her veins. Her vision clouded around the edges, growing so dark that even the ebony color of night around them seemed bright by comparison. As Vagamal swung again, belt whistling through the air, Marek's hand shot out and caught the blow before it fell. She allowed the leather to wrap around her wrist and heaved with all her strength, tearing it from Vagamal's grasp. Her skin felt hot, as if it were alight with fever or a miniature personal flame. Tiny motes of green light filled the air around them and Marek clenched her teeth against the rage within her. She met Vagamal's stunned expression and raised her free hand palm forward, extending it toward the monster who had claimed to be her master since he'd purchased her as a child.

Blue-white light burst outward from her palm, then surged toward Vagamal. Before it hit him, more of the blue-white light leapt out of his chest and poured from his eyes and mouth. It merged with the light coming from Marek's hands and raced back toward her. Vagamal's eyes went wide with shock, fear, or terror, then became as black as coal, all color burned out of them in half an instant. The light poured into Marek in a steady stream. Other streams of light, smaller than the one leaving Vagamal and racing from a half dozen different locations, joined with his as they entered her.

She felt them all within her, mingling in a bittersweet, chaotic pool somewhere deep within the pit of her stomach. It swelled there for the space of a dozen heartbeats. On the thirteenth, energy burst from her in an explosion of blue-white light that blasted Vagamal back off his feet and through the air to crash into wooden crates some ten feet away. Marek, already on the ground, slid a few short feet back as well.

The strange power she'd felt within her faded away and left her gasping for breath, head pounding, not quite sure what she'd just done. The anger, the rage that had overtaken her was gone, leaving her feeling hollow inside, empty and broken. She pushed herself up onto her elbows and looked around, blinking owlishly. The night seemed strangely darker than it had been only a moment before. Vagamal lay unmoving in a pile of broken crates near the apothecary. He didn't get up.

Oh Gods, I killed him.

Marek got to her feet, peering blearily around at the eyes staring back at her from nearly every doorway in the village. They stared at her without words, though she saw the horror in their expressions and the way they gripped various objects in their hands as if to defend themselves against an attacker. Several shifted from foot to foot as if unsure what to do in the face of what they'd just seen. Marek bolted for the apothecary door.

Inside the shop, Marek stumbled across the room as fast as her bad leg would take her. Ragged gasps rattled through her throat. She reached for the shelf, her mind half made up to gather a pack and run, then realized her hands were trembling and seized the lip of the counter in a white-knuckled grip instead.

What have I done?

She swallowed hard and forced herself to think. There was no staying here now. The other villagers would eventually call for the Vitalions and she'd be charged as a spell caster. On top of that, she'd attacked her owner, her master. The law wouldn't be on her side. She had to leave.

She grabbed a sack and started shoving things in it, starting with some food and a number of powders and vials. What was a little honest thievery on top of everything else? Action drove out enough of the fear that she was able to focus, though enough remained that when she heard a small noise from behind her, she rushed to the table and grabbed a knife, holding it point-first before her. The tip of the blade shook in small, irregular patterns.

Egan pushed through the canvas doorway at the back of the room, his face ashen and wan. His eyes held a haunted look deep within them. When he stepped toward her, his feet dragged against the tile floor. It was as if he'd woken from a deep sleep and was now only half awake as he moved across the room. Marek lowered the knife, swallowing the sour taste of fear once more.

"What was that?" Egan asked. The haunted look in his eyes rose toward the surface and, for a moment, Marek wondered if he was even seeing her at all, or if he saw only the act she'd committed repeated in his mind's eye.

"I—I don't even—" Marek stammered. What could she say?

Egan shuffled over to the window and peered out into the gloom. "He's still alive."

For an instant, relief welled up in Marek so profound it nearly brought her to her knees. Then a bitter, icy note crept through. A living Vagamal wasn't a good thing for her. They'd hang her.

Egan turned back from the window and stared at Marek. The look he gave her made her feel as if he'd never seen her before. As if he was afraid of her.

No!

"You used no powders and you said no words,"

Egan said, stepping closer, though still not meeting her eye. "It was like no magic I've ever seen."

Shouting rang out from just outside before Marek could answer. She distinctly heard the words "conjurer," "demon," and "after her." She stared out the window. Almost a dozen shadowy forms bearing lanterns were striding down the street toward the apothecary. Even as she watched, shouts of "Where is she?" and "Get her!" joined with the indistinct rumble of a mob out for blood.

No!

Marek spun back to the counter, ignoring her pains. Her hands darted from item to item, shoving a few last minute necessities into the sack she'd prepared.

"I have to go," she said over her shoulder to Egan. "I'm going to Hammerhead's Inn." The words were out of her mouth before she even realized she'd made that decision. Now that she'd said it, however, she seized onto it and the seed of a plan started growing in the back of her mind.

She turned back to Egan. The blonde-haired youth's face was still ashen, though he looked far less afraid than he had been a moment before.

"Come with me," she blurted. "I can't do it alone, Egan."

He looked away and Marek's heart dropped down into her stomach. If she couldn't even convince Egan . . . A part of her felt like it had died inside, smothered and suffocated by a covering of leaden despair.

"Wait," Egan said, then hurried over to the other end of the room and bent down in front of the unwashed clothes there. He rummaged through some things, then stood and walked back to Marek with an odd contraption of metal and leather held in his hands.

"I made it," he said, looking down at the device. "It will help you run."

He held it out to her and Marek took it, turning it over in her hands. Several stiff metal rods stretched between a pair of iron rings, with a cup-like structure at the bottom beneath the smaller of the iron rings. Leather straps hung from several places, clearly meant to be used to hold it in place . . . on her leg.

"I—I don't have your courage," Egan said. "I would never make it."

Marek didn't know what to say. She held the brace in one hand and watched the younger boy stare sheepishly at the ground. She'd never given him the credit or attention he'd deserved. The hours he must have spent fashioning the brace, making sure each piece fit together perfectly and working the metal on his own. She had no idea he was so skilled a craftsman.

"Come on, go," Egan said, reaching out and taking her shoulder to steer her toward the door.

Marek limped forward, glancing toward the window and the sounds of the mob outside and then back to Egan. This was the only life she'd ever known. How could she just up and leave it like this to become a runaway?

What choice do I have?

"Be quick!" Egan snapped.

Marek limped around him, then spun back and threw her arms around him. He bent down and returned the hug. She stepped back, suppressing her feelings enough to look him in the eye. He held her gaze and squeezed her shoulder. Marek returned the gesture.

"Goodbye, Egan," she said.

He let his arm fall away and Marek limped to the door. She opened it a crack and peered out into the night to see if she was clear. Only the darkness greeted her outside. She hesitated and looked back at Egan and the apothecary one last time. Only that very morning she and Egan had been preparing spells in this room without a care in the world, outside of hiding what they were doing from Master Vagamal. Now, their entire world was in chaos.

"Go," Egan said.

Marek swallowed and then rushed out into the

night.

She was spotted before she'd even taken her first step.

"There she is!" someone shouted.

Marek staggered through the snow, running as fast as her leg would allow. She glanced over her shoulder once as she raced down the main road. Bobbing lanterns held in the darkened clutches of shadowy townspeople followed her. She bowed her head and kept running.

CHAPTER 6

Outside the city, Marek slowed enough to pull the hood of her cloak up over her head before continuing on down the road. Each step was a fiery blaze of the purest agony, but she couldn't afford to stop, not with the mob behind her. She couldn't see them anymore, but she swore she could hear them. Even if it was only her mind playing tricks on her, Marek decided it simply wasn't worth taking that chance. It wasn't until nearly a half an hour later, when the lights of the city disappeared behind the curving arch of a large hill, that she allowed herself to stop and flop down onto the side of the road. Her lungs heaved, pulse raced, and her foot throbbed with a fiery pain so intense she very nearly wept.

Once she got her panic under control, Marek fished the brace out of her pack where she'd stowed it. She hoped trying to work out how the thing functioned would keep her mind off the terrors of the day, but exhaustion and shock were proving even more of a distraction. Marek shook her head in an attempt to clear it, then pulled the contraption close, peering at it in the moonlight. Up close, the brace looked far more similar to an elongated saddle stirrup than anything else. She went to try and put it on and got tangled in her long skirt.

Stupid thing.

Marek set the brace aside and pulled out a small knife. A few deft strokes later, the skirt now ended just below her knee, allowing her full range of motion and access to her boots. Tossing the extra cloth aside and putting down the knife, Marek retrieved the brace and fitted it over her boot, working with fingers made clumsy with cold. The stirrup part fit against the heel of her boot right in the middle of where a normal foot's arch would have been. The smaller metal ring wrapped around her heel and ankle and straps up the sides secured the rest of it snugly against her calf. She got to her feet and tested her weight against it. It held. She took a few hesitant steps. Not even a twinge of pain came from her leg, at least not from her deformity. The dull ache of sore and tired muscles remained, of course.

Gods bless Egan!

A small chuckle escaped Marek's lips, a bright, happy sound that chased away the night's darkness for an instant. Marek couldn't remember the last time she'd laughed like that. She also couldn't remember a time when she hadn't walked with a severe limp. Walking normally would take some getting used to.

She stepped back, testing her weight again and then took a few more steps, this time with haste. She lost her balance and would have fallen, but her arms hit something cold and hard and she twisted toward it. An instant later she realized what she'd run into and let out a gasp of mingled surprise and horror.

A headless corpse hung from a chain, suspended by its feet. The arms hung down by where its head should have been, nearly touching the ground. Marek's touch had sent the body rocking back and forth like some sort of macabre puppet on a string. A disconcerting screech of metal grating against metal filled the night air as the chain shifted in its socket. The stench of it, even in the severe cold, was enough to make her gag. Only the shock of her run and laxity of her mind afterward had kept her from noticing before. Marek stared at the body for a long moment, barely registering what she was seeing through the veil of the day's events. Without taking her eyes from it, she pulled up her hood and stumbled back to the road, mind now as numb as her frozen fingers.

Only a short distance farther down the road, a metal cage shifted in its wooden supports, suspended by a chain. Marek recognized the place, though she'd never seen it in person. Death Hill, they called it. The place where thieves, murderers, and runaways were taken to die.

The road took her straight by the cage. Marek told herself not to look, but found her eyes peering inside it anyway as she passed. A bearded, long-haired man stared back at her, eyes hard and very much alive. He was dirty, stank like a week-old cut of meat left in the sun, and looked as if he'd been beaten, but Marek recognized him almost immediately, even without his red Vitalion armor. The soldier who had rescued her from the men in the alleyway.

She kept on walking.

Gods take this cursed place.

Hammerhead's Inn lay atop a large rise, nestled back among the trees. Marek clambered up the steep slope, grateful that the brace on her twisted foot kept her from tripping and stumbling back down the path. The slope was steep enough that she would have rolled a goodly distance before stopping. That is, if she hadn't run into a tree or slammed against a boulder first.

Even with the brace, exhaustion slowed her step to almost a crawl. Her eyelids drooped and her pains had shifted from individual burning lines into a single dull ache which covered her from head to foot. Her mind felt as if it were covered in a thick fog, or else half frozen over, like a lake mostly covered in ice. She focused on each step, watching her feet moving along the ground.

Reaching the crest of the hill, Marek allowed herself to stop and look up, surveying the inn. The inn was multiple stories tall, fashioned of brick on the lower sections and whitewashed plaster and wood on the upper portion, and sat in a pool of murky light cast by a dozen crackling braziers set about the grounds. Lights shone from the windows around the main door, which was closed, though the other windows were dark squares set in the lighter backdrop of the pristine walls. Smells and sounds wafted out from the inn and Marek breathed it in, feeling the pulse of life wash through her, cutting through the fog in her mind and easing some of her pains. A half dozen figures stood near the doorway, and the bray of horses mingled with the sounds of their low chatter and the ingress and egress from the inn. Marek waited there, at the edge of the light, for a long, long moment.

You can do this.

She took a deep breath and let it out again, mist pooling around her from the cold. Then, back straightening, she walked forward.

Men stared at her as she approached and it was all Marek could do to try and swallow her anxiety and keep walking toward the door. In this part of the Outlands, only the worst kind were out so late at night. Her mind kept playing over what had happened earlier, and that had been during the light of day. How much worse would she receive under the covering darkness of night?

She kept going. She looked back over her shoulder more than once and pointedly ignored the man relieving himself near the door when he leered at her and winked. The smell of the act was harder to ignore, but she did her best. Still, her stomach kept turning about in writhing knots that tied and untied themselves inside her. She paused at the door and looked around, but no one was even looking in her direction. She pushed the door open and stepped into the inn.

A wall of sounds, smells, and sights hit her with greater force than any of Master Vagamal's blows as soon as she stepped over the threshold. Counters and tables covered almost every inch of the main area, with enough people around each that Marek wondered if there were more here than in her entire hamlet. Conversations boomed from every direction. Every space that could possibly hold a body was filled. In just the few seconds it took for Marek to catch her breath after the initial shock, she noticed at least one dwarf, a handful of men who were clearly thieves, a half dozen armored warriors, a number of brutish-looking thugs, a dog, and even what appeared to be an orc. There were a few women as well, though they were either barmaids or foreigners whose sole intent in life appeared to be seducing vile-looking men who were already drunk enough to be free with their coin.

You can do this.

Marek pushed forward, making for the bar. A heady accumulation of smells spun around her as she moved through the crowd, the stink of sweat, dirt, and unwashed bodies most prominent among them. Behind that, a thin haze of smoke added a thickness to the air which left Marek feeling as if she'd spent far too long next to the hearth.

Men stared at her as she passed. Some of them peered at her owlishly around heavy wooden tankards, eyes barely staying in focus as they blinked in her direction. Others gave her hard looks as if wondering what she was doing there. Others still gave her the look of merchants assessing wares. She avoided those as best she could, but the thickness of the crowd was such that she didn't have much choice in the matter, really. Why would Gojun have sent her here, of all places?

Hugging one wall, Marek trudged onward. She noticed a slate writing board affixed to one wall. The orc she'd seen before was writing on it with a piece of chalk. She caught a glimpse of what it said before the press of the crowd moved her along.

Bounties.

She smiled at a large man standing near the hearth, attempting to be friendly, but he simply stared at her blankly for a few seconds before blinking and starting to sway where he stood. She stepped around him and noticed a vaguely familiar figure caressing the cheek of a tall, blonde-haired woman across the room. Was that the rogue from the cart?

A shout from one side warned her just before a pair of figures hurtled in her direction. Marek dodged to one side and narrowly avoided getting bowled over by a man locked in combat with—was that a woman?

A golden-haired woman landed a blow on the man's chest. She wore leather armor and metal bracers that glinted in the light as she struck. Since the man too was wearing leathers, the blow did little actual damage, though it knocked him back a half pace. His one remaining eye—the other lay hidden behind a massive, leather eye patch—narrowed in obvious anger. Marek staggered back against the wall as the fighting pair exchanged a few more blows, then stepped forward as their fight carried them away from her. She watched them with a strange, twisted eagerness as the fight continued.

The woman grabbed a tankard from a nearby

table as she dodged a few wild swings from her opponent. Eye Patch, for his part, pressed forward as the crowd roared, but the woman swung the tankard and struck him a resounding blow to the side of the head. He didn't even slow. His chain mail clinked as he swung again, though the woman was quick enough to duck beneath the punch. She was up again in a flash and punched him right in the eye patch before swinging both hands up over his head and pulling it down to meet with her rising knee. The sound of her knee striking flesh made Marek cringe.

Again, the man didn't slow in the least. He continued his downward motion and grabbed the woman behind the knees and lifted her clear off the ground. The crowd roared in approval as he slammed her down onto a table and whipped out a long knife. Marek's breath caught in her throat as Eye Patch lunged for the woman. She managed to pull her legs up and kick him back against a wooden support beam, though he didn't let go of the knife.

Something whirled by Marek's face in a spinning jumble of metal and wood. Her eyes tracked it even though they didn't register what it was until the axe passed clean through Eye Patch's neck and buried itself in the wooden pillar behind him with a heavy thunk. Silence fell over the room as the toppling, headless corpse hit the floor. Every eye zipped toward the bar, Marek following their look a moment later, shock slowing her reaction time.

A dwarf stood atop the bar, one thick-fingered hand still outstretched and pointing in the direction of the quavering axe. He growled low in his throat and his massive, bushy beard quivered as his deep voice broke the silence.

"I won't be sayin' it again," he growled, pointing a finger. "No fykin' blades in the establishment."

A booming roar of approval sprang up from the crowd. Marek spun around to look at the occupants of the nearest table as they raised tankards and fists into the air. She'd been so close to death today, she marveled that she could still stand with all the jumbled emotions running through her. A headless body lay only a few feet away from her boot, the sheer violence of the act that had put it there leaving her numb. At the same time, a thrill of excitement battled against the shock. This was the sort of place where things actually happened, where adventures and quests had a chance to germinate, and where life and death courted one another like lovers after a quarrel. Marek swallowed hard and watched a woman pick up a couple of feathers from off the table and then run a hand over her hair where the remaining stub of the plumage sat wrapped in her braid. The woman's face blanched white.

An old, hunchbacked orc moved toward the

body.

“Feed that mess to the pigs,” the dwarf, most likely the “Hammerhead” in “Hammerhead’s Inn,” ordered.

Marek swallowed again, tasting bile, and looked away. The soft hum of conversation returned and the busy sounds of the inn drowned out the uncomfortable noise of the orc at work. She pushed forward toward the bar, though a crowd of men wanting drinks now stood in her way. She attempted to squeeze between two of the warriors, but couldn’t even get her head past their arms. She ducked around the one on her right and tried again with a different pair of men but got similar results.

“Hammerhead!” she called. Maybe he’d hear her.

Hammerhead kept pouring drinks, spilling a fair amount onto the bar.

She opened her mouth to try again, shoving at the man next to her, but then found herself pushed roughly aside by the man on her other side. A tall, lithe, one-eyed man forced his way to the bar and slammed a gorgon’s severed head onto the bar. Marek felt her mouth drop open. How much more shock could she handle? She studied the head with morbid curiosity, though both the sight of it and the smell made her want to gag. Gorgon Slayer raised his hands to the roar of the crowd and then strode over to the large slate board with a confident swagger in his step. He planted a fist against a line on the board and then wiped it away.

"A round of drinks for the Blood Clan," Hammerhead roared, then added, "On the house." The assembled men cheered again. Did that ever stop in a place like this?

"Hammerhead!" Marek called, trying to push forward again. She jumped, but barely managed to look over the arm of the man in front of her. Why wouldn't anyone just move?

"Hammerhead!" This time he noticed her.

"Move it along now!" he shouted.

Marek pushed at a man, but got knocked aside. Frustration welled up within her and before she could really think through what she was doing, she snatched a dagger from someone's belt and, stretching over a shorter woman at the counter, slammed it down into the bar with a shout.

"Hammerhead!" she shouted.

Let him ignore that.

The dagger rang as it sank into the wood, vibrating dully. Hammerhead looked over at her and his eyes glinted beneath bushy eyebrows. He reached out and pulled the dagger free, then held it up between them in two thick fingers.

"I'm going to assume that you're new here and this is a gift so that orc over there doesn't have to polish the blood off the blade of my axe again."

Hammerhead's voice carried the rough burr of the dwarf race, though it rumbled with suppressed danger.

"I'm looking for work," Marek blurted, ignoring the shiver that ran down her spine at the matter-of-fact way Hammerhead had threatened to kill her.

"You can talk to Narne over there." He gestured toward the room behind her. Marek turned to look. One glance told her all she needed to know about Narne's occupation.

"No! Adventuring work . . . I want a chance at a bounty." She said the last part while looking down at her hands, her voice diminishing to almost a whisper. She couldn't believe she was being so bold, but now that she was in the middle of it, why not? She'd just established that this was a place for adventures, after all. She smiled up at him and said with more enthusiasm, "I do magic."

"Oh," Hammerhead said, moving around the bar toward her, voice lilting, the surprise overexaggerated. "Why didn't ya say so? A magician? Well, I had no idea that all this time I'd been playing court to a real fykin' magician." By the time he got to the end of his sentence, he was standing directly in front of Marek. She was surprised to find he was taller than she, if only by a few inches. He grabbed her by one arm and spun her about roughly.

"Now get out, afore my temper turns."

Marek struggled against him, her motions desperate and as fierce as she could muster. She had nowhere else to go. If she couldn't get a bounty here of all places—well, she *had* to get a bounty. Hammerhead pulled her by one arm, his grip so strong Marek wondered if her arm would show bruises in the shape of his fingers.

"In the name of the Goddess, Ana-Sett, I demand an audience with Orrin Tuck." A clear, feminine voice rang out over the noise, silencing it as easily as Hammerhead had with his axe.

Marek turned to look at the speaker and saw Hammerhead do the same out of the corner of her eye. The woman stood in the exact center of the room, garbed in white robes that covered her from neck to foot. Long red hair cascaded down each shoulder and an amulet glinted in the flickering light where it hung from a cord around her neck. She wore a long white travel cloak that draped over one arm. One hand gripped the end of a thick, ironbound staff. The likeness of an owl, the symbol of the Goddess Ana-Sett, rested on top of the staff. The woman looked weary, yet resolute, and while Marek watched, the priestess noticed them and started walking in their direction. Marek glanced up at Hammerhead, who had released her, and upon noticing he was distracted promptly stole back the dagger he'd taken and dropped to the floor and out of sight.

"The fykin' women tonight . . ." Hammerhead grumbled.

The priestess came to stand before Hammerhead. Where Marek hid beneath the table, she was able to hear their conversation without any difficulty whatsoever.

"Are you Orrin Tuck?" the priestess asked. Her voice was soft and melodic.

"Hammerhead's what they be callin' me now."

"I am Teela, of the order of Ana-Sett, sent to plead your help. Orcs raided my temple two nights past and my people were slain or taken by foul beasts. I seek heroes to win their freedom."

"Have you any gold?" Hammerhead's voice was hard. Unfriendly.

Marek couldn't see Teela's face from where she hid beneath the table, but Marek could sense her hesitation when she spoke.

"I have some," she said, in a halting voice. "Two hundred silver."

Hammerhead laughed. "That's not gold. That might get you a fykin' fingernail and some hair from a hero."

"Please. You and your kind were friends to the order in times of old."

Marek felt impressed that despite the clear pleading in the words, Teela kept any sign of desperation from her voice.

Hammerhead's thick eyebrows came together over his nose and he frowned. "Times of old are olden times now, and those heroes lie shriveled in the dirt. I have no use for causes and neither does any man here today."

"They have my sister!"

Hammerhead pursed his lips as he considered her words, then raised his chin and shouted out over the noise. "Does any man here want to help save this lass's sister who was kidnapped by a band of marauding orcs? The pay is two hundred silver pieces."

The room exploded into laughter. Marek peeked out from beneath the table to look at Teela's face. Unshed tears made her deep blue eyes look like cool springs on a summer's day. Marek bit her lower lip, a plan forming in the back of her mind. It was a foolish plan at best, suicidal at worst, but it was the only chance she had.

"There's the door," Hammerhead said to the priestess with a nod toward the exit. "I suggest ya use it."

Without a word, Teela turned and pushed her way through the throng toward the door.

Hammerhead growled low in his throat and walked back toward the bar. As soon as he had passed where she hid, Marek scrambled out from under the table. Hammerhead stopped suddenly in his tracks.

"If I just fykin' saw who I think I fykin' saw," Hammerhead said, freezing Marek where she was, "she'd better be here to sell herself as a whore!"

Marek leapt to her feet, plastering a confident smile on her face that she didn't actually feel.

"I'll take that bounty," she said.

Hammerhead gave her a flat look. Marek turned and ran to the nearest table and then clambered up on top of it. The men at her table leered up at her lecherously. Marek grinned out at the crowd as every eye in the place turned toward her.

"I am forming a team," she said in a loud voice that carried to the far corners of the room. "Any of you is welcome to join my team. I bring the skill of magic."

Laughter was her only answer.

CHAPTER 7

Teela clutched her amulet in her left hand, eyes closed as she prayed to her Goddess.

Bless me, Goddess. Please. I must find a way to do this—help me find heroes who can help me save my sister. She's one of your daughters too.

The door to the inn opened, and a roar of raucous laughter rolled out of the common room. She shuddered at the mere memory of the depravity and debauchery she'd witnessed within that place. Men drinking, cursing, and fighting as if they had no dignity or honor left in them. The looks they'd given her made her skin crawl and yet at the same time made her flush. The women she'd seen in there were, if anything, even worse. Teela thought she'd even seen the vilest of all sinners: harlots. How could those women sell their virtue for a taste of hard iron coin? She felt sick.

Booted feet thumped on the landing and Teela opened her eyes, letting her amulet fall to her chest. She started walking away, her step firm though she didn't yet know where she was going. Something thumped to the ground just behind her and someone let out an undignified squawk amidst an uproar of laughter, but Teela didn't bother turning around to see what had happened.

"Careful," a voice called. "She's got magic."

Teela ignored the voice. She'd come here because it was the only place she could think to start after tracking the orcs that had taken her sister and several of the others from the Goddess's holy temple. As a young acolyte in the order who ran away from her home to escape an arranged marriage, Teela had sated her boredom and curiosity with stories of the adventurous Redthorns from decades past. They'd been a group of warriors so renowned and feared throughout the land that even the great dark wizard Szorlock had fallen before them. She'd heard one of the elders once say that the great Orrin Tuck had retired to this inn and, having nowhere else to go after discovering what had happened to her sister and the others who'd been taken prisoner, had come here. Orrin Tuck. He was no hero. The world had changed. The Vitalion Empire had enslaved this corner of the Outlands and broken the wills of any would-be heroes long over ten years before.

"Wait!" The sound of footfalls rushing up behind her made Teela turn.

A young woman, perhaps only nineteen years of age, with black hair and full, wide-set eyebrows rushed up to her, face flushed. Teela gave her a critical look up and down, noting her abnormally small stature.

"You need help," the girl said.

Teela frowned. Of course she needed help. That much was obvious to anyone who'd been listening.

"In there. I heard you," the girl continued.

"I require seasoned adventurers," Teela said. "Heroes even. Not young girls."

She hiked up her skirts and prepared to leave. She felt tears well up in her eyes again and turned away. Why were the Gods tormenting her so?

"I have a team," the girl blurted. "My name is Marek. I lead a team."

Teela turned back, using every ounce of her remaining will not to roll her eyes. As she turned, she noticed a strange metal contraption strapped to one of the girl's feet.

"You have a limp." Teela turned away again.

"No one else will help you," Marek said. The words struck Teela like a blow and she stopped, though she didn't turn to acknowledge the girl, but Marek continued anyway. "Hammerhead said it. The mission is too dangerous and you have too little to pay."

Teela turned back. "And you," she said. "You do not fear it?"

"No. Should I?"

"Yes." Teela stepped forward, feeling the odd burning in her chest that she'd always understood to be the Goddess whispering to her.

Though she rarely understood why it came when it did, or always exactly what it meant, Teela had learned to trust it when it came. She reached out a hand and placed her fingers on the side of Marek's head, index and middle finger above and thumb below.

Images flashed through Teela's mind. An owl, the symbol of the Goddess, sat in front of smoldering embers that danced through the air like little insects. Then images of the Goddess herself. Death greeted her next, and a vision of Marek consumed by magic as she used it, and then other images still that flitted so fast through Teela's mind that she couldn't even begin to describe them. She was left with a strange swelling of emotions within her, both fear and confusion chasing each other through her chest. Beyond that, however, the Goddess had left her with a clear, burning answer to the girl's entreaty.

"Two hundred silver pieces, full sum upon completion," Teela said. "It will be dangerous, but with care, we may anticipate survival."

Marek's mouth widened into a delighted smile. How could the girl be smiling in the face of everything Teela had just seen and everything she'd just told the girl about the quest?

"You won't regret this," Marek said.

"I very much doubt that."

"Give me until fourth watch," Marek said, pulling up her cloak and moving around Teela.

"We'll meet at the stone circle at dawn."

Marek nodded and dashed off down the road, looking entirely too happy about the whole thing. Teela spun to watch her disappear into the darkness, wondering if she'd just made a serious mistake. The Goddess, however, had made her will clear. Teela would not stop trusting her now.

Marek crouched in the long grass in the darkness, fighting a yawn and simultaneously wondering if she were just a little crazy. Gojun had told her to find herself a party to join as a conjurer. She'd simply seized on the moment presented her. The situation with the priestess hadn't been an ideal opportunity, but, considering she was a nobody slave girl on the run from nearly killing her former master, it was better than she likely deserved. Now, all she had to do was gather a team and be back to meet with the priestess before dawn. That wouldn't be too hard, would it?

In the back of Marek's mind she laughed at herself.

Down below, on the road itself, two Vitalion

guards laughed and poked their swords into one of the cages suspended over the road. The corpse into which Marek had bumped earlier that night swung slightly in the mild breeze near them. Inside the cage, a man dodged the penetrating swords and kicked them away.

"Dance, man, dance!" The two guards laughed as the man inside the cage executed a particularly energetic maneuver to avoid getting cut.

Marek bit her lower lip, considering her options. The man in the cage was the one who had saved her from the man in the alley and his thugs earlier. Despite that, or maybe because of it, he was now suspended in the cage at the mercy of men who'd likely been his peers up until now. If she was to free him, she'd need to distract the two guards and . . .

The guards gave one last great guffaw of laughter and then sheathed their swords. After a moment, they spat into the cage and started walking down the road. Marek waited for the space of thirty heartbeats before hurrying down the hill toward the caged man. What she was about to attempt was probably stupid. She could get caught, or worse. She had no guarantee it would work or even that the man would help her if she released him, but it was a place to start at least. Every adventuring group of which she'd ever heard had at least one true warrior in it. He or she was the one who could take the beatings and dish it back out, protecting the healers and conjurers from harm. This man seemed to have a particular knack for that sort of work.

As soon as Marek reached the swinging cage, she started turning it so she could look the soldier in the eyes. He'd taken a seat in the bottom of the heavy iron contraption, arms held limp over his knees. What was left of his clothes was dirty and torn, smeared with mud, sweat, and the red-brown mar of rust from the cage itself. His face was scuffed, bloodied, and bruised, and his eyes had the half-closed look of one who was simply biding his time without a care in the world. Before Marek had even finished turning the cage, however, he began speaking.

"I know you," he said in a slow, deliberate voice. "You're that slave girl who got me thrown into this cage."

"Marek." She glanced over her shoulder at the two guards, who appeared to be chatting down at the end of the road. They weren't looking in her direction, but Marek felt sweat bead on her forehead anyway.

"Peregus had some influential friends in my regiment."

Marek turned back to the soldier, meeting his deep, powerful eyes. There was a depth to them

Marek hadn't expected. It was like the look Gojun gave her when talking about the history of the Deiran kingdom and its fall to the Vitalion Invasion. It was the look of a man who'd seen too much and spoken of it far too little.

"I'm here to free you," Marek said. The soldier continued to meet her gaze with the same haunted expression in his eyes. "All I need is for you to swear an oath to me."

The soldier flicked his eyes to the side in a sort of visual shrug. "Why not?"

"I need a swordsman. For a bounty. Join me and we'll win it together."

The soldier laughed. It was a somewhat broken sound, almost a cough, but the grin which covered his bruised face left little doubt of his true intent.

"You're joking." He looked over at her and the smile faded. Marek gave him a hard look as if to say *that's right, I'm serious,* but wasn't entirely sure she managed the expression properly.

"You're not joking."

Marek shook her head. Of course she wasn't joking. Why else did he think she was here? Insecurity welled up within her, sticking her tongue to the roof of her mouth and refusing to let her speak. She simply waited, holding the soldier's gaze. He looked down at her over the end of his too large, very broken nose and a faraway look came into his eyes.

"Long ago, I swore an oath to the Vitalion Empire," he said. His hands grasped the sides of the cage and wrapped around the cool, dark iron bars there as it swayed. "That oath took me across the world and into this cage. I'm done with oaths."

Marek stepped forward, seizing the bottom of the cage to keep it from moving. She pressed her face closer to the bars.

"I saw you in the alley. You're a brave man." She felt a lump well up in her throat. If it hadn't been for him, this night would have gone very differently for her. She'd still have been awake, and just as tired, most likely, but for entirely different reasons.

"I wouldn't go that far."

"No more masters or magistrates," Marek said, leaning closer still. "We'll create our own destinies."

"And what would those destinies hold for us, little marmot?"

Marek tightened her jaw and said with as much conviction as she could muster, "A life of dignity."

The soldier pursed his lips and looked thoughtful. A long moment passed between them and Marek felt her heart work its way up her throat and flutter there. Eventually, he nodded and stuck a thick, calloused hand through the bars of the cage.

"Well, friend," he said, "for a life of dignity."

Marek grasped his hand and felt her heart

plummet back into her chest and light a fire of pride and victory there. She squeezed his hand and then released it, stepping back from the cage and moving along the side until she found the chains and lock holding it closed.

Inside the cage, the soldier laughed, head tilting back toward the stars.

Marek picked up the lock in one hand and then stepped back, preparing herself to do magic. Unlocking things was a simple enough spell, under the right conditions. Given the current circumstances, she prayed to the Gods it would actually work.

"Eleno Respar," Marek muttered, intoning the words of the spell Gojun had taught her.

"Oh Gods . . ." the soldier pushed himself back in the cage as far from her as he could get.

"Eleno Respar."

Nothing happened.

Why isn't this working?

Down the road, the two soldiers who'd been tormenting the caged man noticed something was going on and shouted something incoherent. Marek ignored them, clearing her mind as she'd been trained. A small seed of doubt worked through her mind, but she managed to stomp on it and fully clear her thoughts.

"Oh," the caged soldier said, glancing back and

making the cage rock back and forth. "Here come the guards. Maybe one of them has a key."

Marek ignored his vain attempt at humor and focused on the lock, forcing her will into it through her mind and upraised hands. It *would* burst. It *would* open.

It will!

The lock exploded in a massive flash of flame and smoke. Marek leapt back, surprised as much by the spell working as by the sudden, blinding light. Inside the cage, the soldier scrambled to his feet.

"Rathos's balls!" he swore and leapt from the cage.

Marek waited long enough for his feet to hit the ground and then started running, her new companion only a step behind. The guards chased after them, closing the gap at an incredible speed. Marek ran a few paces, flush with the success of freeing the man and the spell actually working like it was supposed to, before she noticed that her companion wasn't with her any longer. She turned just in time to see the soldier, clad only in a white tunic top and breeches, face down two fully armed and armored opponents.

The soldier ducked down under the first guard's strike and let the man roll over the top of him, leaving the guard sprawled on the ground behind him. The second guard rushed in, but the soldier stepped forward into the charge and grabbed the man by the wrist, stopping the sword stroke. In the space of half a breath, the soldier brought his forehead down into the guard's face once, twice, and then a third time. Marek marveled at the sheer brutality of it. The soldier caught the guard he'd been beating by the back of his head and brought his knee up into his chest in a mirror of the move he'd used on one of Peregus's men earlier that day. The man fell without a sound.

The first guard was getting back to his feet, but before he could even make it to his knees, Marek's companion was upon him. He kicked the guard in the face, knocking him to the ground, and grabbed his sword as he fell. In one smooth motion and with a roar, Marek's companion brought the sword down and ran it through the man's chest, chain mail and all.

Marek held a hand to her lips and then let it fall toward the ground. She'd seen a lot of death and violence today, both as a witness and as a participant. But the sheer brutality of it. This man she'd just saved had killed not just one man, but many, and done it with the ease of a horse relieving himself on the road. When she'd imagined fights such as these before, she'd thought of them as a glorious contest of strength and will, a mighty dance between foes with exchanges of blows following some sort of code of conduct. This had been a violent, quick thing, over and done with in less than the time it took to heat up a pot of water for Master Vagamal's morning tea. Marek swallowed and stumbled over toward where the soldier had stopped by one of the fallen men. He had grabbed the man's sword and was testing the heft of it in his hand.

"The name's Thane."

Marek searched for something to say as Thane rummaged through the man's pockets and helped himself to a number of the man's possessions. In the end, she simply said the first thing to come to mind.

"We need a thief." It was a stupid thing to say, really, even if it was true.

"Well," Thane said, removing a scabbard and belt from the fallen man. "It's Thore's day. I believe there's one coupling with my commander's wife."

CHAPTER 8

The trip back into the city was relatively uneventful, though it came with more than a twinge of unease inside Marek's gut. She worried that word of what she'd done to Master Vagamal would have reached this far already, though they didn't encounter a single sign of the mob which had chased her out of the village or even a heightened alertness to the watch. If anything, the Vitalion guards they passed seemed as lax as they always did, lounging at their posts and idly chatting among themselves. They didn't even give them a second glance as they entered the city.

Thane led Marek through the narrow streets, avoiding the main roadways as much as possible. The sounds of the city at night were different than those of the day, if no less unique and foreign to Marek as the sounds at Hammerhead's Inn had been. The daytime city carried the sound of a broken, chaotic master beating slaves. At night, insects buzzed and chirped and, near homes they passed, the soft crackle of flame in well-tended hearths could be heard. It was a quiet, subdued sound, like what Marek had always pictured a loving family would sound like.

They passed down the street where Gojun Pye's house stood. The door was closed fast and not a single light shone through the windows. Marek swallowed her disappointment and pointedly ignored the alleyway where she'd first met Thane earlier that day. Thankfully it was dark enough to hide the blood which stained the cobbles red.

As they continued to pass through the city, Marek let her mind wander back over Gojun's sudden exit. The wizard did tend to leave from time to time, off on one errand or another, but each of those had been planned excursions. They were always some sort of journey with a clear and present task to be accomplished. They were thought out and planned in advance. This . . . this had been a chaotic jumble of decisions and hasty departures. If Gojun was to be believed, he didn't have any intention of returning, or else why would he have burned his things? It didn't make any sense. Marek felt a pang of regret mixed with a surprising amount of anger. Gojun was the one she usually turned to when things went ill with her master. He would have been able to help her figure out what she'd done and how she'd done it, perhaps even show her how to master it. He could have saved her. But no . . . now he was gone, and that was fine with her. She could do this on her own just as readily.

I will!

Thane held up a hand and Marek almost ran into it before managing to pull herself out of her own thoughts. A boy played in the street ahead of them, but that couldn't have been the reason he'd stopped her, could it? She shot him a quizzical look. He motioned for her to crouch and they inched forward toward a large manor house in almost the exact center of the city near where the Vitalion Garrison lay. Once they'd managed to partially secret themselves behind a cart, Marek was able to pick out the rather raucous sounds coming from an open window in a second story tower near them.

"Well," Thane said matter-of-factly, "there's our thief."

Marek hissed at the boy playing down the street, attempting to get his attention. He threw a stick at the ground and didn't look in her direction.

"Boy," Marek called, then again more insistently, "Boy!"

He glanced at her and then looked away, throwing a small stone after the stick. Was he purposely ignoring her? Marek felt a small rush of irritation take her and wrinkled her nose, brows coming together above it.

"Boy!" she said again, almost as a growl.

The boy looked over at her and then half walked, half crawled over to her. He looked rather sheepish and he knelt before them.

"Go around the corner and tell the guards you saw a man climb into that window."

The boy looked up over his shoulder toward the direction she indicated. More sounds flooded down to them which were probably not appropriate for the boy to be hearing, but he didn't seem at all surprised to hear them.

He looked back at her and the skin around his eyes crinkled in confusion. "What's on your leg?"

Marek frowned. That's what he was curious about? Her leg?

"Go!" she snapped, making a shooing gesture.

The boy got to his feet and scampered off, retrieving his stone as he passed it, though he left the stick behind.

"What *is* that on your leg?" Thane asked, as the boy ran off.

Before Marek could answer, distinct voices suddenly came down from the window above. A feminine voice cried out in muted alarm.

"My husband's back. Here, take these."

The words drew Marek's gaze like a moth to flame and she looked up at the window in time to see the shutters pushed aside and a half-naked man appear at the window's edge just after a bundle of clothes hit the cobblestones of the street below. Marek recognized the man immediately.

The thief from the back of the hay wagon.

She felt her lips curl into a silent snarl. She looked over at Thane, but then flipped her head back as she heard movement from the window. A woman clutching a sheet over herself kissed the thief and then stepped back into the room out of Marek's sight. The thief, for his part, stepped up onto the window's ledge with surprisingly lithe grace. Thankfully, he was wearing both his boots and a pair of tight leather leggings. He turned back into the room for half a moment and blew a kiss back in the direction of the woman, then threw himself from the window. He dropped the twenty or so feet and landed with ease on the street next to the pile of loose clothing, bending at the knees to absorb the force of the blow. He immediately leapt back to his feet and turned back to the window, where the half-naked blonde woman held one hand to the sheet around her chest and used the other to blow a second kiss down to the thief.

Gods, she looks hideous.

The thief bent and gathered up his clothes and Thane pushed forward. Marek almost laughed aloud as the thief righted himself just in time for his nose to meet Thane's club-like fist. The thief dropped to the ground and Thane promptly placed a booted foot against his throat to keep him from getting up. Marek smiled to herself. Thane might be brutal, but he sure was effective. She placed a foot, her braced one to be precise, on the thief's wrist.

"What is that thing on your foot?" he asked in a strained voice.

"Where's my money?

"I have no idea what you're talking about."

"In the hay wagon." Marek kept her voice even, but she spoke each word deliberately and accentuated them with wide eyes and an expression which she hoped clearly said she didn't believe him.

"I meet a lot of women in the hay," the thief said with a grin, somehow managing to still look relaxed and unconcerned despite having Thane's foot poised to crush his windpipe. "No offense, but I can't say I remember you, sweetheart."

Fine.

Marek stomped her other foot high up on his thigh, the heel digging into the space between his legs. He winced and tried to squirm back, but Thane's foot held him in place.

"I think it's coming to me," he said. His voice had gained a much higher pitch for some reason.

Marek held back a small laugh, but then once again her eyes were drawn upward as shouting sounded from the open window above.

"What manner of insult is it that you bring to me, to this house?" A man with short-cropped hair and fine clothes which spoke of money leaned out the window. The half-naked woman that had been kissing the thief only moments before screeched something at the man, but he shoved her aside with a shout of "Get away, you whore!"

"Can we maybe discuss this somewhere else?" the thief said, eyes meeting Marek's. Above them, the well-dressed man's shouting continued.

"Take your time," Thane said and, by way of response, lifted his foot for long enough to kick the thief in the chest, then placed it back against his throat.

"All right, all right," the thief said between fits of coughing. "Given my very limited knowledge on thieves I would assume your money is gone, gambled away or spent on very, very expensive women."

Marek dug her heel into his arm. "You bastard!"

"Most probably."

The thief twisted to one side and, before Marek even registered the movement, whipped back the other direction and swept Thane's legs out from under him. Thane toppled to the ground with a shout. Marek felt like she should do something, react somehow, but the thief had a foot planted in her stomach in the very next moment. She stumbled back, and twisted, suddenly off balance. She sucked in a breath and let out a gasp of pain.

The next moment, one of the thief's arms was around her throat and the other held Marek's own dagger against her flesh there.

Marek blinked. How had he gotten to his feet so fast? His grip around her neck was stronger than she'd expected, so strong, in fact, that she could barely breathe. She wrapped her hands around his forearm and tried to pull it away from her, but it was like trying to push against stone.

"Sorry, sweetheart," he hissed in her ear, "but I'm a harder catch than that."

"We're here to make you an offer," Marek said. She twisted so she could see his face out of the corner of her eye. "I need you for one mission."

This close to him, pressed against his warm flesh and smelling the scent of him, Marek found herself more than a little distracted. The knife at her throat proved useful in reversing some of that distraction, as did the shouting from the window above, but even together they only partially helped.

The thief chuckled softly. "No chance, m'lady."

"Then we'll let the magistrate have you," Thane said, his bearded lips curling into a mocking sneer. "And she keeps your clothes." Thane pointed at him with his sword—a rather direct threat, even for Thane.

"What is the pay?"

"Fifty silver," Marek replied. She regretted the

words almost as soon as she'd said them. She'd turned the phrase upward at the end, making it almost a question rather than a statement. She cursed herself as the thief clearly sensed her insecurity and pounced.

"A hundred." He countered.

Of course, his voice was firm.

A warning bell sounded in the distance. Marek recognized the sound as the signal calling the guard. Shouts of alarm came from down a side street. The thief's grip shifted slightly but didn't loosen as he twisted to look in that direction. Then his hands tightened and he pressed the dagger more firmly against Marek's throat. She felt his body twist behind her and felt a flush creep across her face and warm her chest.

"A hundred," he repeated, more firmly this time.

"Is now really the time to haggle?" Marek asked. She wasn't sure if she was trying to buy time or if the question was some sort of odd haggling strategy of her own. Either way, the thief didn't seem bothered in the least. He shrugged, and the dagger's tip dug into her throat. Searing pain shot through her.

"Seventy-five!" she almost shouted.

"What?" Thane asked.

Above them, the well-dressed man appeared in the window and shouted down the street toward the sounds of the alarm bell.

"Have him destroyed!"

The thief sucked in a breath and the dagger disappeared from Marek's throat almost at the same instant as he shoved her forward away from him.

"I'm in," he said, then grabbed his clothes off the street and dashed down an alleyway.

After sharing a startled looked, Marek and Thane hurried after him.

CHAPTER 9

Gojun leaned low over the neck of his horse. A light rain covered his hands in a fine mist where they clutched the reins and stained his gray cloak a darker, more somber hue. The steady clop of his horse's hooves against the stones of the ancient path was a hollow, muted sound. The air hung heavy with the smell of dampened earth, greenery, and the press of trees close about him. Gojun shivered and blew a droplet of water off the end of his nose, then straightened in his saddle, a flicker of movement catching his eye.

He reined in his horse, keeping a hand on its neck to keep it quiet. Goose bumps formed on his arms and crawled across his skin until all the hair there stood on end. Gojun peered into the mist around him, watching for movement. Tree branches devoid of leaves made black smudges in the gray mist, looking for all the world like the polearms of orcs or other weaponry. After a moment, Gojun relaxed. He was jumping at shadows again.

Clicking his horse back into motion, Gojun slumped back over in his saddle and pulled the hood of his cloak down low. He rubbed a hand across his chin, feeling the rasp of stubble against his palm and scowled. The beard itself didn't bother him. He'd worn a beard for years before the Vitalions came. Since then, he'd been forced to go clean-shaven and inauspicious, hidden in plain sight in Merren's backwater hellhole. Gods take that place. No, what bothered him was that in the twenty years he'd lived in relative seclusion, he'd grown soft as a newborn babe. How had he missed the signs of Szorlock's machinations?

He wondered idly if Marek had made it back to her little hamlet safely. The Vitalion guards were, among other things, a rather harsh lot toward slaves as a whole, even more so when that slave had a deformity like Marek's. He would have been worried about her if he hadn't spent almost her entire life helping her learn the harsh realities of living under the rule of an unkind master. He'd been there to guide and direct her, but never to defend her. Even if he'd wanted to, that sort of thing would have hurt more than helped her. No, this way she knew how to defend herself, knew how to hold her own, and had the street smarts and wisdom to get herself out of most situations. The only thing she lacked was a bit of confidence. Perhaps Orrin Tuck would be able to help her out with that. Gojun made a mental note to send a missive to him at some point in the future, then dismissed the entire train of thought. Marek would be fine either way, whether his departure had saddened her or not and whether she'd made it back before nightfall or not. Such was the life of a slave.

Something moved in the gloom to one side of him and Gojun reacted without thinking. He brought up one hand in a curt chopping motion. A hissing, whirling something struck a spot in the air only a foot or two from Gojun's head, stopping midair in a cascade of cold, white light. The thing hung there for a moment, sizzling, then dropped to the ground. A smell of char lingered in the air.

"Get down offen that horse, wizard," a rough voice bellowed from inside the tree line opposite where the attack originated.

Gojun grinned. "I think not. Show yourself, you great, ugly brute."

A boom of laughter rolled out from the gathering fog. Gojun turned in the direction of the sound as a massive figure materialized from the gloom. Even in the wan light which pierced the clouds, the man's grizzled hair shone with the luster of being wet, plastered to the side of his wide, craggy face. It hung well past his shoulders, though it was in a braid, as was his long, salt-and-pepper beard. If it hadn't been, Gojun knew from personal experience that the beard would have been so large and bushy as to cover his entire chest, which was quite the feat. At a few inches over six feet tall, Gojun was no small man himself, but the mountainous man before him made him look like a child.

"Gojun," the man said. He lifted a dinner-plate-sized hand in greeting, the hand clutching an axe so large it could cleave an ogre in two with a single blow as if the axe weighed less than a walking staff.

"Kynall." Gojun nodded over at the man, unable to keep an amused grin off his face. "What's with the theatrics?"

"New kid."

Gojun arched an eyebrow. New kid?

A low, whistling hum was the only warning Gojun received before something hard slammed into him. Pain exploded across his back. Ropes coiled around him as a large metal sphere spun around his arms and upper body. The ropes got shorter and shorter until the metal sphere at the end smacked hard against his chest. His horse reared up in fright, and the momentum of the horse and the force of the blow knocked Gojun free of the saddle. He hit the ground hard and the pain which flared in his side was only rivaled by the anger that surged up with it.

His arms were pinned to his sides by the rope—he recognized the weapon now, a bolas—but, as a wizard, his true strength didn't lie in the use of his arms. He stilled his mind, ignoring the pain and forcing his will toward a single purpose. He hadn't seen his attacker, nor had Kynall so far betrayed even the slightest sound, but that didn't matter now. What mattered was freeing his hands.

He spoke a single word. The ropes around him split and Gojun rolled to his feet. Even as he stood, he turned, facing the direction from which the attack had come. He spread his hands wide, ready to dart into motion or else reach for spell components hidden within secret pockets in his cloak. Pain still gripped him, but it was a small nuisance now, masked by the anger and focus burning through him.

"Kynall," he growled. His gaze flitted through the trees, searching for any signs of movement that would give away his attacker's position. "Circle around to the left and get behind . . ." He trailed off.

Is that my horse?

Gojun's horse had bolted when he'd been tossed free, but Gojun could just make out its blurry form appearing through the drizzling rain. Someone was leading it.

The sound of Kynall's booming laughter made Gojun groan. He turned to his friend of forty years to see the giant of a man bent over at the waist, hugging his stomach as he shook with laughter.

"Pranks like that are going to get you killed

someday," Gojun said drily. He brushed himself off and prodded his arm and then his ribs one at a time to make sure none of them were broken. "And I'll be the one to do it, most likely."

Kynall waved a hand and straightened, snorting as he met Gojun's gaze. "I've missed you too. I don't trust you, mind, but I've missed you."

"I'd hate to see what you'd do if you didn't," Gojun grumbled. Mud spattered his cloak both where he'd landed on it and where he'd then rolled while getting to his feet. Most of the pain had subsided to a dull ache, but as he'd been cold and mildly damp before, he was now cold, completely wet, and irritated. Still, he couldn't help but return the smile when Kynall grinned at him.

"A right bad time of it you'd have, I'm sure." Only a small touch of malice darkened the otherwise jovial tone. Gojun supposed he deserved that at least, considering the circumstances of their last meeting almost twenty years ago.

Kynall's head turned to look down the trail and Gojun followed his gaze.

The man leading the horse stood straight and tall as he regarded Gojun, hard eyes belying his youthful, clean-shaven face. His sandy brown hair hung down past his shoulders, and his face was one ladies might call handsome. He walked with the grace and poise of a man accustomed to battle, though his hands only had a few scars. A cloak hung over his shoulders, though it did little to hide the brace of knives strapped horizontally across his chest or the pair of bolas hanging from his belt. As he turned, Gojun noticed several glints of metal beneath his cloak and guessed several more knives were strapped to his back.

How many does he need?

"Where'd you pick him up?" Gojun asked, raising an eyebrow in Kynall's direction.

The big man shrugged. "He's useful to have around. Handy with a knife and silent as the grave when moving through the woods."

The corner of Gojun's mouth twitched upward. "Unlike you, my old friend. You sound like a herd of wild pigs."

Kynall snorted. "Quiet enough to surprise you."

Fair point.

"Come on, we've got a cave up here where we've been waiting for you. What took you so long?"

"I didn't get your missive until yesterday morning," Gojun said, "and I had some things to attend to. You there, fetch me my staff, will you?"

The tall youth scowled. "Fetch it yourself, old man. I'm not your manservant."

He threw the reins of Gojun's horse to him and pushed roughly past him, his face a dark cloud. Gojun retrieved his staff from beneath the girth strap of his horse's saddle and turned back to Kynall, gesturing for the big man to lead the way. Kynall's eyes danced, but he didn't say anything, just chuckled softly. The youth had already vanished into the mist.

"What did you summon me for, Kynall?" Gojun asked as they walked, his staff thumping against dirt and stone.

Kynall growled and spat to the side. "'Tis dark talk to be having out in the open. Wait till we're in the cave by the fire, will you? Besides, you summoned me, you old conjurer, pulling on your strings like some great spider in a web. You always know which strand to pull, and which to cut away."

Gojun felt a chill run down his spine. He pointedly ignored the spider commentary and all the painful, dark memories it dredged up along with it. Kynall was a warrior through and through, almost as skilled in battle as Orrin Tuck, and he'd been the greatest among the Redthorns back in the day. Gojun had personally seen the man stare down a dragon without a trace of fear and defeat an ogre with nothing but his bare hands and then laugh about it afterward. Fear was as foreign to him as fire was to a duck. Only one thing could rattle him so badly.

"Szorlock?"

"Fyke it, man," Kynall sputtered. "I said let it

wait till we're in the cave."

Gojun grunted and Kynall resumed walking, muttering profanities under his breath and swinging his massive axe absently. Gojun made sure to stay out of its reach.

Szorlock.

He'd known that's what it had to be. Nothing else could have brought Kynall this far south, far from where he normally called home. The Redthorns had each gone their separate ways two decades ago, each about their own tasks. Last he'd heard, only Orrin had settled down to any real living, if that's what you could call running a semi-legal inn that harbored magic users, bounty hunters, and the worst of the dregs of all the races which called the Outlands home.

Kynall led him off the path after a moment and toward a cliff face. A cave's mouth appeared in the gloom and Kynall entered without a moment's pause. It was large enough for a horse to enter, so Gojun led the animal in with him. It took a moment for Gojun's eyes to adjust to the gloom, but when they did, he took in the large space, fire crackling merrily in one corner. At some point, someone had crafted a fireplace out of stones and clay, a flue directing the smoke out through a crack in the ceiling. A pair of horses was tethered deep within the cave and they whickered softly to his own steed, who returned the sound. A pair of rumpled bedrolls lay near the fire.

"Jaffin," Kynall said, "tether his horse with ours. He'll be here a night, but then I imagine he'll be off again before first light."

Gojun raised an eyebrow, but let the tall youth, Jaffin, take his reins again. He tried not to smile at the young man.

Kynall gestured to the fire, where a pot of what smelled like a lemongrass tea was bubbling. Gojun followed him and took a seat on the ground.

"What news, Kynall?" Gojun said, accepting a warm cup of steaming tea from the massive man. "Why did you summon me?"

Kynall blew on his tea and took a sip before answering, the cup looking tiny in his large hands. Finally, he looked up and met Gojun's eyes.

"Szorlock is searching for the Darkspore," he said slowly, "and I think he may have found a piece."

"Where?" Gojun demanded, spilling tea over himself in his haste. He cursed as the hot liquid burned his legs and scalded his hand, but he pushed aside the pain. "How? No one knows where all the pieces are, not even me."

The Darkspore. The heart of the Lich King. The power to not just destroy, but to unmake. Power over death.

"A brilliant idea, that," Jaffin said. Gojun turned

his head in that direction, watching the scowling youth walk up to them. "Would've been better just to destroy the thing instead of trying to hide it."

Gojun ignored him and turned back to Kynall. "Speak, friend."

Kynall scowled and peered down into his cup as if searching for answers.

"After the Redthorns disbanded, we all went back to our lives. Orrin became Hammerhead, you became a hermit, others disappeared altogether. It didn't sit well with me, though, the Darkspore. I became a mercenary, but I kept my eyes open, watching for Szorlock and his minions."

"As did I," Gojun said.

Kynall gave a small nod as if in acknowledgement, though it seemed more a courtesy than any real acceptance. "Couple weeks back, I was working guard for the caravan, me and the boy here, when one of them Golgotian mystics attacked us. I recognized him from the days we chased Szorlock across the world. Mekru Nom, sure as I'm living. The boy and me escaped, but we knew he was looking for something, heard him asking the caravan master about a shard and a temple afore he killed him. Sucked his soul right out of his face."

Gojun looked up at this. "Not Kishkumen?"

"Nah, that soul sucker stays as close to his master as a hound."

"And he was looking for a temple? Did he think a shard of the Darkspore lay there?"

Jaffin snorted. "I'd tell you to ask the priestesses at the temple, but they're all dead."

Gojun raised an eyebrow at Kynall. "Why is your little friend so . . . confrontational?

Kynall sighed and ran a hand through his beard, scratching at his chin. He blew out a long breath, looking as weary as Gojun had ever seen him. Jaffin's face became a dark mask.

"Ignore him, Gojun," Kynall said at length, waving a dismissive hand. "I don't—"

"No," Jaffin interrupted. "He deserves to hear it."

Gojun steepled his fingers in his lap and turned to regard the tall, thin youth. The young man stood and took a few steps closer to him, one hand making a cutting motion in the air.

"I don't believe the stories, wizard. Not the ones I hear in the taverns late at night, or the ones my father tells when he's sober." Jaffin punctuated each statement with a swipe of his hand and a marked step forward.

Gojun regarded him calmly, keeping his expression impassive. This wasn't anything he hadn't heard before.

"When he's drunk is when he gets to tales I think are true. Gojun the Betrayer, he calls you. Gojun the Foolhardy. Gojun, the man who was once my friend."

Inside, Gojun winced, though he remained calm otherwise. "Your father must not have a high opinion of himself then, if he would consort with me enough to know those stories. Few do. Fewer still are alive to tell them." Gojun put a little barb in the words on purpose.

"How dare you talk about—"

"Enough!" Kynall roared. "That's enough, Jaffin. Wait outside until Gojun and I are finished speaking."

Jaffin spun on the larger man, expression murderous, but Kynall got to his feet in one smooth motion. Though he kept his hands at his sides, the large man closed them into fists. Gojun clearly heard the knuckles pop. Jaffin didn't back down and, despite the dislike he'd developed for the young man, Gojun was impressed by the steel in his backbone.

"Wait. Outside."

Jaffin's long, thin face grew—if anything—even darker. He spun on a heel and marched from the cave in a few, quick strides. Kynall sighed again. Gojun had never known the man to get overly concerned about anything, but that was the third sigh in as many minutes. Age did strange things to men, even unmovable rocks like Kynall.

"Where'd you find him again?" Gojun asked.

"Birth." The word came out barely more than a grunt. "He's my son."

Gojun's lips twisted into a frown. "Son? How'd that happen?"

"In the regular manner, I expect."

"I mean, when did it happen? You were with the Redthorns until twenty years ago and he's got to be well over twenty-five."

"You're getting old if you think that fresh-faced fool is a day over eighteen." Kynall walked over to the fire and poured himself another cup of tea. "I met his mother a few months after the Redthorns disbanded. I wasn't much of a man then, after what happened, after . . ."

The big man's voice trailed off into a jagged, broken silence, but Gojun didn't need the rest of the sentence to fill in the information. He'd been there. It didn't need words. Even after twenty years, Kynall hadn't forgiven him. Gojun hadn't really forgiven himself either.

Kynall took a long sip of tea and then grunted, produced a flask, and poured an amber-colored liquid into his tea. "Anyway, she helped me forget. We had some kids afore she died. That one's the oldest. Best damn hand with a blade I ever seen."

Gojun raised a clearly skeptical eyebrow.

"By Tek's Great Hammer, I swear it. He's a solid

lad, if a little hard around the edges still. Hasn't had the chance to knock them smooth yet."

Gojun grunted. They'd all had to go through that at one point or another. He just hoped Jaffin lived through the process. He scratched at his chin and shook his head in amazement. Kynall with children? The image just didn't sit right in his mind.

"We're going to have to go after them, aren't we?"

Kynall's question pulled Gojun out of his thoughts. He looked up and met his old friend's eye, then slowly nodded.

"It's the Darkspore," Gojun said. "If there is, or was, one of the four shards in that temple, we have to go after it. We have to know if it was even there to begin with."

Kynall grunted. "I'll take you to the temple in the morning. I'll send the boy after the orc trail we found leading away from it."

Gojun frowned, but Kynall scowled. "Don't misjudge the boy. He hates you, sure enough, but he hates all magic users. The Vitalions have a strong presence in our homeland. They have a sure grip on the young and you know how they feel about magicians of any sort. But you'd be doing yourself a great disservice to think him a fool or even innocent. He's simply passionate. Like I was, back in our time."

Gojun waved a hand in a small circle. "No

offense, Kynall. Yes, we will go to the temple. Have the boy scout the trail and meet us back here the day after tomorrow. That should give us the time to make it to the temple and back."

Kynall took another long sip of his tea, scowled, and then tossed the cup aside. It clattered against the rocks and sprayed the ground with tea. He produced the flask from earlier and took a long pull on it directly before turning his gaze back to Gojun.

"So be it, then, wizard."

CHAPTER 10

Dawn rose through the darkness like a flame burning away a coal. Marek groaned and sat up, having only managed to grab a few hours sleep in a ditch on the side of the road while Thane had kept watch of her and the thief. She was stiff, sore, and felt as if she'd been dragged through the dirt by a team of horses. Though she'd not been able to really tell at the time with the rush of the prior day and all that had taken place, she'd pushed her body to the most it could handle and even a little beyond that. The shock had helped with a lot of it. That was gone now, after her sleep, though the effects of it would linger for far longer still.

She got to her feet anyway.

Thane and the thief were already ready, and so they set out into the early tendrils of dawn. The thief looked different fully clothed. He wore a leather vest sewn with metal disks over a tunic and a green cloak. He carried a bow and full quiver of arrows on his back, and he had a pair of curved daggers at his waist. His hair was long and mostly covered his ears, though Marek had caught a glimpse of them and their slightly pointed tips. Some sort of elf, maybe? Between that, his rugged facial features, and the confident swagger of his walk, Marek had little doubt he was as much a rogue as he seemed to think he was. She'd have to be careful of him.

They reached the base of a large hill and started to climb it. Near the apex of the hill, a ring of short, green stones lay half-buried in the earth. Marek had never been here before, but even she had heard stories of the place. Some said it was steeped in a dark magic from the days before the Vitalion Empire, back when dread sorcerers intent on the destruction of everything living battled the heroes of old and the wizards who aided them. Other stories claimed it was something built for ancient marriage ceremonies, the circle of stone symbolizing both a rock solid foundation and a relationship which would last as long as a circle. Marek preferred the former story over the latter, but regardless of which, if any, were true, its only current function was as a meeting place. Marek could just make out a figure in stark white robes who could only be Teela, the priestess of Ana-Sett, standing a dozen paces from the stones.

Marek limped a little more than she would have normally, even with the brace lending her twisted foot the strength it needed to walk. She hated the limp and the way it made people look at her, but she didn't let it slow her as she walked alongside the two taller, larger men. She simply had to take twice as many steps as they did.

They stopped a few paces away from Teela. The priestess looked over them imperiously, leaning against her staff, wind blowing her deep red hair across her face. Marek glanced at her two companions. Thane looked at the priestess with his mouth half-open, an unreadable expression on his face. Marek hadn't told him much about the job, but hoped he wasn't regretting his decision at seeing who it was that held their employ. The thief, of course, grinned rather lecherously.

"We're here," he said, then chuckled and stepped toward Teela with a noticeable swagger in his stride. "Well, well, allow me." He bowed low and extended a hand, taking Teela's as she offered it. "Dagen. And you are?"

So that was his name.

"Teela," Marek said aloud, before Dagen could try anything that would upset the priestess. "Of the order of Ana-Sett."

"A holy woman." Dagen arched one eyebrow and quirked up one side of his lips.

Teela withdrew her hand from Dagen's grip one finger at a time, as if pulling free of a mire that was slowly trying to suck her back in. She looked away from him, then met Marek's eyes, and then flicked over to Thane.

“A little girl, a Vitalion, and a miscreant,” Teela said, her eyes falling on each of them in turn as she spoke, tone imperious and more than a little skeptical. “I pray the Goddess blesses our worthy cause.”

Marek shifted uncomfortably and glanced sidelong at Thane. Who was Teela to complain about them? Who else was she going to get? Still, Marek had to fight hard to keep her face from flushing.

“Charming,” Dagen said, stepping away from her to stand next to Thane.

Teela ignored him. “There is an orc encampment ten leagues east,” she said. “My sister is held there. We will rescue her under cover of night.”

Marek frowned and looked over at Thane and Dagen. She didn’t have any real experience with adventuring, but the plan sounded like it would work. Before she could say anything, Dagen was talking again.

“You and I under the covers at night?” He tilted his head and looked Teela up and down like a horse trader looking over a new stallion brought to market. “I like it. Except without the dress, all done up and white. You stick out like a lily in a pile of pig shite.”

Thane drew his sword and stared at the hilt intently. Marek fought down a flush of irritation, though she couldn't bring herself to say anything. This was *not* how she'd wanted this meeting to go. Then again, *nothing* had gone the way it was supposed to go since yesterday morning, starting with that stupid vision spell.

"Done up?" Teela's whole face wrinkled, as if she'd actually just caught a whiff of the aforementioned pig leavings.

"Should we head out?" Marek pitched her voice loud, though kept it a question. Her hope that it would successfully steer the conversation away from Dagen's arrogant, ignorant, *male* commentary proved fruitless, however.

"My white robes symbolize purity and show my dedication to the Goddess Ana-Sett. And I will not be spoken to like one of your common whores." Teela's voice was cool and collected, but held the hint of an edge in it.

Marek almost grinned. Maybe she could start to like this one, if she ever actually had a chance to talk to her like a real person.

Dagen grunted and leaned in close to Thane, putting an arm around his shoulder. He spoke in Thane's ear, but it was clearly a whisper meant to carry. Thane kept his eyes affixed to the sword in his hands, turning it over as he inspected it.

"Speak to ladies like whores and whores like ladies," Dagen said. "It's surprising what you get from both." He looked over at Teela and grinned. Marek licked her lips and looked away in disgust and embarrassment. Were all men the same?

Thane placed the tip of his sword into the sheath then used both hands to pointedly ram it home.

"I've ten leagues yet before I test this blade," Thane said, shrugging out from under Dagen's arm. "Don't push me, elf."

Marek looked Thane up and down as the large man strode away. Perhaps she'd misjudged him. He was, after all, the one who'd saved her from Peregus and his men. It was just Dagen who was the scoundrel. Well, Dagen, and Peregus . . . and Peregus's men . . . and Master Vagamal . . . so, Thane was something of a rarity. Still, she felt bad for having misjudged him. Teela, Marek noticed, hid a small smile of her own as Thane strode past her.

Such a strange woman.

"The Goddess leads us," Teela said, and then turned after Thane, walking in the direction of the rising sun. As she turned, Marek noticed her fiddling with a pendant at her neck, though the priestess didn't seem to notice. Maybe Teela was just as nervous about all this as she was. The thought was oddly comforting.

"The Goddess leads us," Dagen said with an outrageous bow and grandiose gesture after Teela's retreating form.

"Ten leagues," Marek snapped, which wiped the silly smile right off Dagen's face in an instant. His mouth worked, though no sound came out. Before he could say anything at all, Marek turned and followed the others. She had no desire to stay behind and bandy words with Dagen this early in the morning.

By mid-morning Marek knew two things with absolute certainty. One, Dagen was, without question, the most annoying, irritating, pig-headed man she had ever had the misfortune to meet, and two, she *hated* walking. Once again, she was lagging behind everyone else as they walked along, following a path Teela indicated for them to follow. Her twisted foot hurt, even with the brace, and her limp grew more and more pronounced the longer she walked. Before today, the longest walk she'd ever taken had been from her own small town into the city and back again. She had covered that distance four times over already.

Teela and Thane walked close together, the burly warrior keeping a hand close to his sword as they walked. Dagen came next, and Marek brought up the rear. She wondered at that. She was, after all, the leader of this company. She worked for Teela, Thane and Dagen worked for her. Shouldn't a leader be at the front of the group rather than at the back of it? She kept silent though. It made sense for Teela to be first, since she was the only one who actually knew where they were going, and it sort of made sense that their only warrior be close to her in case she needed protection. Still, Marek found she didn't like being at the back of the group any more than she enjoyed a beating.

Morning sat almost spent in the sky when they crested a rise and looked down on a structure cut into a cliff face. Smoke billowed up from the open doorway and more than a few bodies littered the ground between their position and the temple itself, a distance of perhaps half a mile. Though Marek had no experience with the way of battles and war, it looked as if someone had attacked the place, then killed any of the runners who attempted to get away. The structure looked as if it had once been fine, a bastion of whatever God or Goddess its members owed their faith to, but had fallen into disuse and disrepair long before it was attacked.

"Maybe we should take a look around down there," Dagen said, gesturing down toward the cliff face with one finger half extended. "See if they missed anything valuable."

Marek turned and gave Dagen a flat look. The

look he returned her made it clear he had no qualms whatsoever about pillaging a temple. *Heartless scoundrel.*

"They were my friends and teachers." Teela's voice held unshed tears within it and she sniffed before licking her lips. Dagen had the decency to look at least mildly embarrassed at that.

"Should we go down there?" Marek asked. She watched Teela's wan expression, noticing the glimmer in her eyes and the slack posture of a woman in grief, before continuing hastily, "To pick up the trail?"

Teela pursed her lips, and her back straightened. She shook her head and started walking again, taking a path parallel to the cliff into which the temple had been carved. Her ironclad staff thumped hollowly against the stones.

"Let's keep moving."

Despite her earlier misgivings about Teela's attitude, Marek had to admit the priestess showed remarkable strength of will. Marek wasn't sure she could have maintained such composure had she been in a similar situation. As it was, only a mixture of luck and willpower had gotten Marek this far. Teela seemed to have made it on will alone. Marek followed the priestess down the trail and, a moment later, she heard Dagen and Thane follow her. At least she wasn't in the back this time.

A subdued group stopped for a meal in the brisk light of the midafternoon sun. Marek set about gathering firewood with Teela, who worked mechanically. She found herself shooting glances at the priestess as they worked, her thoughts a jumble. The temple they'd passed, Teela's temple, lay in ruins. Marek had seen death before, but never such rampant, merciless destruction. Bodies lay strewn about the ground, some of them smoldering where they'd been burned by passing flames. None but the crows remained to care for the fallen. Marek shuddered at the memory, then shuddered again at the guilt that wormed up her throat and then down the back of her spine. They hadn't stopped either. Whatever drove Teela now, whatever lay behind this quest of theirs, it was pressing enough to force Teela to abandon those she'd called friends and companions. Marek wasn't sure how she felt about that.

After she and Teela finished gathering the wood, Thane got a fire going and set a small pot of water over a tripod he pulled from a pack. He fished around in the pack and threw a handful of leaves into the mix, allowing a strong-smelling tea to steep as the water heated.

"What scrumptious meals are we to have on this quest of ours, love?" Dagen asked, cracking open one eye to peer over at Marek. The man lay against a boulder, legs sprawled out in front of him, a long blade of grass dangling from the corner of his mouth. Marek felt an odd little panic flutter through her when she realized she hadn't planned meals.

"Whatever you brought along with you, thief," Teela said, glaring at him with a look so intense it made Marek recoil by reflex.

Dagen chuckled softly and shook his head, closing his eyes. "You could have at least let her squirm a little. Didn't you see her face?" Dagen opened his eyes long enough to wink at Marek before shutting them again.

Marek flushed, but before she could respond, Thane drew his sword. The blade came out of its sheath with a rasp of leather. Marek looked over at the Vitalion soldier, brow furrowing in curiosity, but Thane simply pulled out a stone and began working it over the length of the blade. He didn't look up, nor did he speak, but it effectively ended the conversation.

A few minutes passed in silence. Marek picked at the grass, then fished some dried meat out of her pack and ate it in a few quick bites. While she'd never been starved as a slave, she'd never really been able to eat her fill either, until she learned to eat quickly. She'd have to learn to eat normally again eventually. When the pot came to a boil, Thane set aside his sword and pulled the pot off the flames, setting it on the ground to cool while pulling four metal cups from his pack. The tea steamed in the cold air. Thane poured it with surprising delicacy and passed it around, starting with Teela and ending with Dagen. He then pulled a flask of some sort from a pocket and poured a liberal amount into his tea.

"Here now," Dagen said, sitting up. "If that's spirits I'll have some, myself."

Thane regarded him with a flat expression and stowed the flask back into a pocket. Dagen scowled. Marek watched the pair without comment as she blew on her own tea, cooling it so she could take a sip.

"Don't think about trying to lift it off me either, elf," Thane said. "I sleep with a dagger in hand and one eye open."

Dagen raised an eyebrow and smirked. "Do you now? Well, if I were an elf, as you claim, it wouldn't make much difference, now would it?"

"Do not lie to us," Teela said, her voice snapping like a whip. "We all see your pointed ears. Do not try and deny what is plain to our eyes."

Dagen inclined his head to her slightly, though his eyes narrowed and his expression darkened around the edges. Marek wasn't sure if it was the set of his jaw or the way the corners of his lips dropped almost imperceptibly, but she got the distinct impression that he was in pain of some sort.

"Half elf," Dagen said shortly and leaned back against the boulder.

Teela raised one thick eyebrow, but didn't press the issue. Thane grunted and frowned into his cup. Marek found herself studying Dagen. Perhaps there was more to him than the charismatic bravado he wore like a cloak.

CHAPTER 11

Night's enveloping darkness had already begun to claim the land within its chill embrace by the time they reached a point where Teela signaled them to be quiet. The priestess exchanged a few words with Thane, and the warrior took up the lead as they entered a series of narrow, shoulder-height canyons carved out of the sandstone by the passage of time. Marek wasn't in the rear, though she sometimes traded places with Dagen, who was currently at the back, his mood not much improved from earlier. They walked swiftly and silently, Thane with his sword out. As they crept along, Marek caught the scent of something foul on the wind.

"What is that smell?" she whispered. Her voice sounded strangled even to her own ears and her skin crawled along her arms, forming little bumps.

"We have to stay downwind," Thane instructed, not slowing or answering her question in any direct manner. "Keep low and quiet."

Marek bit back any more questions, though it grated a little that no one had actually answered her. Was she the leader or wasn't she? The question, however, answered itself a few moments later. They crested a small rise which overlooked a small stream, then darted back down behind the rock before they were noticed.

"That's a lot of orcs," Thane said as they all peered carefully back down at the scene below.

Marek felt her heart race as she looked down over the expanse. Dozens of orcs lounged about a makeshift camp at the water's edge. Armored and outfitted, these were nothing like the docile, hunchback beast at Hammerhead's. These were warriors, soldiers, creatures bred, designed, and trained to kill. Her skin crawled.

"Right," Dagen whispered, "time to go home."

Marek didn't really disagree with the sentiment, though she knew she should. Her eyes roved over each of the orcs, gaze lingering on the swords, clubs, and half-moon axes each carried. She noticed the cages sitting half-submerged in the water. Several shadowy figures were in each cage, only their upper bodies visible above the surface of the water. Moonlight glinted off the water and shone off weapons and armor.

"If we fight, we die," Thane said. He turned and met Marek's eyes. With a start, she realized he was waiting on her to make a decision. With a slow sense of dawning comprehension, she realized they were all waiting on her. She expected herself to be afraid and fold under the pressure she now felt around her, but she surprised herself. She actually knew exactly what to do.

"I have a plan," she said, scooting back from the edge. The others retreated from the ledge as well, coming together in a tight group so they could whisper and not have the sound carry down to the orcs below.

"I'll create a distraction on that hill." Marek gestured to their right. "That will draw them that way and get them to chase us. Then Dagen will run in—"

"Whoa, hey, no!" Dagen interrupted.

Marek whipped around to look at him, cutting off midsentence.

"Like hell I will. Are you out of your nut? Those aren't imaginary orcs that your grandmother told you about to lull you to sleep, sweetheart."

Marek turned away to peer over the ledge again at the orcs, Thane and Teela mirroring her movements to one side. Dagen grabbed the back of her cloak and yanked her back down.

"Those are real, bloodthirsty, muscle-bound animals," he continued, pulling Teela away from the edge as well. "And we only have one muscle-bound animal." Dagen threw an arm over Thane's shoulders as if to make his meaning clear. Thane gave Dagen a flat look, but didn't argue the point.

"I can conjure a distraction." Marek made her

voice sound confident and sure, though her insides squirmed. She'd seen Thane kill five men already and come out of a four-on-one situation with only a split lip. If even he was hesitating now, maybe it was for a good reason.

"There's a lot of orcs down there," Thane said. The way he said it made it sound like a simple observation, but Marek could tell he was also giving her a warning.

Maybe they were right, maybe they'd gone and tried to swallow a wild boar whole. This wasn't their fight, not really . . .

No!

Marek snapped her eyes back to Dagen.

"Fine. Well, then, thief. You're going to slip into the water, quietly, hop into those cages, and find out which one has Teela's sister in it," Marek said in a rush, agitated mostly at herself for her moment of weakness. Dagen made a small noise as if considering Marek's words. "Then come ashore when you're in the clear," Marek finished.

"What about freeing the other captives?" Teela asked. Her voice held a plaintive note to it, as if she honestly thought she needed to beg for them to have any desire to do good at all. Marek wondered what sort of religion this Ana-Sett preached which fostered such default hostility and distrust.

"Yeah," Dagen said, "why not? And while I'm

at it I'll swipe some teeth from the biggest gooch's mouth." He made a gesture as if snatching something out of the air with one hand. "Forget it."

"If anything happens we'll attack, causing a distraction." Marek wasn't sure if she said it or asked it, but Thane nodded. Marek felt a rush of relief that she hoped didn't show on her face. Maybe she could do this leader thing after all.

"It's a good plan," Thane said.

"Naturally," Dagen said. He put a little extra emphasis on the beginning of the word, twisting it into a thorny burr. "And what about that guard down there by the cages? Maybe you'll make friends with him. All the while Thane can spend the night up here on the rocks pleasuring you lovely ladies while Teela's sex-deprived Goddess watches on with envy."

He leered at them both in turn. Marek flushed, but Teela's face darkened with perceptible anger even in the darkness.

"Shove your dagger straight up through his bowels," she said.

For a moment, Marek thought the priestess was talking about Dagen doing that to himself, but then Teela continued as her intent became clear. "He won't scream and death is instant." She looked away, though Marek was able to see her forcibly calm herself in profile. "The sisters of my order study principles of combat."

Marek gave Teela a silent cheer inside her mind. "Dagen, if your thieving skills aren't up to it—"

"My thieving skills? No, no, no, no, no. It's fine. I'll do it," Dagen said, then straightened, pulled off his pack, bow, quiver of arrows, and all but one of his daggers, and rubbed his hands together. "Always the thief gets the sodden end of the stick."

To the side, Teela clasped her hands together and muttered something under her breath Marek didn't understand, though it was clear she was praying.

"Teela," Dagen snapped. "Cut that out, all right? It's bad luck."

Teela ignored him, though her lips did move less perceptibly for the next few moments. Marek licked her own lips in anticipation, feeling sweat on her palms and along her forehead. This had the potential to go seriously wrong.

Dagen spat into his hands, rubbed them together, then shoved Marek aside. "All right," he said. "Excuse me." He clambered halfway up the ledge and then hesitated, glancing back at Teela. "What's she look like," he asked, "this sister of yours?"

"Brown hair," Teela replied.

"Is she beautiful?"

"Mmhmm."

"Chances are improving," Dagen said, and then leapt over the side of the ledge.

Marek rushed to the lip of the cliff and peered over the side. She saw no sign of Dagen, but movement down in the water near the orcs themselves drew her immediate gaze. Teela and Thane moved up alongside her.

A form in white robes was being pulled through the water by a long rope wrapped beneath its arms. A handful of orcs stood on shore, pulling the other end of the rope in a strange mockery of fishing. The way the rope was tied, the figure was pulled facedown across the intervening distance.

"What's going on down there?" Thane whispered to Marek's left.

The figure in white robes reached the shore and got up on its knees, though it was clearly unstable and unsteady. Water ran in great streams from the white cloth.

"Teela," Marek said, "is that your sister?"

A pair of orcs grabbed the figure from the water and started pulling it across the rocky ground. The figure stumbled and tripped, but managed to keep its feet amid the grumbling, guttural shouts of its captors.

"No," Teela said, though her voice still sounded pained. "That's a priest."

The orcs pushed, shoved, and cajoled the priest toward another figure a dozen or so paces away, a bald man who seemed at odds among the dark-skinned, pointy-eared orcs. How had they not noticed him before?

"That's him!" Teela hissed. "He led the raid on my temple."

Marek studied the man, though the details were indistinct at this distance. She could make out his bald head, glowing gently in the moonlight, and an odd glow in his eyes. Like a cat's, but without the discerning appraisal contained therein. The orcs inclined their heads towards the bald man while the priest was forced to his knees before him.

Who is he?

"Where is the stone?"

The man's demanding words drifted over to where Marek and her companions lay hidden. Marek noted the odd accent with curiosity. She'd never heard anything quite like it.

"I don't know." The priest's voice was a thin rasp, the sound of a man who'd gone too long without a solid breath and now sucked in air as if it were the only thing keeping him alive.

The bald man raised a hand up alongside the priest's head, fingers bent into a claw. Hauntingly familiar blue-white light began to flow from the kneeling priest and into the bald man's hands.

"What is he doing to him?" Marek breathed. Even as she spoke, the thin band of blue-white light became a solid band, like a thick fog after a chilly night, and the priest toppled to the ground. The blue-white light vanished the instant the priest's body hit the ground. The body rolled and landed back in the stream with a splash, bobbing there like a morbid excuse for a raft.

"Necromancy," Teela whispered. Her voice shook slightly as she spoke. "It's an old, dark magic, which feeds on the life force of others. I'd only ever heard tales of it until now."

Marek swallowed hard. The blue-white light, the falling body. It all rang with solid familiarity within her mind. She remembered Master Vagamal's limp form on the ground. Marek pushed the thought away as she watched the bald man, the necromancer, turn about and stride off out of sight. She swallowed hard and looked down at the white-robed body bobbing in the water.

"I can't see Dagen," Thane muttered. "Any sign of him?"

Right. She'd almost forgotten about Dagen.

"Come on, thief," Marek whispered. "Earn your pay."

CHAPTER 12

Stupid fykin' women!

Dagen waded through the water, feeling his boots tugging at him beneath the surface and weighing him down. How dare that haughty little girl question his skills as a thief. He'd show her. He tossed his head and continued on toward the cage, keeping his movements shallow so as not to disturb the water and make more noise than was necessary. His sneaking skills were good enough that he could have walked right up to the nearest orc and stolen his clothes off him without him even noticing, but he was careful anyway. It didn't hurt to be cautious. He'd certainly get away if the orcs noticed him, but the rest of them back up on the cliff wouldn't.

Typical. That's why I work alone.

With the aid of the distraction caused by the strange sorcerer, he made it to the cage with relative ease, as he'd known he would. Several figures huddled close together within the bars. They wore the remnants of white robes, marking them as members of Ana-Sett's priesthood. At least the so-called symbols of purity and devotion made them easy to identify, even if they did make them a rather boring lot.

"Which one of you is Teela's sister, Caeryn?"

Orcs moved about on the shore not ten feet away, conversing in their guttural, pig-like language.

"Shh," one of the figures within the cave hissed. "They kill those of us who speak."

Out of the corner of his eye, Dagen noticed one of the orcs on the shore lift its head and begin sniffing at the air. *Fykin' luck!*

"I'm here to free you."

"The ogre came," a woman said in a shrill voice that made Dagen want to wince. "He took—"

An orc jabbed a long spear at the cage. Dagen dropped below the surface and heard a muffled exchange above him. The water's chill clung to him beneath the surface, making his lungs scream for air far earlier than they would have normally. Why in the name of all that was good and worth stealing was he doing this again? He should have bolted the first chance he'd gotten. Seventy-five silver wasn't worth all he'd have to do to earn it. There were far easier ways of making that little money. Lifting it off a fat nobleman seemed like a good choice, especially if he happened to have a fair-looking wife . . .

He broke the surface and flipped his hair back out of his face, sucking in a deep breath with a sound he hoped didn't carry too far. He glanced around the side of the cage as he forced his breathing to calm. The orc with the spear had his back to the cage now, and a few others had moved closer as well. This *was* proving a challenge now, wasn't it? He fished in his pocket beneath the surface for his lock pick with one hand and found the cage's lock with his other.

"Let's see what we got here," he whispered to himself. The occupants of the cage remained silent, though they moved back away from the door, as if to give him space to work. Dagen suspected a far more pragmatic reason. If he was caught, they didn't want to be seen in a position that looked as if they'd been helping him. He took another deep breath and pushed the lock pick into the lock.

"Put it in, nice and easy," he said to himself. He fiddled the pick back and forth, feeling for the tumblers within the mechanism itself. He'd spent years honing his fingers to a dexterity and sensitivity so acute they could pick up even the tiniest resistance in the movement of his pick. "Bit deeper," he continued, probing with the pick, "and there she is."

The lock gave without a sound. The spear-wielding orc hunched down near the shoreline and sniffed at the air again. Dagen pulled open the cage's door, which swung open on rusty, protesting hinges.

"Right, let's have a look at you, then," Dagen said, and pulled the hood back on the nearest figure. A woman's face was revealed. A woman with brown hair. "Are you Caeryn?"

The woman shook her head. *Figures.*

"Right then," Dagen whispered. "Go on and get out of here. Head back up the cliff and away from here as fast as you can, all right?"

Several of them pushed past him into the water, swimming toward shore. Dagen cast a glance at the spear-wielding orc on the shore, but the creature didn't seem to notice.

"They'll see we've escaped and come after us." Dagen recognized the owner of that voice. It was the same man who'd told him that the orcs killed the talkers. Dagen gave him a little shove toward the others and closed the cage door after him. *Coward.*

Still, the fool priest was probably right, damn him. What the poor sods needed was either a distraction or time to get away. Part of the orc party had left with the strange sorcerer, but enough still remained to be a problem. And that spear-wielding one at the water's edge—it was definitely going to be trouble, and not just because it smelled like a well-used latrine . . . a glint of steel at the orc's feet caught Dagen's eye.

Before stopping to think it through, Dagen moved forward, pulled himself free of the water, and grabbed the thick, curved dagger off the ground. He hesitated there for half a second, and then looked back over his shoulder to the ridge where Marek, Teela, and Thane were probably watching him. It was too late to change his mind now. Dagen shoved the dagger right up the orc's bowels.

The orc howled in pain even as it fell.

Stupid, fykin', lying priestess!

Dagen spun and stared up at the spot where Teela lay hidden on the cliff and threw his hands up in the air. Orcs raced toward him, weapons drawn. Arrows flew by his head.

"Marek!" he shouted, retreating. "Whenever you're ready, just join in!"

He dove back into the water, allowing it to hide him from watchful eyes. Arrows splashed into the water on every side.

"We've got him," Marek said, leaping to her feet.

Thane was already moving, pushing past her as he hurried down the narrow canyon toward the open expanse below. Marek looked out into the water, but couldn't see Dagen anywhere. She raced after Thane and Teela.

Blood pounded in her ears and she felt the rush of anticipation coursing through her veins. Her hands shook with it and her body almost seemed to hum with nervous energy. Thane pulled to a stop near where the canyon opened up on the orc encampment below, his back up against the sandstone wall. He unlimbered his shield, face grim even in the moonlight.

"Do we have a plan?" Marek asked, stopping alongside him. Teela waited on her other side, knuckles white where they gripped her staff.

"We fight."

"I thought you said we'd die," Marek tried to keep the sudden rush of fear that shot through her out of her voice, but failed on a grand scale.

"We'll see now, won't we?" Thane said. He drew his sword and charged.

Teela hesitated for a moment, then raced after him.

Marek hung back a few moments longer. Her hands shook and her lungs already heaved as if she'd spent all day lugging a heavy weight around. Her mouth was dry, and inside her mind a small voice told her to run. This was no place for a slave girl, no place for a nobody like her. She never should have done this in the first place. This group, these people, they were all going to die because she'd gone and done something far above her place in life. Slaves weren't meant to be important. They were simply things, not worthy of grandeur.

Thane screamed. Marek recognized the agony in his voice and all thought simply melted away. She spun around the corner and raced into the fray. She pulled to a stop only a few steps away, peering down a small rise. Almost a score of orcs was racing toward her.

"That is a lot of orcs," she said, lamely. It was a dumb, obvious thing to say, but it was all she could think in the moment.

An orc swinging a massive mace charged her. Marek scrambled for her dagger and pulled it free a moment before the orc reached her. Instead of trying to avoid the blow, Marek stepped into it, reacting on impulse and stabbing the orc in the neck. The blade sank up to the hilt in the soft flesh there. The orc's dead weight pulled at her arm as the creature slumped forward, mace falling from limp fingers. With a grunt, Marek pushed the body to one side and let it slide off her dagger and onto the ground.

She staggered back. Sounds of battle, the smell of blood, and the intense chaos of the battle assaulted her senses. Part of her recognized that she'd just killed, but that part was hidden beneath the shock and intensity of the moment. Marek stepped back again and looked around, trying to get her bearings.

Thane lay on the ground a dozen feet away, an orc on top of him. Marek could see an arrow sprouting from one of his shoulders. Even with that, Marek watched him throw the orc aside and, with a shout of mingled rage and pain, ram his sword down through the orc's chest before staggering to his feet.

Teela stood closer down by the water. A group of the orcs had broken off and surrounded her, possibly having recognized the white robes she wore and the symbols of Ana-Sett from their earlier raid. Six of them formed a ring around the priestess, who gripped her staff in one hand still. Moonlight revealed her terrified expression, though she stood erect and proud before the orcs surrounding her.

Out of the corner of her eye, Marek noticed an orc standing only a few feet away from her, his back to her. The orc seemed focused on Thane. Marek crept toward the orc, dagger held low, then threw herself up onto its back and wrapped her arms around its neck. The orc immediately started thrashing, a guttural scream tearing from its throat. Marek held on as tightly as she could. Thane let out another scream, which sounded more like an extended grunt. Marek spared him a glance even as the orc beneath her pitched and scrabbled to pull her free. Thane's hand held the arrow that had, until only moments before, been lodged in his shoulder.

"Are you all right?" she shouted.

"Of course I'm not all right!" Thane bellowed something inarticulate and then rammed the arrow in his hand into an orc's throat.

Marek managed to get her dagger down near the orc's throat and slice it open. The orc started to fall, and Marek leaped back as the creature slipped to its knees and then toppled to the ground. She looked over at Thane just as he tore the arrow free of the orc's neck and slammed it back with enough force to send the creature spinning through the air. The orc landed in a crumpled heap at his feet. Marek froze, mouth hanging partially open.

"Help Teela!" Thane shouted at her, yanking Marek out of her shock.

Marek raced toward the priestess as Thane engaged with another orc. She ignored the pain in her foot, trusting the brace to do its job. Teela was surrounded by six or seven orcs, but she kept them at bay with long swings of her steel-clad staff. Several of the creatures already lay still at her feet.

"Hey!" Marek shouted, and leaped onto the nearest orc before it could charge Teela.

Marek wrapped her arms around its neck and allowed her momentum to carry them both to the ground. She rolled to the side as soon as she hit, getting up to her knees and then onto her feet while Teela used the distraction to race around the other orcs. She rushed passed Marek, who slowly retreated as the orcs regrouped and started trudging toward them, dark blades making small circles in the air. A pair of the creatures advanced ahead of the others.

A figure appeared behind the two lead orcs. They both grunted over the sound of metal scraping against metal and leather, then lurched forward. For half a moment, Marek wondered if they were charging and reached for the spell components she had in a pouch at her waist. In the initial chaos of the battle, she'd forgotten about them completely. Terror, however, made her thoughts sharp, if myopically focused.

Her fingers stilled as she recognized Dagen standing behind the two orc bodies, curved short swords dripping with orc blood. He shoved the corpses to one side and rushed toward Thane as more orcs charged toward the two women. Marek and Teela followed without a word.

They met up with Thane in the middle of the encampment, each putting their back to one another as the orcs formed a large ring around them, pinning them in. Marek's lungs heaved and her hands shook, though she kept her left hand close to her spell components in her belt.

"You had to fyking stab him," Thane muttered to Dagen. The warrior looked a little unsteady on his feet and the smell of fresh-spilled blood—his own to be precise—hung like a cloud around him.

"Teela," Dagen said, "your combat training is

shite."

An orc wearing a studded leather breastplate stepped in front of the others and raised a bloody, gloved fist. Marek felt her mouth go dry.

When the creature spoke, its voice was a deep rumble so heavy with accent that the meaning nearly dropped away entirely. "Leave us your women and you can live."

Dagen grunted. "How very orcish of you."

A long pause spread between them. Marek felt the tension swell to the point of bursting, then Thane roared and charged. He leaped for the orc who'd been speaking, sword swinging down in an overhead chop. The orc stepped to the side, forcing Thane to swing his sword back up at an awkward angle. The orc dodged again. Thane stepped forward into the next swing, bringing his sword down in a diagonal cross from right to left. The orc didn't even attempt to avoid the blow. Instead, it stepped into it, batting Thane's sword aside with one hand. The other drove a heavy mace directly into Thane's ribs.

Marek heard the rush of air leaving Thane's lungs, then the sickening crunch of breaking bones. Thane folded over, sword toppling to the ground an instant before he himself slumped over. Teela rushed forward, but the orc moved in for the kill.

Seeing Thane like that, broken and bloodied, something inside Marek snapped. She reached into a pouch at her waist and pulled out a vial in the space between two heartbeats. She glanced at it as she popped off the cork with one hand and dropped the contents—a red powder—into her other hand. Discarding the bottle, Marek cupped her hands together and began the spell, praying to whatever God was listening that it would work.

"*Domah noesthis kaspil,*" Marek began and—much to her delight—a small spark appeared between her hands. She threw her hands into the air as she finished off the spell, voice rising to almost a shout. *"Fu-eni!"*

A ball of fire the size of a man's head shot into the air and then exploded outward in a vast ring of flames. Marek flew backward off her feet, tossed by the force of the blast as if she were a rag doll. She hit the ground hard, but blinked away the blaring pain. Her ears rang with the sound of it and her vision was blurry and spotted from the sudden light in the darkness, but she managed to stumble to her feet. Near her, Marek was able to see Teela and Dagen standing as well. They'd *all* been knocked over by the explosion. A few of the orcs stirred.

"Come on!" Marek called to Dagen and Teela. Secretly, she felt a surge of pride at the success of the spell, but pushed the thought aside as she found Thane among the still orc forms on the ground. He didn't look good. She reached down and helped the burly warrior to his feet, pulling his arm around her shoulders. Thane bit back a shout of pain.

"Let's go!"

Chapter 13

Teela led the way through the trees, the owl statuette atop her staff glinting in the moonlight and granting Marek a beacon by which to follow the priestess in the darkness. Dagen ran at the rear, bow out with an arrow ready on the string. Marek still supported Thane in the middle of the group, though the task was proving more and more difficult the longer they ran along the rocky, mountainous trails. She was, after all, not entirely whole herself. Even with the brace, her foot and leg ached so badly that they were almost numb with the pain. What was more, the weight of his arms around her shoulders grew greater and greater with each step, and the scratch of his long beard and blocky chin against the top of her head grew more annoying. The sounds of their pursuers spurred them on.

"Leave me," Thane moaned for perhaps the tenth time in as many minutes. "I'm not afraid to die."

"Then just do it, already," Dagen snapped from behind them.

They rushed along a narrow path. Marek grunted away her pains as she twisted to let Thane through a thin stretch of the path. He groaned in pain and almost fell, but Teela was there with a helping hand at just the right moment, pulling them both along to safety.

Thane glanced over his shoulder at Dagen. "You had to fyking stab him, didn't you?"

Marek didn't hear Dagen respond. She was too busy focusing on staying upright herself to pay much attention to anything else. Dagen moved up alongside her and took Thane's arm, Teela appearing on the man's other side. It was so much easier to walk without carrying his burden that Marek wondered how she'd managed it at all. Her foot and ankle burned with a dull pain. She took the lead ahead of the others, limping heavily.

After what seemed an eternity, they entered a small wood and Marek strained her hearing. Everything sounded muted in the dark, enclosed space. The only sound which broke the stillness was their own belated breathing.

"Must have lost them," Thane groaned. Teela and Dagen still supported him. Marek wondered at his grit and willpower. His ribs were definitely broken, likely in several different places, yet he still managed to move and not slow them down too much.

An arrow zipped through the air and thudded into a tree just to one side of them. Marek swallowed hard.

"Right," Dagen said, pulling on Thane hard enough to make the stolid man cry out in pain. "Marek! We could really use some magic right now!"

Marek didn't disagree, but couldn't force her mind to think of anything except running. Her arsenal of spells was small to begin with and she couldn't remember even one of them at the moment. Her mind felt as if it were a block of slowly forming ice, the temperature and movement dropping at an alarming rate. She rushed back to them and took Dagen's place at Thane's side so he could use his bow.

"Leave me," Thane groaned. Teela made a small noise that sounded almost like a groan, though neither she nor Dagen slowed. "I'm slowing you down."

"No," Marek said, grunting with effort. "Our oath goes both ways!" In the time she'd been without his weight on her shoulders, he seemed to have gained a hundred pounds. Was she getting weaker or did he need that much more support?

Marek heard the thrum of Dagen's bow and a howl of pain that could only have come from an orc throat behind her. War cries and angry bellows pelted her back. Her heaving lungs worked harder, answering the call of her quickening heart. Fear made her grip on Thane's arm so tight her own knuckles hurt.

"Move him faster or drop him!" Dagen shouted from behind them.

A buzzing noise filled Marek's ears and Thane lurched forward with a scream, almost wrenching free of Marek's grip. Marek twisted to see how close the orcs had gotten and noticed the arrow sticking out of Thane's shoulder. Dagen loosed an arrow of his own and dropped one of several orcs Marek could just barely make out on the trail behind them. She turned back to the trail ahead of her, careful to watch her footing. Her breath came in shallow gasps and her mind lay shrouded in numb emptiness.

"Wait," Thane gasped. For a moment, Marek wondered if he was getting delirious, telling them to wait with orcs just behind them, but then he continued. "I know this place. Up there." He gestured with the hand that was draped over Teela's shoulder toward one side of the narrow, wooded canyon. "We raided a camp here once. There's a cave. It's hard to get to."

Marek turned Thane in that direction without a second thought. Teela copied her motions on Thane's other side. Hard to get to or not, they really had no choice. It was only a matter of time before the orcs caught up to and killed them all. The thrum of Dagen's bow sounded repeatedly behind them, then stopped abruptly.

"I'm out of arrows!" Dagen shouted.

Marek didn't slow. She scrambled up what felt like the side of a cliff itself, half dragging Thane behind her. Somehow, she and Teela managed to clamber up the rocks without killing themselves or Thane, but it was a near thing. Dagen rushed up behind them, the sound of orc pursuers filling the air.

"Hard to get to?" Teela said in a breathless, exasperated voice. "If it were any harder, we'd be dead."

"Quiet!" Dagen hissed.

The cave lay behind a massive boulder, the entrance nothing but a narrow slit in the canyon wall. They pushed in and nearly slipped on the steep incline. Marek went first, careful to support as much of Thane's weight as she could. The warrior's head sagged against his chest, flopping about like the head of a dead chicken.

"I'm not going to let you die!" Marek said with a gasp, pulling him down the steep slope into the cave.

It seemed like an eternity before they reached the sandy cave floor. Marek and Teela slipped out from under Thane's arms and let him drop to the ground. He caught himself on his arms with a moan of pain and held himself up as if ready to stand

“The bolt,” Thane said, then shouted, “Pull the bolt!” The pain in his voice was sharp enough to cut.

“Quiet!” Dagen ordered. The half elf stood at the cave’s mouth, moonlight glinting off the long, curved knife in his hand.

“Okay,” Marek said, trying and failing to keep her shaking hands still. She stepped up to Thane and wrapped her hands around the thick black shaft sticking from Thane’s shoulder.

She swallowed hard. This wasn’t anything like the adventuring she’d imagined. She was supposed to be the leader, and she’d gotten Thane beaten to a pulp and shot so full of arrows he looked like a practice target. Steeling herself, she yanked on the shaft. It pulled free with an odd, squelching sound. Thane bellowed out a roar of purest agony, back arching and mouth opened wide enough to show all of his teeth.

“Keep him quiet!” Dagen called down from the cave’s mouth.

Thane rolled over onto his back, low moans spilling from him as readily as the blood staining both the front and back of his clothes. Marek leaned over him, unsure what to do. She placed a bloodstained hand on his shoulder and made comforting noises.

"I've got you," she said. Blood poured from Thane's shoulder and rolled down his side to mingle with the pool forming there from the arrow wound on his back.

"I'm bleeding too fast." Thane's voice was terrifyingly weak.

Marek's mouth worked, but no words came out. She didn't know what to do. Thane was dying, Marek could feel it in the weak, fluttering cadence of his broken breaths. She saw it in his eyes. Hands grabbed Marek around the shoulders and shoved her to the side with surprising strength.

"Move aside!" Teela said.

Marek stumbled and tripped, rolling across the sandy cave floor. She felt a flash of irritation, but pushed it down as the redheaded priestess knelt by Thane's side and tore away layers of clothes to expose his wounds. Thane moaned and whimpered, though Marek could tell he was doing his best to hold the sounds back.

"Embrace the pain," Teela said to Thane, "and welcome death should she beckon you."

What?

Marek spun her head to look at Teela just as the priestess whipped her right hand back and then thrust it back downward, her fingers entering Thane's wound with a flash of golden light. The sound her fingers made, parting the flesh and slipping on the blood, made Marek want to gag, but she couldn't look away. Thane screamed, and the sound dwarfed all previous cries of pain like the sun snuffed a candle's light.

"No! No!" Marek screamed, starting forward. Strong arms wrapped around her and Marek struggled against them, even after realizing they belonged to Dagen, who had slid down into the main chamber. Thane screamed again, back arching and entire body convulsing as the golden glow swelled within his breast, sprouting from the wound and Teela's fingers therein. What was the priestess doing? She was killing him!

Teela rocked back and forth, eyes closed and lips moving without words. The hand not inside Thane clutched the talisman which always hung from her neck, the symbol of her Goddess. Behind closed lids, Teela's eyes spun about, contorting like they would in a deep, dream-filled sleep. The gold light flickered and grew, pulsing like the beating of a heart. Teela's rocking grew more pronounced and Marek realized she was in communion with her Goddess, Ana-Sett. Teela's mouth came open as Thane continued to scream. Marek heard Teela's sharp, shallow intake of breath over the screams.

The wound sealed itself back up, the flesh knitting back together before Marek's eyes.

Teela pulled her fingers free a moment before the

wound closed up altogether, though a thin line of red still remained, marking where the gaping hole had been only moments before. Thane's screams slowly ebbed, dying down to nothing more than a quiet moan.

"I couldn't get it all," Teela said, voice a weak, gasping mockery of her earlier arrogant tone. "It will take time to fully heal you, but you will live."

Her red hair slid down across her face, almost like a curtain, except for where it stuck to the sweat on her forehead. She slid a hand across Thane's bearded cheek, turning his head slightly as if wanting to check him for signs of comprehension.

"You are so beautiful," Thane mumbled.

Beside Marek, Dagen made a small sound. She glanced at him out of the corner of her eyes, noticing the hand cupped over his mouth and the wide, disbelieving eyes.

"Sleep now," Teela said. "I will watch over you."

"Thank you." Thane took one of Teela's hands in his own and pressed it to his lips despite the tremble in his grip. "Thank you."

Marek looked away. Thane was safe, no thanks to her leadership. If not for Teela, things would have ended very differently. Guilt struck her with a blow so fierce she had to look away. Why were they even following her? She'd managed a single spell, yes, but when they'd really needed her, when *Thane* really needed her, what good had she been?

"I'm going to go see what else is in this place," she said to no one in particular. She had to get away from here, away from the emotions writhing within her. No one stopped her. She assumed the orcs had passed or else Dagen wouldn't have left his position near the cave mouth. She paused just long enough to retrieve a clay lantern and a flint before she was off, almost running down a side passage. Thane's soft moans raced after her, like the condemning shouting of the village she'd left behind.

Chapter 14

Jaffin mimicked the movement of the grass, slipping in and out of the shadows and trusting in the amorphous nature of his cloak to hide him from prying eyes. He'd found the body of a priest back near the river, and judging by the burned out, blackened eyes, he wondered if he'd stumbled upon the Golgotian again. Something had happened there, at the stream, judging by the number of bodies and the tracks. The cages he'd found in the stream were empty, though they'd clearly contained victims as recently as a day before. The attackers, whoever they were, had run off, drawing the larger part of the orcs there with them. But another part had headed west. Jaffin had followed his hunch and tracked the smaller party to a small canyon several leagues to the west of the stream.

In truth, he wasn't too concerned about being spotted as he approached the valley's lip. Orcs were, as a rule, the least intelligent and observant of any of the races—outside of politicians and bureaucrats that is—but his father's incessant badgering over the years had honed within him a habit of being over-prepared and extra cautious. That may have been why he'd left two orc sentries lying still at their posts, knives buried in their backs. He hated leaving the weapons behind, but there really was no sense in retrieving them. Orc blood never came out.

Grass gave way to stone beneath his booted feet, though it could have been gravel for all Jaffin knew. He'd spent so long moving silently, so long in the wilds of his homeland, his body knew exactly how to respond to each shift in terrain and adjusted accordingly without much conscious effort. He shifted into a crouch as he neared the top of a rise, slowing down so that only his forehead and eyes appeared over the lip at this quarry.

Firelight blinded him almost instantly and he looked away with a silent curse. Only fools looked directly into a fire at night. It left one blind in the darkness. Blinking rapidly to allow his eyes to adjust, Jaffin looked back down into the narrow valley, making sure to keep his line of sight roving so as not to fixate on the glowing orange ball that was the fire.

A narrow carriage crafted from a fine, dark wood rested in the sheltered confines of the thin valley below. A pair of horses lay picketed a short distance away, grazing on a small patch of grass next to a pool of water. Jaffin wasn't familiar with this area, but he would have bet his last coin it was a natural spring of some sort. He only rarely lost bets.

A handful of orcs sat around the fire, oddly still for their race. Jaffin expected to see them drinking, or wrestling with one another, or even torturing some small animal with fiendish delight. Instead, their eyes remained downcast, fixed on the fire, or else darting furtive looks down the valley toward the carriage.

They're afraid.

The thought made the end of his nose twitch. Anything that would make that many orcs *that* afraid was worth pausing to consider very carefully, even if orcs were easily frightened by their own shadows. Jaffin glanced in the direction they were looking.

A tall, bald man Jaffin instantly recognized stood just beyond the carriage, arms clasped behind his back. Looking down at Mekru Nom, he was glad he had followed his earlier hunches.

For a moment, Jaffin contemplated moving closer or shifting around to the other side of the valley, but then light flickered down below and all other thoughts fled. He shifted his eyes in that direction, focusing intently on the spot of light pulsing in front of Mekru Nom. It cast a pale, blue-white glow, which grew steadily stronger. Jaffin dropped a hand onto one of his favorite knives, pulling it free of its sheath as a gust of wind tossed up enough noise to cover the sound.

A solitary, hooded figure dressed all in black resolved out of the darkness. In one hand he held a small sphere of glowing energy aloft from which the light emanated. With a small flick of the wrist, the figure tossed the sphere aside as soon as he came within a few feet of Mekru Nom. It vanished as soon as it left the figure's fingers.

A small breeze swirled through the valley below and brought the scent of smoke to Jaffin's nose. He heard blood pounding through his ears and took several deep breaths to steady himself. The hooded figure raised its hands and slowly pulled back the hood. Firelight shone off a bald head, thin face, and deep, deep eyes which seemed to glow with a golden-orange light, almost like a cat's.

Another fyking Golgotian. I'm going to kill you, old man.

Kynall knew how Jaffin felt about magic users. The hatred that coursed through him became an almost unreasonable thing, like it had earlier with that fyking monster, Gojun Pye. He still didn't believe half the stuff his father said about the wizard. A single magic user had been bad enough, but three? Jaffin ground his teeth together and passed his thumb along the length of his blade.

"Kishkumen," Mekru Nom said, his voice loud enough to carry back to Jaffin's hiding place.

The other Golgotian, Kishkumen, inclined his head slightly in Mekru Nom's direction.

"Where is the shard?" Kishkumen's voice was a sibilant hiss, soft and unctuous enough to make Jaffin shiver, but strong enough for him to still hear clearly.

Down below, the orcs pointedly looked away and made a rather obvious show of looking into the fire or anywhere but back toward the two magic users facing one another. Could they really be any more stupid?

"It's with one of the priestesses," Mekru said, voice calm and steady. Despite himself, Jaffin felt a modicum of respect for the man for facing his peer so calmly. "I thought she was with those we'd captured, but the ogre must have taken her."

"You lost it?" Kishkumen's voice cracked like a whip. The orcs all flinched in unison.

"I know exactly where it's at. Something cannot be lost until its location is no longer known."

Rathos's balls, Mekru must have ice running through his veins.

Kishkumen's eyes flashed, literally flashed, the golden-yellow glow illuminating his face enough that the twisted scowl of his lips looked macabre by comparison.

"Szorlock grows weary of your excuses, little man," Kishkumen said. "How many years have you been out here? You must have searched all four corners of the known realm by now."

Mekru said nothing. Jaffin steeled himself. His father had taught him young to listen to the absences as much as to the actual sounds of the forest. Silence meant danger, meant a recognition of fact. It meant something bad was coming.

"Now Mekru," Kishkumen continued, tapping a finger to his lips. "What would you do if you sent one of your lackeys out on a task at which they repeatedly failed?"

"At least I've been doing something other than licking at Szorlock's boots like an errant pup," Mekru said, though his voice was level and calm.

Kishkumen clicked his tongue and then smiled, showing teeth. "Now, now, old friend, don't start avoiding the question. Face it with courage, like all those would-be heroes we've left to fill graveyards over the years." He stepped around Mekru and clasped his hands behind his back, walking in a complete circle around the man. Mekru kept his face forward, eyes fixed at a distant point on the horizon. Jaffin felt the skin of his back threaten to crawl up into his hair.

"What would you do to one of your lackeys who repeatedly failed you?" Kishkumen repeated.

Jaffin almost missed it. One moment Mekru appeared stony and resolute, eyes fixed down the valley, the next he'd spun about and his hand rested on Kishkumen's throat. Mekru's closed fingers shook where they gripped flesh. Kishkumen bent at the knee and Mekru pushed him back so he was leaning at an angle where the man could have easily overbalanced and fallen over.

"I would kill him," Mekru growled. "Slowly, with my bare hands. I'd wrap my fingers around his throat and squeeze until his lungs screamed for sweet release and then squeeze harder. I'd wait until his body went limp as a boned fish and then I'd snap his neck and leave his body for the orcs."

Mekru's voice grew lower and lower until it descended into a guttural hiss at the end. Jaffin had to strain to hear. Kishkumen's face reddened, but he didn't struggle or even appear to be unduly distressed. Cries of warning sounded in Jaffin's mind. The orcs around the fire leapt to their feet. Several of them drew swords.

"That may be too good for you, little hound," Mekru continued, pushing Kishkumen down to his knees. "Maybe I should just—"

His voice cut off abruptly and he pitched forward as a soft whistling noise cut through the night. Mekru's hand slipped off Kishkumen's throat. Kishumen leapt to his feet, sucking in a deep breath. Mekru lurched forward and then sprawled face-first onto the ground. Three black-shafted arrows rose up from his back like silent flags of death.

Jaffin hunched down as the orcs below bellowed in apparent pain. More hissing sounds split the night air. Arrows took down four of the orcs in rapid succession. Jaffin considered ducking away then, but dismissed the thought almost immediately, keeping himself perfectly still. For the archers to not have spotted him already was a miracle by itself. If he moved, even a little, it would draw their attention and—likely—their fire. The remaining orcs didn't even have time to get to their feet before they were struck with enough arrows to have brought down a rampaging sow protecting her brood. They fell without a sound.

Kishkumen stepped up to Mekru's fallen form and looked down at the body with a curious expression on his face. One hand absently rubbed the side of his neck. Jaffin licked his lips, knowing that from his eyes down he was still hidden from view and the motion wouldn't betray him. Something important had just happened here, he knew. A power struggle that had clearly been building for years had just been resolved.

Figures materialized out of the darkness. Black-cloaked archers appeared along the tops of the hills surrounding the other side of the narrow valley. Jaffin felt sweat bead on his forehead and slip down toward his eyes despite the chill winter air. He couldn't tell if the archers were orc, human, elf, or demon taken flesh, but they stood at rapt attention, unmoving except for the shifting of their cloaks in the breeze.

"Ah, Mekru," Kishkumen said, voice barely loud enough for Jaffin to hear over the soft caress of the wind. "You never did learn to wait for the right moment to move. Patience is the key to lasting victory."

Another figure materialized out of the darkness, walking up to Kishkumen as the man—no, the *monster*—stood for several long minutes more over the body of his companion, regarding it with lowered brows and pursed lips. The archers remained motionless as the new figure approached. Jaffin kept waiting for the figure to come into sharper focus, but it remained shadowy and unfocused, as if made of shadow itself. The figure's cloak looked as if it had been cut into long, ragged strips which danced in the wind, floating around him like a dark cloud of despair. Jaffin swore he felt something almost palpable and decidedly malevolent oozing from the figure even from over two-dozen paces away.

"I have found the trail to the Darkspore, my lord." The sound which came from beneath the figure's dark hood would never have been described as a voice. At the initial sound, Jaffin thought his ears would bleed. By the time the words ended, he felt as if his very soul had been violated in a brutal, bloody fashion.

Kishkumen slowly turned to regard the other figure, eyes lingering on the body at his feet. Only the corners of his eyes betrayed a frown.

"Ah yes. Good work, sniffer," Kishkumen said after a moment. "Let us be off."

The Golgotian turned on a heel and started away, the sniffer—whatever hellspawn that was—taking the lead. The archers fell into rank behind them in perfect unity, forming two lines that marched in absolute step with one another. They left the still-burning bodies lying where they'd fallen.

Jaffin waited where he was for the space of one thousand heartbeats, counting each one as he allowed his mind to process what he'd just seen and heard. Sweat dripped down his face in a steady stream. By the time the thousandth heartbeat passed, he still hadn't been able to come to any conclusions about the encounter. Outside of one . . .

He needed to tell his father and, though it pained him to say so, Gojun Pye what he'd heard.

CHAPTER 15

Marek held the clay lantern aloft, index finger cupped around the clay ring. The lantern cast a pale yellow ball of light which barely fought back the darkness enough to see. Still, it was better than nothing.

Marek wasn't sure how long she'd been walking. It could have been a few minutes, but it could also have been as long as an hour. Her battling emotions had calmed somewhat, though the guilt, fear, and—honestly—doubt, still lay like a lead weight in her chest. But the emotions weren't threatening to kill her any more.

Light glittered on the wall in the passage ahead of her, though it wasn't the pale orange light of flame, more like the pale white of stars reflected off of water. Another entrance perhaps? She crept forward cautiously. If it was, in fact, another way into the cave system, she'd need to go back and tell the others. They'd have to make sure to watch both places for the orcs . . . Her thoughts trailed off as she rounded the corner and looked out at the sight before her.

The passageway ended at a steep drop off, though

the room opened up into a massive chamber that could have held Marek's entire village with room to spare. Stalactites and stalagmites dripped from the ceiling and bloomed from the floor. Pools of luminescent water filled pockets in the floor and cast strange flickering beams across the entire expanse, like stars captured underground but still allowed to dance. Moonlight filtered down from cracks in the ceiling as well, reflecting off the water and adding to the majestic glow of the room itself. The sight took Marek's breath away and banished the darkness.

She turned, looking for a place to sit down on the narrow ledge, and her eyes fell on a wooden chest. It lay shrouded in dust a few feet from her, resting against the stone at the edge of the ledge. Marek placed her clay hand lamp on a small promontory of rock and knelt next to the chest, hands once again trembling. It wasn't locked.

The lid creaked as she forced it open. Marek reached inside, pulled out something heavy on a chain, and held it up before her eyes. Lantern light revealed it to be a headpiece of some sort. Marek held it up to her own forehead, imagining herself as one of the nobility, a fine lady striding down a city street wearing a fancy dress and jewels that drew the eye of everyone who passed. She smiled, picturing the faces they'd make. With finery like that, maybe they wouldn't even notice her foot.

She snorted and allowed the headpiece to fall into one of her hands. As long as she was dreaming, she might as well wish for the Gods themselves to appear to her.

Marek placed the jewelry back into the chest and ruffled through the contents. Her hand wrapped around something hard and somewhat large and she pulled it free. A carving, worked into the likeness of two figures locked in a lovers' embrace. She couldn't tell if it was carved from stone or wood, but it was white and well worn. Who would have left something like this here? She stroked it with one hand, thoughts growing distant. The two figures held each other close, appearing to look deeply into each other's eyes even though the carving didn't have any facial features at all. They were locked together, as if the thought of ever letting go was as foreign to them as death. Another thing she would never have.

"It's a faltic."

Marek jumped and sucked in a gasp, looking up to see Dagen standing just inside the passage leading out onto the ledge.

How long has he been standing there?

Marek felt herself flush, though she hoped Dagen would take it simply as surprise. She sucked in a couple more breaths, allowing the silence to stretch a little. Dagen gave a soft chuckle and sat down next to her, getting uncomfortably close to the edge of the ledge.

"It needs to be placed on a shrine," Dagen said in a soft voice, taking the carving from Marek with gentle fingers. "It's a gift to the Gods to grant a wish for love."

Marek looked down at her hands, then up at Dagen's subdued face. "How do you know that?"

Dagen didn't meet her eye. "Ah. Personal experience, I'm afraid." He sighed softly, then looked up at Marek and gave her a pert smile. He gestured around the cavern before them with the carving. "It's far too pretty a thing for this place."

Marek let her gaze wander over the cavern, watching the lights dance from place to place across the ceiling and over the ground. The sound of falling water punctuated the silence of the space.

"I don't even know where we are," Marek said. "What is this place, a house?"

"Oh no." Dagen gave a wry chuckle. "No, it's a runner's cache. Deiran smugglers used to keep them up and down the trade routes, but that's long forgotten. Vitalia took care of that." He paused for a moment, glancing around the cavern again. "But, um, what wish will you ask the Gods for, being a slave and all?"

Slave? She felt a small rush of anger well up

within her and she narrowed her eyes at him. So they *did* question her leadership. They doubted her. Though she'd known it already, hearing it outright still burned like the sting of a wasp.

"No, I just—" Dagen obviously realized he'd said something wrong as he stumbled over himself trying to get the words out. "I just saw the mark on your neck." He reached out and laid a hand on Marek's neck. Marek had to suppress a shiver as Dagen leaned in closer and his fingers gently caressed the tattoo at the base of her skull. "It explains a lot."

He leaned in even closer. Marek felt her heart pounding within her chest, felt her skin flush with heat. Dagen's head tilted to one side and his lips parted. Marek felt herself respond and her own chin came up, positioning itself for the kiss. His nose brushed hers.

Marek pulled away, looking down and silently cursing and praising herself at the same time. She'd barely known him longer than a day, barely even understood the wash of confusing, conflicting emotions making battle within her. Longing threatened to force her back toward him. Confusion kept her at bay. Dagen simultaneously held all the charisma and charm of a characteristic rogue and, now that she'd pulled away, Marek realized that *that* is what made her hesitate.

"I'm going to go make a fire," she said and got to her feet.

She knew the excuse sounded forced, even to her own ears, but she didn't know what else to say.

Back in the main chamber, Marek found a fire already crackling merrily in the center of the room, a cauldron suspended above the flames. Candles had been lit and placed around the room to provide light. Whatever was on the fire smelled good, though the scent was dampened by the smoke. The cavern provided a natural flue, carrying the smoke out the cavern's entrance or up through small cracks in the ceiling, but the smell still lingered.

Thane rested on some blankets near the fire, chest covered in neat white bandages. His face still held little real color and his beard and hair were a disheveled mess, but his chest rose and fell with steady, untaxed breaths, which gave Marek no small relief.

She entered the chamber and took a seat next to the fire, her back up against a rock. Teela sat near Thane, though she appeared to be dozing as she leaned up against the rock, staff held in a loose grip and balanced across her knees. Marek wished she felt as peaceful as Teela looked. Her own emotions were a bubbling mess of guilt, confusion, and anger, though she wasn't entirely sure where that last bit had come from. Teela opened her eyes and glanced at Marek, then looked down at Thane before leaning her head back against the wall again.

Marek heard Dagen enter the chamber a few minutes later. She heard him pause at the shallow pool just behind her and dip his fingers in, flicking the water back into the pool from whence it had come.

"Well, Teela," Dagen's voice echoed softly in the cavern. There was a hard edge to it now, though, one Marek hadn't heard before, which sent shivers down her spine. "I presume the mission's over."

Marek turned to look at him, frowning.

"Unless you have some idea where your sister might actually be?" Dagen leaned against his bow as if it were a walking staff. His face lay mostly concealed in shadow, only the hard outlines of his jaw and profile visible.

Marek licked her lips, unsure what to say, though not entirely disagreeing with what Dagen was saying. She'd been wondering similar things herself in her wanderings through the cave complex, though she hadn't yet figured out how to broach the subject. She turned to regard Teela, who was hugging her knees.

"My sister may have been taken by the ogre."

Teela didn't meet anyone's eyes when she spoke.

Marek looked up sharply. "The ogre?" she asked.

"Ah yes," Dagen hissed, "the ogre. And not just any old ogre, but the one that attacked your temple with the orcs." Teela kept her eyes fixed on the floor. "A little—or should I said a *huge*—detail that Teela left out." By the end, Dagen was nearly shouting. His last word echoed off the chamber walls, reverberating back like a damning cry of many voices.

"That's probably why she didn't want us to go down there," Dagen continued. Marek noticed tears forming in Teela's eyes, but the priestess blinked them away as Dagen kept going. "We'd have noticed all the evidence."

"No!" Teela shouted, and though her face was stricken, her pale complexion blanched even paler. "I mean, I didn't know the Goddess led us to—"

"Oh, the Goddess be damned," Dagen interrupted. "I did my part whether your sister was there or not! Now I want my silver and then I'll be going."

Marek felt the color drain from her own features, and her heart plummeted out of her chest and into the pit of her stomach. She'd failed and, more than that, she couldn't even keep the team together.

Still, a small voice in the back of her mind did congratulate her on not having kissed him. *Stupid, selfish man.*

"I do not have your silver, not yet," Teela said, voice still soft, though her expression had become cool and almost collected again. Marek admired her strength and wished she could possess it herself.

Dagen's expression darkened and the lines around his eyes deepened as his lips curled into an expression that was halfway between a frown and a scowl. He let the silence stretch for several deep, heavy moments.

"Well, that's just perfect, isn't it?"

"The Goddess has promised to provide you with payment." Teela's voice was firm with resolve and an absolute faith.

"Okay, I'm done with you lot." Dagen spun on his heel and clambered up the steep slope toward the cave's mouth.

Marek watched him leave, though she didn't stir. She knew she should go after him, say something, anything. It was her responsibility as the leader of this team to step in and resolve situations like these, but she simply didn't know what to say. She felt like the foolish slave girl constantly beaten by Master Vagamal for disobedience, then going back and being disobedient all over again. Would she never learn?

"I know in my heart that my sister is alive," Teela called after Dagen. "I still have to find her."

Dagen paused at the mouth of the cave and turned back to her, rolling his eyes. "Yeah, well, good luck with that, priestess." He picked up his bow and vanished into the night.

Marek leapt to her feet. "Dagen, wait!"

She clambered up the steps as fast as her bad foot could carry her, but Dagen was already gone. She reached the cave's mouth and rushed out into the night, feeling the chilled air bite at her cheeks and remind her of winter's stranglehold on the outside world. She rushed down the slope, limping more than running. Even with the moon nearly full in the sky, it was hard to see and she stumbled more than once.

Where is he?

Marek hurried down the path, not entirely sure what she was going to say when she caught up to him or even why she was chasing after him in the first place. She knew she wasn't a very good leader, but the sight of him actually leaving, of giving up and walking out on them, that had awoken something within her. Anger and sheer force of will pushed her onward. As she'd raced up the cavern's stairs she'd decided that she wasn't going to let him go, not without doing everything she could to persuade him to stay. He was a part of the team, and their job was not yet finished. The attempted kiss had nothing to do with it.

Didn't it?

Part of her wondered if her rejecting the kiss had been what set him off to begin with, though she pushed that thought aside as she raced down the path. Her cloak snagged on a branch, but she simply tugged it free and kept going. A low fog rolled through, obscuring her vision even further, though it was not enough to keep her from *hearing* the orcs ahead of her even before she saw them. She came to sudden stop, hoping they hadn't heard her.

A hand wrapped around her neck and covered her mouth. Marek struggled, heart thumping in her chest, but whoever had her was stronger by far and dragged her off the path a moment before a pair of orcs trudged past. Marek's captor pulled her to the ground and made a shushing sound. Marek recognized the voice, even with such a small sound.

Dagen released her and she rounded on him, not even trying to keep her anger and frustration out of her voice.

"What are you doing?" she demanded.

"I am leaving," Dagen whispered. He wore his hood up, obscuring his features, and his bow was over one shoulder. He kept pivoting his neck, looking around at the passing orcs from where they hid among some low trees and brambles. "This mission is suicide."

Marek gave him a flat look. "It's suicide alone."

"I'll take my chances." He paused and met her eyes. "Come with me, if you like."

For half a moment, looking into those eyes, Marek considered it. Like before, when he had tried to kiss her, Marek felt her insides go hot, her skin burn. The thought of his lips against hers, of their togetherness, nearly convinced her right there, but then she shook her head.

"I want to see this through." She had to know. Had to know if she could really do this. If she was more than just a slave girl. It wasn't about being a good leader anymore. It wasn't even about being a good conjurer anymore. Somewhere in the last few hours it had become simply about finishing what she'd started, about keeping her word. About honor.

Dagen looked at her for a long moment, his expression unreadable, then he got to his feet.

"Take care of Thane," he said, then raced off into the night in a half crouch.

"Wait!" Marek called after him, but he was already gone.

Marek made it back to the cave without much difficulty, outside of the actual climb itself. As she stepped into the cave, her eyes adjusted to the light of the fire. She paused in the entryway, looking down at Thane's still form lying prone near the fire. His chest rose and fell in measured, rhythmic movements, unimpaired by his wounds. Teela crouched near the fire. She stirred a pot which hung over the fire with a long ladle. Even from the entryway, Marek could smell the simmering broth, and it made her mouth water and her stomach rumble. She ignored it.

She clambered down the slope into the cavern proper and made her way over to Thane. She knelt down next to him, ignoring her protesting foot. Dried blood stained his face, and his cracked lips looked swollen and split in a number of places. Blood matted his beard. Marek reached out and ran a hand through his long hair, doing her best not to disturb him. He stirred and his eyes fluttered open. He stared up at Marek, though she could tell his eyes weren't in focus.

"Teela?" he murmured.

Marek let out a small sigh. "No."

"Mmmm," Thane muttered. He blinked and as his lids rose, his eyes came into focus.

"I'm sorry," Marek said.

Thane shook his shaggy head. "Nothing has changed." He took one of her hands in his own, though his grip wasn't nearly as strong as it usually was. "My promise is good," he said, giving her hand a squeeze. "One bounty. We leave at dawn."

Marek smiled and her own vision blurred as tears welled up in her eyes. Thane made a small, reassuring noise deep in his throat and—despite everything else that had gone terribly wrong—for a moment, everything was right in the world.

CHAPTER 16

Gojun looked over the side of the ridge and down at the temple of Ana-Sett. Rather, what was left of the temple. A few fires still smoldered among the discarded husks of outbuildings and wagons of some sort. Though the temple itself had been carved into the cliff face, other structures had been erected along the ground. It all lay in rubble now.

Gojun rubbed a hand over his stubbly chin and ground his teeth together. He remembered a time when the order of Ana-Sett had been a grand and glorious thing, a group of healers, priests, priestesses, and caregivers devoted to a well-respected Goddess. Now the order was as broken and spent as the temple below. The core of it remained, but it was only an empty shell.

"I told you there wasn't much left," Kynall said.

The mountainous man stood a few steps to one side, leaning against his giant axe and fishing inside his cloak for something with one hand.

"There never is. Not when Szorlock is involved."

"Didn't get them all though, looks like."

Gojun looked at Kynall and raised an eyebrow.

The man pulled a pipe from an inside pocket of his cloak and jutted his chin down toward the temple with a grunt. Gojun looked in that direction.

Where moments before there had been only desolation and stillness, Gojun now saw signs of movement among the outbuildings. A few figures in red scrambled about, going from building to building. Light glinted off armor and weaponry.

"Vitalions?"

Kynall grunted. He produced a phosphorus match and lit his pipe with it, puffing with single-minded purpose for a long moment. A small cloud of pungent, bitter smoke pooled around him.

"Maybe they're looking for survivors."

This time Gojun raised both eyebrows and gave Kynall a look which quite clearly said that the man was either an imbecile or insane. Kynall grunted again, though this time it sounded more like a throaty chuckle than an actual grunt.

"Fine, Gojun, fine," Kynall said. The man pulled his pipe from his mouth with his right hand and pointed it at Gojun, leaving a small trail of smoke behind. "If this goes to hell and there's fighting though, I'm blaming you."

It was Gojun's turn to grunt. "When have you ever not?"

"When have you not deserved it?"

Gojun didn't have an answer for that. He looked

down at the Vitalions and then straightened, lifting his staff off the ground.

"Come on then," Gojun said. "Let's go see if the shard of the Darkspore really passed through here."

Kynall ran a hand the size of a dinner-plate over his face and muttered something under his breath around his pipe stem, which he'd returned to his mouth. But he picked up his axe and followed Gojun down the switchbacks toward the temple.

The Vitalions noticed them well before they reached the bottom of the cliff face. Gojun surreptitiously shifted his staff from his right hand to his left, testing the weight of it in his grip. He also shortened his stride and added a small limp. Kynall shifted closer to him and adjusted the axe on his shoulder, assuming a more menacing posture as he walked, as if he were a guard of some sort. Gojun suppressed a small smile, memories of similar strategies in potentially volatile situations passing through his mind. That had been a different day, a different era.

The Vitalions clumped together near one of the smoldering outbuildings as Gojun and Kynall approached. Gojun studied them through half-closed eyes. Rust stood out on armor, patches adorned once fine cloaks, and the hard, wooden gaze of the soldier who stepped forward to intercept them bespoke a recent history distant from comfortable. The polished hilt of the man's sword colored that uncomfortable past with a darker hue.

"Move along, strangers," the soldier said, voice like cold iron and heavy with authority. An officer, perhaps? Or at least he may have been, at one point.

"We come in need of aid, friend." Gojun kept his voice soft and put a small quaver in it. "In times of old, this temple held healers. Does it not, anymore?"

The Vitalions laughed.

"Are you fyking blind, old man? Can't you see what happened to this place?"

"You must forgive an old man," Gojun said. "My eyes, they aren't what they used to be, you see. I can smell smoke, and the salty, putrid stench of death, but I thought . . ." He trailed off for a moment and made a small gesture with one hand. "Well, even the best healers lose someone every now and then."

"The zealots here are all dead," the lead soldier said. "The temple is abandoned."

Several of the other soldiers laughed softly, a low murmur of whispers dancing between them. Gojun shifted slightly, recognizing the sound of men preparing to do something decent people wouldn't have even considered.

"And you're here to investigate who did it, then?" Kynall said, his deep, rumbling voice making the soldier's appear soft by comparison. "Good for you,

Vitalion. And here I thought you folk were looters, come to pillage from the dead."

The soft hum of conversation died. The laughter cut off and broke into a dozen sharp shards that fell away like shattering glass. Silence rushed in to take its place, leaving the air thick with sudden tension. Gojun licked his lips and took a mental inventory of the spell components he had close at hand. A few soldiers' hands strayed toward the hilts of their swords. The hair along Gojun's arms stood on end and the skin along his lower back squirmed in an unpleasant upward motion.

Kynall made the first move. He shrugged and let his axe roll down his arm, catching the long handle just beneath the head with his left arm. The soldiers jumped back, three of them drawing swords.

"Last warning," the Vitalion ex-officer said, hard lines forming around his eyes and along his jaw. "Move along and there'll be no need for anyone to get hurt."

Kynall grunted, but didn't respond. Gojun realized that Kynall wanted to see what he would do. After all the good Gojun had done as part of the Redthorns, the one bad but necessary decision he had made was the only thing coloring their relationship now. So be it then.

Gojun straightened and raised a hand to push the hair back out of his eyes, fixing the leader with an iron stare cold enough to shatter ice.

"I feel it only fair to offer you the same chance," Gojun said, voice so devoid of warmth he expected it to solidify into an icy spear as it rushed toward the man. "Go now and leave the dead in peace. Do not desecrate their resting place further."

The Vitalion leader, for his part, seemed slightly taken aback for the space of a single heartbeat, then he laughed and drew his sword.

Gojun didn't even bother waiting for the man to take the first strike. He simply stepped forward, staff already swinging, and struck the Vitalion such a resounding blow to the side of his head that Gojun's staff reverberated with the impact for several long seconds. The Vitalion blinked several times as Kynall roared and charged past the man, his axe spinning in his hands. Gojun watched with a strange sense of satisfaction as blood slipped down the man's cheek and his eyes glazed over. The sword slipped from his fingers and he toppled to the dirt, landing at almost the same instant as the blade.

Gojun stepped back and glanced sidelong at Kynall's battle with the five remaining Vitalions. A large brute of a man, Kynall intimidated even the most seasoned, hardened warriors. The five remaining soldiers seemed anything but that. Kynall hadn't even raised his axe yet—he stood a few paces away from them, looking menacing and twisting his axe about in his hand—but one of the soldiers, a ruddy-faced fellow with a sparse collection of red hairs on his chin, simply dropped his sword and fled in the opposite direction. The remaining four closed ranks, but the wavering of their sword points and the way they huddled close to one another spoke volumes about their own courage. Kynall could easily take them, but Gojun decided there'd been enough death on this hallowed ground already.

Gojun stepped over to Kynall and put a hand on his shoulder, stilling him. With his other hand, Gojun pulled a glass vial from a loop on his belt and tossed it at the soldiers' feet. They leapt back as a small cloud of red powder—dried basilisk blood—burst up from the shattered glass.

"*Domah noesthis kaspil fu-eni!*"

Flames leapt up in a wall of heat, smoke billowing out where none had existed only moments before. One of the soldiers screamed a rather feminine wail and dropped his sword. The others were more dignified in their retreat, dropping weapons and running like young acolytes after a scolding from a priest. The flames died down, but by then, the last glint of Vitalion red had already vanished around a bend in the road.

"You take all the fun out of everything," Kynall complained. "You know that?"

Gojun shrugged, his irritation not fully spent. "It's a wonder Vitalia conquered as much of the land as they have with soldiers like these."

"Deserters, most likely. Give them some credit though. You did throw a fykin' fireball at them."

Gojun snorted. "That was hardly a fireball. Just a show to give them a little scare. Basilisk blood isn't nearly a strong enough reagent for any sort of lasting fire magic. Most magic is just showmanship and trickery. The rest of it is just a knowledge of reagents and how to activate them."

Kynall grunted and Gojun felt himself deflate, the irritation and tension draining out of him as he realized Kynall probably didn't understand a word of what he'd just said. Kynall wasn't stupid, not by any sense of the word, but he did lack a certain knowledge of the finer, more intricate workings of the world around them. One couldn't hope for a better companion in a battle, though.

"Come on," Gojun said, voice heavy with the weariness of knowing far more than he wished he did. "Let's get this over with. If the shard was here for any length of time, I'll sense its presence when I get close."

The fallen Vitalion officer behind them groaned and Kynall raised a bushy brow in Gojun's direction. "What should we do with him?"

Gojun shrugged. "You decide."

A few minutes later, they entered the heart of the temple, stepping over the body of a fallen priestess who lay in the entryway. A small totem of an owl lay clutched in her lifeless fingers. Gojun tried not to look at the red stain on her back, as he had been trying and failing to do since encountering the first body just beyond where they'd met the Vitalion looters. He'd seen each of them as he walked by, and would have the images of them lying frozen and lifeless in the dirt burned into his memory forever.

A cold anger smoldered in his chest.

"Sense anything?" Kynall asked.

Gojun shook his head, blinking several times as his eyes adjusted to the gloom within the temple. He tapped his staff on the ground in a specific pattern, activating the spell he'd woven into it for occasions such as this. A soft glow flared to life at the tip of his staff, a white, heatless flame that flickered and danced but produced a solid, unmoving white light.

"Useful," Kynall grunted.

Gojun moved deeper into the temple without answering. His light, though small, illuminated the sweeping columns inside the entryway which had been worked into likenesses of the Goddess with owls and forest creatures wrapping up around them like stony vines. Skilled artisans must have toiled for years and years to craft the hundreds of perfect carvings Gojun could see. It was almost beautiful enough to hide the dark smears of dried blood along the column bases and to mask the stench of bodies just beginning to rot which filled the musty air. Almost.

"This way," Gojun said, gesturing toward a side passage with his staff.

Though he'd never been inside this particular temple, all of Ana-Sett's edifices had a similar construction. The world saw the outer sanctum, with its finery and frippery. Only the holy and pure saw the real heart of the temple.

Gojun moved through the hallway with reverent steps. Even if he didn't particularly care for the Gods as a whole, he knew enough to treat their holy places with the respect they deserved. Behind him, he heard Kynall mutter a prayer for the dead in a soft, reverent whisper.

There.

A small burr of dissonance fluttered through Gojun's senses, tugging him toward yet another side passageway. He quickened his pace and Kynall thumped along behind him. The fine carved walls gave way to rough, natural ones, the hall occasionally lit by light filtering down from cracks in the ceiling where stones met unevenly. Gojun's skin started crawling along his arm, seeming to bunch up near his shoulders. A deep feeling of unease swept through him, one he recognized from a time he'd hoped to never remember again.

"It's been here," Gojun whispered, turning a corner and finding himself in a small room fashioned of unmarked stone boulders left in their natural position. "Right there, in fact."

He pointed at a spot where two boulders met and formed a crevice into which something small could be placed. Several books and golden cloths lay scattered across the ground next to the body of an old man in the white robes of Ana-Sett's priesthood. The evil in the room was thick enough that Gojun found he had difficulty breathing.

"There're no marks on him, Gojun," Kynall said in a soft voice.

Gojun looked closer at the man, tearing his eyes away from the small crevice in the rocks.

"Necromancy." The word slipped from Gojun's lips as a hiss. He spun on a heel and hurried back out of the temple, his quick steps turning into a run the closer he got to the temple entrance.

Kynall thundered along behind him. "Wait!" Kynall huffed, his gasping breath loud enough to be heard over the sounds of their boots hitting stone.

"No time. We need to know what Jaffin found. We'll follow him if we have to. If Szorlock gets his hands on that shard . . ."

He didn't finish. He didn't have to. Kynall offered no further argument. He simply ran.

CHAPTER 17

Teela awoke to the sound of crackling flames and the soft murmur of a voice from somewhere nearby. Her eyes immediately went to Thane, who was dozing only a few feet from her. His lips moved as if he was about to speak, but no words came out. She'd been positive he'd said her name not a moment before. Now he looked peaceful and still, the only movement the steady motion of his chest as he breathed. She took comfort in that. More than that, she took comfort in his presence so near her. Despite the fact that he was still weak, she felt safe with him around. Not like that rogue of a half elf, Dagen. She certainly wasn't sad to see him go.

The voice murmured something again and Teela looked up, noticing Marek sitting on a ledge on the other side of the fire, her hands extended out over a clay pot on the ground before her.

What in Ana-Sett's holy name is that girl up to this time?

Marek's face twisted, but the heat from the fire distorted the air between her and Teela and the priestess couldn't tell if the expression was a grimace of frustration, concentration, or pain.

The clay pot vanished.

Teela's breath caught in her throat. Marek's face split into a wide grin and she immediately began looking around, as if expecting the pot to reappear somewhere around her. Teela looked as well. She found the pot at about the same time Marek did, half buried in the stone wall to Marek's left. Marek's upper lip curled into what was unmistakably a grimace, though there may have been a wry twist to it. Teela had always thought the girl a little odd, even for a sorcerer. What slave would go out of their way to learn magic in a land where sorcery itself was outlawed? Why take that risk? According to Teela's logic, it meant Marek was clearly mad. Still, looking at the disappointment on Marek's face, Teela couldn't help but be moved. She got to her feet and picked her way over to where Marek sat.

"You should rest," Teela said, voice pitched low and soft so as not to wake Thane. *He* needed rest more than anyone, and Teela still felt the lingering exhaustion and ache deep within her bones that she felt each time she used her link to the Goddess to heal another.

"I have no need." Marek fiddled with a bit of cloth in her hand. Was that a scroll or spell perhaps?

Teela made a small, disbelieving sound. She'd handled this wrong. Teela wondered how she always ended up saying the wrong things. It was a habit of hers that had begun when she was a child. It had gotten her into trouble more than once. There was far too much fire within her, Caeryn would always say. So much, in fact, that it had to bleed out into her hair.

"Nor I," she said, softly. "Sleep doesn't come so easily now. Before all this, I would sleep like a babe."

Teela found her gaze wandering toward the fire in the silence that followed. After a moment, she realized her eyes had drifted to Thane once again, examining the contours of his face beneath his beard and admiring the firm line of his jaw. She felt her cheeks grow hot and turned away from the vision of Thane, pointedly searching for something else upon which to focus her attention. Her eyes fell on the odd metal brace Marek always wore on her leg, but which now lay on the ground beside the girl. She picked it up and turned it over in one hand, examining the leather straps and metal frame with puzzled interest. She'd seen a lot of interesting things in her years inside the temple of Ana-Sett, despite the order's waning influence in this corner of the world. The order itself was one of service and healing, and much of her time had been spent assisting the elders in caring for the sick and wounded. Even then, she'd never seen anything quite like it.

"This is very clever," she said, looking up at Marek.

Marek sucked in a breath, turning her head from side to side, then whipping it around to stare intently at Teela. She leaned forward, eyes intent.

"Teela. You're a healer. Are you able to heal anyone?" Marek said the last word with a measure of fear in her voice, as if she were dreading the answer, but was unable to keep the words contained.

Teela looked down. She'd wondered if Marek would ever get around to asking that question. She *was* a priestess, and she had great power, yes. But that power was complicated.

"Those with pure intent and who have faith to heal and be healed." Teela met Marek's eyes, seeing the eagerness within them like the swirling storms of a tempest raging across the sky.

"Yes," Marek whispered, pulling up her skirt to reveal her twisted, dirty ankle and foot. "Am I pure enough? Can your Goddess—can she heal me—my leg?" There was a long pause, broken only by the sound of the crackling fire. "Please?" Marek finished.

Teela heard the desperation in her voice. The emotion was there just beneath the surface, a raw, bitter thing clawing to get out. Teela sighed. Ana-Sett was sometimes a fickle mistress. As much as

Teela wanted to heal people, sometimes the Goddess decided otherwise.

What harm is there in trying?

Teela reached out and wrapped her hand firmly around Marek's swollen leg, pressing her palms against the ankle, and then reached out to the Goddess. Warmth immediately sprang from her hands and a light erupted from the gaps between her fingers. Her eyes snapped closed. For half a heartbeat, Teela felt the thrill of the Goddess's power surging through her, then everything somehow shifted. Her arms began to tremble and her breath screamed in ragged bursts through her throat.

An image of the Goddess flashed through her mind. Her eyes were wide in the vision, gold tiara hugging her brow and tracing down over her ears. The vision flickered, then came back even stronger. The Goddess seemed even closer now and Teela sensed her anger, her disapproval. It washed through Teela like the thundering of her blood within her veins. The image flickered again and was replaced by a vision of Marek with ebony tears dripping from black, pupilless eyes.

Teela released Marek's leg, fingers springing open almost of their own accord. Her arms and hands still trembled, though her breathing had stilled. The Goddess's will was plain.

"I'm sorry, Marek," Teela said, shaking her head.

"It is not the will of the Goddess."

"What?" Marek shook her head, face contorting through a half dozen different expressions. "Why?"

Teela was half surprised to realize she knew the answer, as if Ana-Sett herself had left the words embedded in her mind. Perhaps she had. The thought made Teela want to shiver, though she managed to keep her composure.

"Your leg. It's a deliberate mark from the Gods . . . a reminder of the darkness inside you."

"I'm good," Marek protested immediately. "I know I am. There's no darkness inside of me." Marek rocked back and forth gently, like a mother rocking her small child to sleep. Except there was no child.

"We all harbor darkness inside, and light."

Marek got to her feet, snatching the brace up off the stone with one hand as she pushed past Teela and stepped closer to the fire. A few feet from it, Marek spun back to face Teela.

"Then why am I different?" Marek threw her hands into the air. "Why can't I be healed?

Teela didn't have an answer for that one. *See, the Goddess is fickle.*

Marek scowled and spun about, tossing the brace into the fire before stalking off down a side passageway. Teela leapt to her feet in a panic and rushed to the fire, plucking the brace out of the mess with a ginger grip. She dropped it a couple feet back from the fire and stamped out the remaining flames.

Crazy, foolish, stubborn girl.

CHAPTER 18

Marek adjusted the strap on Egan's brace, tightening the metal bands near the top and loosening the clasp near her ankle. It eased the pain there, somewhat, but did little to diminish the lingering emotional pain of the previous night's encounter with Teela's Goddess. Her fingers very briefly brushed a singed portion of one of the straps, though Marek forced her mind to pass on to other things. She looked up at Teela and Thane, who stood close together among the trees ahead of her.

"How recent do you think this ogre trail is?" she called.

After a little discussion that morning, they'd decided to continue the mission without Dagen. Since Teela's sister hadn't been with the others, and Teela assumed the ogre may have taken her, the consensus had been to double back to see if they could pick up any signs of the creature's passing. Luckily, they had.

"Less than a day, I'd wager." Despite his wounds, Thane didn't so much as limp. He wore his Vitalion shield strapped to his back and the heavy furs and pack he normally carried without even a trace of discomfort. Teela's healing had all but returned him to normal. Apparently the Goddess didn't see any hidden darkness in *him.*

"Are Vitalion soldiers trained in tracking?" Teela walked close enough to Thane to touch him if she turned too quickly. Her voice wasn't pitched any softer than normal, but the pair was far enough ahead that Marek had to strain to hear her words and even more so to hear Thane's reply.

"Aye, but men, not ogres."

Marek grimaced and got to her feet, hurrying after them and scowling at Teela's back and, by association, Thane's as well. Was there really that much difference between tracking men and monsters? She'd known the dynamic of their group would change without Dagen, but she hadn't truly realized how much she'd feel excluded when left with just Thane and Teela. The two had always seemed to gravitate toward one another, now that Marek was thinking about it, but something had changed last night. It sparked a deep, twisting mass of unpleasant emotions which writhed in Marek's gut.

Stupid priestess.

"Why'd you become a soldier?" Teela asked.

Marek climbed up a fallen log behind them, listening so intently to their conversation that she nearly tripped, and then leapt down the other side. She knew so little about her companions, she realized. She should have thought to ask these sorts of things herself, but it had simply never occurred to her. Living life as a slave hadn't necessarily taught her much about the social niceties normal people seemed to grasp instinctively.

"Chance to see the world," Thane said. "And swing a sword at it. And you?"

"Why did I choose the order of Ana-Sett?"

"Aye."

Marek hurried to keep up, staying just close enough to listen without appearing to eavesdrop. "It was my sister who was first called, greatly upsetting our father," Teela said.

An owl hooted in the distance, drawing Marek's gaze. As she sought out the owl, her eyes fell on the broken husk of a tree, recently shattered by the passing of something very large. The ogre, most likely.

"I promised I would never follow in her footsteps. Nor did I desire to. Then I found out he planned to trade me to a nobleman for a tract of land. I refused and ran to Caeryn and the order. The Goddess has been my life ever since."

"Not many girls would pass up a chance to marry a nobleman." Thane's voice held a small measure of curiosity in it. Marek found she agreed with the sentiment. Marrying a nobleman didn't sound like an unappealing life.

"I refused to be traded like property."

"Well, we all sell ourselves for something in the end."

"That's rather bleak," Teela said.

"Life is bleak," Thane said, though his voice sounded distracted.

Lost in her own thoughts, Marek looked up at the change in tone, noticing that he'd stopped and crouched down to look more closely at something on the ground. Tracks, perhaps?

"The imprint is deeper here," Thane said, looking up and peering through a curtain of his own hair toward the path ahead of them. Marek and Teela walked up alongside him. "And it lengthens. The ogre was running."

"Running?" Marek asked. "For what?"

"From what," Thane corrected. He straightened from his crouch, but remained on his knees.

Marek suppressed a shiver and licked her lips, feeling suddenly nervous. From what indeed? What would make an ogre run?

Teela moved over to Thane's other side, head turning this way and that as if expecting to find the answer lying about near them. Marek followed her in that direction.

"I have little experience with these creatures,"

Thane said. "Following blindly is reckless."

Teela took a seat on a fallen log and Thane sat down next to her, adjusting his sword so it wouldn't catch on anything. Marek studied the tracks on the ground, trying to puzzle out what had made the ogre start running. The whole thing made her uneasy.

"What do you suggest?" Teela asked.

For a moment, Marek thought she was talking to her, but then Thane replied, making it clear she'd not been the target of the question at all.

"I say we get up high."

Marek looked sidelong over at him. Thane looked as nervous as Marek felt, which only served to make Marek even more uneasy. "Spy out the land. Learn what might be waiting for us."

Really?

"We don't have time," Marek said. "If your sister's still alive there's no telling how much longer she has. We have the trail, let's keep going."

She started walking in the direction of the tracks, pointedly ignoring the pair as she passed them sitting on the log. She only made it a few steps before a flash of reflected light on the ground caught her eye. Bending to pick it up, Marek realized what it was a moment before her hand wrapped around the dagger's hilt.

Dagen.

The curved blade was covered in blood, some of it still fresh. Marek's hands trembled slightly as she righted herself again.

Dagen.

Marek only half noticed Thane get to his feet, his eyes fixed on the blade in her hand.

"Orcs," Thane muttered. He made the word sound almost like a curse.

"He chose his own path," Teela said, getting to her feet and walking closer to Marek and Thane.

"He may have been taken captive," Marek said, letting her hands drop to her side and peering into the trees that surrounded them. There was no sign of him. She didn't really expect there to be. She looked anyway and hoped he'd only been taken captive. "He's likely still alive."

Please don't be dead.

"Maybe." Thane didn't sound hopeful.

"The Goddess has her purposes," Teela said softly. "Dagen's fate is no longer our concern."

Marek spun on the priestess. "I've heard enough of your damn Goddess!" she snapped. "What good is she to me, to you, to anyone?" Anger piled up within her, mingling with resentment, pain, and bitterness that still lingered from the previous night's encounter with the Goddess's *purposes.* She let it pour out of her. "You know, maybe Dagen had it right." Marek stepped closer Teela, meeting her cold green eyes. "Your temple is burned, your sister is probably dead, and chances are we're probably going to die here too."

Teela frowned, but Marek didn't give her a chance to speak.

"Maybe I'm not good enough," Marek continued, "for you and your Goddess to care about, but I know this. I'm not like your Goddess. I wouldn't leave a friend to die alone in the wilderness." Marek spun away from her, ignoring Thane entirely.

"Just like Dagen left us?"

Teela's words struck Marek like a blow. Her lips curled into a snarl and she was about to turn back to the priestess when a low growl ripped through the silence.

"What was that?" Teela asked. Marek looked in the direction from which she thought the sound originated. What could be out there this time?

"We need to move," Thane muttered, hand on his sword. "Now!"

All thought of argument vanished as Marek raced after the man. Teela ran close to her, though they both stayed a step or two behind Thane. Marek cursed her foot as more growls split the air. She limped as she ran, working twice as hard as either of her companions just to keep up.

"We need to find a clearing," Thane yelled over his shoulder over a sudden, terrible howling which left Marek's skin crawling across her arms. "We'll have a better chance of fighting it if we can see it."

Fighting what? The thought sent shivers down Marek's spine as she ran. More howls split the air, this time coming from even closer. Marek caught a glimpse of something darting through the trees out of the corner of her eye, but didn't see enough of it to know what it was. They ran on.

Thane suddenly pulled to a stop. Teela let out a whimper of fear and Marek looked up. A creature the like of which Marek had never seen before, but immediately recognized, stood before them. Narrow, beady eyes stared hungrily out at them beneath massive, bony brows. Dozens of teeth jutted from a thick, wide jaw. Spikes as long as Marek's arm ran in three long lines down its back. Its hairless skin was, if anything, the worst part of it all. Dull gray flesh shone with a strange reddish luster in the right light. It lay tight against muscle and bone, appearing for all the world like the rotting remains of a corpse. A hellhound.

It growled deep in its throat and regarded them with obvious unconcern. Marek nearly gagged at the smell wafting from the creature. It was the single most disgusting scent she'd ever encountered, though the nausea lay smothered beneath a layer of fear so intense and unadulterated it was barely recognizable.

"Don't look in his eyes!" Teela screamed.

Marek felt her mouth go dry and forced herself to look away. Almost as one, Teela and Thane spun around and dashed back the way they'd come, Marek a step behind.

"I may have looked directly into his eyes!" Thane yelled.

"If you truly had, you'd be dead."

"Do we keep running or make a stand?" Marek shouted. She glanced back over her shoulder as she ran, a motion so involuntary she didn't even realize she was doing it until the third or fourth time she did.

"Keep running!"

The hellhound roared as it leaped into pursuit.

"I thought we needed to find a clearing!" Teela shouted.

Marek ran as fast as she could, though she quickly fell behind the priestess.

"I'm trying!"

Marek forced herself to run faster, practically dragging her bad leg behind her. The foot snagged on a stick and she sprawled headlong into the ground, the weight of her pack forcing her to one side. Pain flared up from her foot and shot up her leg, but Marek ignored it. Panic made her heart race, her lungs sucking in great gasps of earth-scented air. Teela and Thane raced on ahead of her, oblivious to her plight.

The hellhound appeared on the trail behind her. Marek rolled onto her back, feet digging into the ground and scrambling for purchase. Her hands went to her waist, grasping for anything that could help her. The hellhound growled low. Marek may have imagined it, but it seemed the creature licked its lips as it began to crawl forward.

No! Not like this!

Her hands found a vial and she yanked out the stopper as she brought it over to her other hand and dropped a quantity of the white powder into it.

Which spell? Not many used only a single component. It came to her in a rush of sudden clarity. The hellhound's clawed foot struck the ground only a few inches from Marek's foot. The smell of its breath nearly made Marek heave.

"Manu kespa dem gusti!" she shouted, and hurled the powder at the hellhound's face, noticing Thane running back toward her out of the corner of her eye.

The powder ignited in the air as the spell took effect. It hit the hellhound in the face and exploded in a cascade of sparks and smoke. The beast reared back with a whimper, raising a foot to paw at its face.

"Stop playing around and run!" Thane bellowed.

"Run!"

Marek scrambled to her feet and took off at a sprint. Thane ran just ahead of her. Marek felt a rush of gratitude toward Thane battle with the terror which threatened to consume her. The hellhound growled behind her and Marek heard it leap into pursuit. Teela joined them, letting Thane take the lead again. Her heavy staff thumped against the ground, in time with Marek's beating heart.

The hellhound let out an earsplitting squeal, which cut off abruptly with a strange crunching noise.

"What was that?" Marek asked. Dread filled her. The sound of the hellhound's squeals—of pain, or fear, or utter and complete agony—left her imagination running wild at what else lay out there among the trees.

"I don't want to know!" Thane said through belabored gasps. "There's a clearing ahead."

Marek looked up. The trees opened up ahead of them, revealing a clearing covered in snow. Marek pushed herself to run faster. If they could just get there, they may have a chance. Her foot protested the abuse, slowing her even further. She started to fall behind.

Not again!

Thane and Teela burst into the meadow a dozen yards ahead of her, leaving wide tracks in the snow.

They fell to their knees just outside the tree line, gasping for breath, mist pooling around them. Marek limped toward them as fast as she could manage. Her ankle gave out.

Once again, Marek found herself sprawled on the ground, foot and ankle screaming in pain. She rolled onto her back and pulled on the straps on her brace. Maybe if she tightened it . . . one of the straps broke off in her hand, the charred section pulling free and crumbling into small, blackened bits.

"We should have scouted." Teela's voice carried back to where Marek sat.

Marek knew the complaint should irritate her, at the very least, but she simply didn't have the energy for it. She rolled to the side, fully intending to stretch out in the snow and let it cool her.

The ground shook.

Marek looked up into the face of a twenty-foot-tall, monstrous, green-skinned ogre. It stood, looking down at them with eyes as large as Marek's head, a rictus smile on its bloodied lips.

"Get to the trees!" Thane shouted.

Marek pushed herself up, testing her weight on her foot. It held, barely. The ogre rumbled and started toward her. Marek limped forward, then felt a hand on her elbow. She turned to see Thane.

"Leave me," she snapped. "I can make it."

Thane simply scooped her up and threw her over one shoulder as if she weighed less than a sack of meal. He took off toward the trees, Marek's stomach digging into his shoulder.

"Put me down!" She grimaced as she jounced with each of his steps. Pain from her leg, which Thane's arms held in a vice-like grip, lanced through her.

"Shut up and hold on!" Thane gasped.

"Leave me!"

The ogre lumbered toward them, massive strides eating the distance between them like a starving man ate a meal. Marek looked into its eyes, seeing the hunger there, the black pits of a ravenous need to destroy and conquer, and the leering, unconcerned grin of a creature born and bred to kill. She stared into the face of death and it scowled back at her.

"Faster!" she yelled. "Run faster!"

Thane screamed, but Marek felt him speed up. She bounced and jostled on his shoulder, but she no longer cared. The ogre gained on them still, not even seeming to try. Marek watched it in frozen terror, unable to do anything but watch its unyielding advance. She felt completely and totally helpless, like a calf being carried to the slaughterhouse for a festival meal.

They weren't going to make it.

Thane turned and looked back at the ogre.

Marek twisted her head to keep it in her line of sight as well. The creature was close enough that its stink washed over her, a smell even more putrid than the hellhound's had been. Thane roared and Marek found herself flying through the air. She hit the ground hard, scattering snow across the meadow. She looked up in time to see Thane race the other direction, clearly attempting to distract the ogre long enough for her to get away. The ogre flicked out a long hand and knocked Thane to the ground. He didn't get up.

The ogre turned and leered at Marek, who'd managed to roll onto her back. Cold snow numbed her hands and back. Fear numbed the rest of her. The ogre chuckled, a sound so deep and sinister it broke through Marek's numbness. She scrambled back, fingers scrabbling through the snow. The ogre advanced on her, legs like tree trunks rippling with muscles beneath a tattered kilt or loincloth. In the back of her mind, Marek knew she should try to escape, to fight, to do something, *anything*.

She just kept backing away.

Teela burst from the trees behind the ogre, rushing to Thane's side. She knelt down beside him.

"Over here, you brute!" Teela yelled.

The ogre turned, looking down at her with a lecherous sneer. "Pretty," the creature rumbled, lumbering toward her now instead of Marek.

What is she doing?

Marek watched in horror as Teela struggled to lift Thane, pulling on his shoulders, tugging at him. The ogre growled and reached out a hand toward them. Marek watched, unable to force herself to move as the ogre pulled them both up into its arms and lumbered away, massive strides carrying it a great distance with each step.

"Marek!" Teela's voice carried toward her over the sound of the ogre's footfalls. "Forget about us! You must find the stone! Find my sister! The Goddess will aid you!"

Her shouts cut off with a shriek and the ogre disappeared among the trees, a throaty, deep chuckle that could only have come from the ogre drifting back toward her on the wind. The sound of the ogre's footfalls lingered on for several more minutes until they too disappeared.

Marek lay on the ground for a long time. She wasn't sure how long, though it was long enough that a light snow began to drift down from the sky above and the chill of the snow soaking her clothes no longer even bothered her. Her mind struggled against absolute disinterest and her heart felt like ice had completely consumed it. Despair weighed down her lungs and made breathing a difficult task. She recognized the signs of shock, though it was a detached recognition, as if she were observing herself through someone else's eyes.

Marek got to her feet, some part of her realizing it would be night soon. She looked around, trying and failing to come to terms with the knowledge that she was now completely alone. She limped over to where Thane and Teela had been taken, the snow crushed into the ground or else missing entirely where they had been. Small flakes filled in the depressions, as if trying to wipe away their memory.

Something caught Marek's eye. Lying in in the snow and dirt that had been churned together under the ogre's feet was a necklace.

No, a pendant.

Marek bent down and picked it up. Simple beads of different colors and shapes ran along the length of leather cord. At its center, a golden pendant hung, shaped like an elongated arrowhead but worked into the likeness of an owl. The pendant of a priestess of Ana-Sett.

Teela's pendant.

Marek felt a single, solitary tear slip from her eye and run down her cheek.

CHAPTER 19

Marek lay as close to the small fire as she could get, turning the small, gold pendant over and over again in her fingers, head against the frozen ground. The cold night wind howled, tugging at her hair and chilling her to the bone despite the fire. The fire's flames danced and the pendant, the amulet really, glittered with the strange pattern of light reflecting off its surface. Marek traced the lines of the owl carved into the gold surface with one finger, though it was too numb to feel anything at all.

"Why won't you heal me?"

The words sprang from Marek's lips, though she hadn't realized she'd spoken them aloud for several moments after she'd said them. Her thoughts drifted, mind as numb as her fingers, though Ana-Sett, the Goddess herself, was present in almost all of them.

Whispered voices sprang up around her. Marek sat up, sucking in a surprised gasp. She peered around her, glancing from the cliff that sheltered her back to the barren limbs of the trees that surrounded her on all other sides. Blood pounded in her ears like the beating of a distant drum. No other sounds greeted her but the distant wind and the crackling flames.

Am I going mad?

She found the amulet clasped in one hand and wrapped her palm around it, enclosing it inside her other hand as she'd seen Teela do too many times to count.

"Ana-Sett," she whispered, closing her eyes, not knowing what to expect. "Hear my prayer."

The whispers deepened around her. The image of an owl bursting from a ring of flames, wings beating against the air, raced through her mind. Marek jerked her eyes open, glancing around again, before realizing that both the whispering voices and the vision in her mind were coming from the amulet in her hand. Had Ana-Sett actually heard her? Was Ana-Sett actually *real*? Marek felt her mouth go dry and swallowed hard, wetting her lips with the tip of her tongue.

The image of an owl swiveling its head around and regarding her with deep, round eyes met Marek in the darkness as she closed her eyes again. She forced them open, but the vision didn't end. The owl's feathers shifted, becoming the headdress of a beautiful, crowned woman whose eyes reflected the same deepness and power the owl's had only moments before.

"I have failed, Goddess." Marek's voice seemed to echo endlessly, the words overlapping with one another. Inside the vision, the owl hooted and beat its wings until flames leapt up again. Where had the woman gone? Marek felt anger, disappointment, and judgment within those growing flames. "My friends are going to die. I'm alone. I'm alone."

The owl turned away from her in the vision. Even though she knew it was a vision, Marek felt the sting of rejection, the pain of being spurned.

"Heal me," Marek pleaded. "Heal me so I can save my friends."

No vision. Only the blackened night sky filled her eyes, the dancing flames of her fire a strange counterpoint on the edge of her vision.

"Ana-Sett if you hear me, answer." Marek forced her thoughts inward. Her grip on the amulet tightened until her nails dug into her palm. Had they not been numb from the cold, the pain of that alone would have made her shout.

"If you hear me," Marek repeated, "answer me."

The woman appeared in her mind's eye again, gaze cold and imperious. Her perfect face lay half cast in shadow, though the visible part showed milky skin, round eyes, and a firm jaw. Marek reached out, seeing her own dirt-covered hand extended toward Ana-Sett's flawless fingers in the vision, seeing the tremble of her own hand as it strained to touch the

Goddess.

"Answer me."

Her hands trembled in the vision, but grew no closer to the Goddess.

"Answer me. Answer me!" The last came out as a scream, both mental and real.

Marek looked down at the amulet in her hands. The numbness was giving way now to something else, something far colder. Despair.

"Answer me."

Inside the vision, the Goddess tilted her head as if considering Marek's request. Marek's hand trembled and moved the smallest fraction of an inch closer to the Goddess's. Hope flared up deep within Marek's chest.

The Goddess closed her own hand and turned away. The visions faded slowly to blackness. She'd been spurned. Rejected. Again.

Just like always.

Something inside Marek shattered.

"You're wrong," Marek whispered, eyes narrowing, shaking hands slowly steadying until they lay like rocks in her lap. "You're wrong about me."

Images flashed through Marek's mind. An owl, Ana-Sett, the owl again. Marek pushed them aside, swallowing hard and steeling her resolve. The Gods hadn't helped slave Marek escape beatings; she'd survived despite the beatings. The Gods hadn't taught her magic; she'd learned it on her own, with only a little guidance. The Gods hadn't saved Teela, or protected her sister from the ogre, or protected the temple from the orc invaders.

"To hell with the Gods," Marek said, voice becoming as firm and hard as she'd ever known.

The amulet slipped from her fingers and landed in the dirt at her feet. She resisted the urge to stamp it underfoot. She looked up at the sky, noticing the faint tendrils of purple inching across the eastern horizon. Dawn had come. Had she been at this all night?

She packed quickly and stamped out the fire, using a spare belt to tighten the brace around her foot where the straps had been weakened by flame. She paused, making sure the last embers were fully out before pulling up her hood and tossing her pack over her shoulders.

"To hell with the Gods," she repeated, and started walking in the direction of the ogre's tracks.

CHAPTER 20

Darkness hugged the land. After a full day of walking, Marek knew she should stop and rest for the night, but she kept going anyway. She'd stumbled across orc tracks earlier that day which had intermingled with the ogre's larger footprints. She followed them both now, stumbling along in the gloom. The moon shone bright in the sky and gave her enough light by which to see, but she still watched her step rather pointedly as she walked, only occasionally looking up at the path ahead.

She sighed, shaking off her weariness and glanced up. Her eyes widened. A bit of cloth fluttered on the end of a branch where it had snagged and torn. Marek limped toward it and pulled it free with one hand. Her exhaustion vanished as excitement kicked in. The cloth was of a fine weave, thick, like from a cloak. She brought it up close to her face, fingering the material. Was it green?

Dagen.

Recognition hit her. A wash of emotions swirled through her chest. Dagen had abandoned them. He'd run away from the quest, from duty. From her.

She still carried his long, curved knife in her belt.

Something caught her eye as she looked back down the path. Light flickered in the distance, very faintly, then vanished. She wondered if she'd been seeing things for half a moment. Then it came back, flickering through the trees.

Firelight?

She shoved the scrap of frayed cloth into a pocket and started toward the light. As she got closer, she heard voices muttering to one another. Low, guttural, almost animal voices. Orcs. The camp looked to be secreted behind a number of smaller hills, though there were enough gaps through which she could see the fire when she was closer. Thankfully, the orcs were either too stupid or too arrogant to post guards. Still, Marek slid onto her belly and inched the last few feet up the side of one of the hills until she could look down and survey the entire camp.

Marek counted ten orcs in all, seated around a fire, passing around flasks of something Marek was sure she never wanted to taste. The smells that reached Marek, still over ten paces away, were enough to make her gag. The orcs laughed and called out raucously to one another, bellowing and shouting as if they had nothing to fear. They probably didn't, for all Marek knew. Several sat about idly sharpening weapons or else wrestling with one another, ignorant of being observed. Their guttural voices sounded almost like the grunting of swine with only the occasional intelligible word tossed into the mix.

One of the orcs moved, revealing a framework of logs erected along the far side of the camp that she hadn't noticed before, almost like a crude sort of cross. A man had been strapped to the framework, hands bound out to each side of him. Bruised, bloodied, and devoid of weaponry, Marek still recognized him as easily as she would her own face.

Dagen.

Come on, Marek. Think.

She didn't know what to do, but she couldn't just leave him there. Her eyes fell on a snake resting on the lingering warmth of the stone upon which she was leaning. An idea coalesced in her mind.

Orcs, Dagen mused, were decidedly similar in both nature and smell to pigs. They sounded the same, looked relatively similar if one were to ignore their dark gray complexion, and both had the rather unfortunately tendency to smell like their own shite. His arms ached, tied as they were above his head, and his back and neck throbbed from where they'd struck him a few days ago. He was relatively positive that they planned on killing and eating him at some point in the near future. All told, he wasn't having too bad a time of it.

"What about a last meal or something?" he said offhandedly, directing his words at the nearest orc, a burly, ugly fellow in the process of swallowing a whole skin of grog by himself. "Some meat, perhaps?"

A few of the orcs laughed.

"Some ale would be nice," he continued conversationally.

The orc he'd been addressing spat a mixture of grog and Gods know what else across his face. Dagen jerked away by instinct, disgust filling him with the sudden desire to slam a dagger through the fykin' orc's gut. He shook his head and twitched his nose, pointedly ignoring the stench of whatever horrendous liquid now adorned his face and stuck in his beard.

"Thanks very much," he said with a mocking smile. If his hands were free, he would have gone for an elaborate bow or perhaps a rather rude gesture, but, seeing as his hands were bound tight enough that he was starting to lose feeling in his fingertips, the smile would simply have to do.

Stupid fyking orcs.

What good was having the Vitalion Empire's soldiers everywhere, mucking up the perfectly respectable Outlands with their laws and uniformity movements, if they couldn't at least stamp out the foul trogs? Fyke, even Thane should've been able to accomplish that much, and he was as Vitalion as they came.

To be fair, though, the Vitalions did have a few redeeming qualities. Dagen had yet to find one that wasn't open to the right sort of bribe. The thought made him smile, but the motion sent pain up his bruised cheek and the smile slid into a grimace. He licked his lips, tasted the filth the orc had spit on him, and almost vomited right then and there.

Fyking trogs.

The ugly orc that had spit on him sauntered over, muttering something guttural under its breath. Dagen forced a smile onto his face, meeting the creature's soulless black eyes. Something shimmered there, a deep, fathomless distaste for all, but even more specifically for Dagen in this moment. The creature dropped a blackened hand onto the hilt of a sword at his waist and stroked it in small, familiar circles. Dagen twitched his nose, and tested his bonds again, feeling the rope dig into his skin. Pain lanced through his arms. For half a moment, Dagen wished Thane had been there right then—the poor fool made an excellent meat shield, if nothing else, and would likely have provided at least a half-decent distraction—then a hissing sound erupted from the direction of the fire.

Flames burst outward in a ring that engulfed the stone barrier and sent smoke billowing into the blackened night sky. All seven orcs seated around the fire and the ugly brute standing next to him leapt back, most drawing weapons as the flames seemed to undulate and twist back within themselves, rising with the smoke. At first, Dagen thought he was imagining the smoke twisting into the form of a serpent as it rose, but then realization hit him at about the same time as it hit the orcs.

A massive, hooded serpent rose out of the flames. It reared back, neck forming a perfect "s" shape, and hissed a warning down at the orcs around it. The snake's body slid down into the flames, merging with the fire that still burned within the ring. Dagen didn't wait to see if it was real or illusory. The orcs were distracted, some already running for cover or else taking swings at the beast with whatever weapons they had at hand. Dagen, ever the opportunist life had made him, turned his attention to his bonds.

The orcs paying him no mind, Dagen threw his whole weight against the ropes holding his left arm in place. He threw his hip into a quick, snapping jerk, hoping it would either pull his arm free or else topple the framework to which he'd been tied. He succeeded in nearly ripping his arm from its socket.

Biting his lower lip against the pain, he swung his head around and studied the ropes around his other arm. This was his only chance. Whatever that snake-creature was, if he didn't do it now, there was no way the overly superstitious orcs would leave him alive when they fled from this place to escape the demon. It was a wonder they'd kept him alive this long. He gritted his teeth and jerked on his arm.

Gods take it all!

Dagen bit back a groan. What the hell was he going to do now? A hand closed around his shoulder.

Dagen jerked away, heart pounding in his chest. He whipped his head around, ready to twist away from the orc he knew would be there, or else jerk his head back to slam into his assailant. Marek stood behind him, face intent, hands extended out over Dagen's shoulder. Relief poured through him like a bucket of icy water tossed over his head.

"Ah," he breathed, lungs fluttering and making him gasp for a few breaths before they regulated themselves. "Thank fyke."

He looked up at her, noticing her face in profile. Her pale white skin glowed with the firelight, brow wrinkled in concentration, lips pursed. A small shadow played beneath her cheekbone, accenting the smooth curve of her jaw and the sharp angularity of her brows, so unlike his own. In that moment, she was the most stunningly gorgeous creature he'd ever seen.

"Quiet," she said, not looking at him, "I'm concentrating."

Moment gone.

Dagen looked to where her eyes were fixed, realizing only then that she was the one who had created the serpent in the fire. That meant it was most likely just an illusion, but still, he felt his mouth go dry. He didn't like magic users, especially not powerful ones, unless, of course, he was stealing from one of them. They made his skin crawl. When had Marek grown so powerful?

Several orcs jabbed swords at the creature to little avail. The snake, for its part, hissed and struck out at them in return, though its attack—while effective in making the orcs leap away in obvious fear—clearly did just as little real damage. Still, it gave Marek enough time to pull out a dagger and slice through the ropes holding one of Dagen's arms in place.

"Thank you very much," Dagen said, and took the dagger from her to free his other hand.

The ropes parted easily enough, and Dagen was relieved to feel a tingling sensation of pumping blood returning to his hand. He glanced at Marek out of the corner of his eye—she was once again forced to focus all her attention on the illusion of the snake keeping the orcs at bay—then he darted in the direction of the fire.

"Don't mind me," he said, scooping up his pack and weaponry, minus his favorite dagger *(fyking orcs)* and scampering back toward Marek and the safety of darkness outside the firelight. "Just keep focusing."

As soon as he reached her, Marek spun on her heel, a neat trick considering that odd little brace she wore, and started running with him away from the camp. Only a few seconds later, a massive explosion of sound buffeted their backs. Something had happened to the illusion Marek had conjured. Dagen had no interest in stopping to take a look, though. Together, he and Marek raced into the night.

CHAPTER 21

Marek slowed, panting, as her foot screamed in pain. She hobbled down the steep slope of the hill, pushing through branches and brambles, Dagen only a step behind. The sounds of the orcs in their camp were faint but hadn't stopped completely.

"You have impeccable timing, Marek," Dagen said, scrambling nimbly down beside her. She'd stopped at the bottom of the slope and taken a seat with her back against a large boulder. "The ugly one had a look in its eye I didn't like."

Marek sucked down a lungful of cold air and looked back the way they'd come. She glanced at Dagen, then looked away just as quickly. That was probably the closest thing she'd get to an actual "thank you."

Her hands shook from the effort of maintaining the illusion. She tried to steady them, but the trembling simply didn't stop. She'd used up the last of the spell components she'd stolen from Vagamal's apothecary, and she still had no idea what she was going to do apart from rest at that exact moment, but she felt a warm swelling pride burn within her chest. She'd done it. She'd rescued Dagen from a band of orcs. And she'd done it completely on her own. She pulled Dagen's long, curved dagger from where she'd stashed it behind her belt and proffered it—hilt first—to Dagen.

"This is yours," she said with a small smile in her words. The warmth spread inside her at the sudden light in Dagen's eyes when he saw the weapon.

Well, good to know he's glad to see that at least.

"Oh." Dagen took the dagger and turned it over in his hand, eyes examining the blade with the attention Marek had only ever seen before on the face of young lovers staring into each other's eyes. "Oh my Gods. I thought you deserted me."

Marek made a face. Dagen was too focused on crooning over his dagger that he didn't notice. Maybe she should have kept the thing after all.

"Where are the others?" Dagen asked. He laid the dagger across his knee and glanced sidelong over at her.

Marek opened her mouth, unsure how to respond, then closed it and looked down at her fingers, making herself busy by checking what supplies she had left. She'd wondered how long it would take him to get around to that question. Of course he wouldn't have thought she could have made it on her own.

"You left them. Smart." A wry note crept into

Dagen's voice. Marek looked up from her busy hands.

"No," Marek said firmly. "We're going to rescue them."

Silence stretched between them. Marek wondered if Dagen was going to make some sort of snide comment or hurl one of the stinging sarcastic barbs of which he was so fond. She hadn't made it a question, but she wondered if Dagen really would stay and help her. He'd already deserted them once under far less perilous conditions. Part of her, still flush with the success of rescuing him, hoped he'd changed and dared to think he might come along. A small voice in the back of her mind, the same voice which had made her turn away from his kiss all those nights ago, told her she was being a fool.

"The ogre?" Dagen's voice lay almost in the realm of a whisper.

"Uh huh."

"Oh fyke, Marek." A plaintive tone, like that of a parent attempting to dissuade a child from their favorite course of action, turned his voice into almost a whine. "Why?"

"Because they're our friends." Marek busied her hands with checking the ties on her brace and didn't look in Dagen's direction. "And I don't have many friends. And neither do you."

Dagen looked at her, mouth a thin line. He

didn't argue the point, though.

"I spotted the ogre trail not far from here," Marek said. "It's just over that ridge."

Dagen sighed. "You know it's suicide, don't you?"

Marek nodded. She was willing to take that risk. Thane had done as much for her, and so had Teela for that matter.

Dagen blew out a long breath and ran his fingers through his hair. "All right."

Marek smiled.

The trail wasn't hard to find and, before the morning sun had fully crested the horizon, they'd covered enough distance that Marek no longer looked back over her shoulder to see if the orcs were still following them. She was pleasantly surprised that Dagen didn't hesitate even once or look like he was going to try and run for it again. It seemed that once he made a decision, he stuck with it. They didn't talk much, but Marek found she preferred it that way. Too many emotions warred within her each time she looked at Dagen for her to even know where to begin any sort of a conversation. Why did he have to be so complicated? For that matter, why did she have to be as well?

Well before noon, Dagen suddenly held up a hand and closed it into a fist, signaling Marek to stop. She did so immediately, looking around. She'd been too wrapped up in her own thoughts to really notice where they were going. Hills surrounded them on either side, thick, scraggly brush the color of sand growing all about them. In the distance, a dark, gaping blackness swallowed up a section of a hill. Dagen signaled for her to drop, which she did, copying his movement. They inched forward, crawling on hands and knees. Marek licked her lips. The hair on the back of her neck stood on end and she had to fight down a shiver.

"Is this the ogre's cave?" she asked. She knew the answer, but she needed to hear Dagen's confirmation to make it real. If someone had told her, even a fortnight past, that she'd be in a situation to ask that today, she would have called them mad.

Dagen propped himself up on his elbows and looked over at her. Marek was suddenly aware of just how close they were.

"I'd bet my magic wand we're at its doorstep," he said, gesturing toward the cavernous opening with one finger.

He met her eyes and then gestured for them to fall back a ways. That seemed like a wise course of action. They retreated behind a small hill. Marek realized she was clutching her arms about herself and forced her hands down to her sides. They could do this, right? She could do this. Dagen shifted about, making a show of checking his knives.

"You know you're asking the impossible, right?" Dagen asked. The whites of his eyes showed bright as he met her gaze. The green irises shone with an intensity Marek hadn't seen before now.

"Surely not impossible for you." Marek tried to keep her voice disparaging, but didn't know if she succeeded. Questioning Dagen had worked remarkably well the last time she'd needed him to do something difficult.

"I just want to make sure you'll appreciate my success."

Marek forced her face into a frown, but thought the humor in her eyes might betray her. She turned away, but his hand wrapped around her wrist in a powerful grip and pulled her back toward him. She spun a complete circle, and suddenly Dagen's hands were on either side of her face, wrapped around her ears and tangled in her hair. His lips crushed against hers, his breath hot inside her mouth. Marek closed her eyes, too stunned to do anything but melt into the kiss, feeling the urgency, the passion, and the deep, powerful longing in his lips.

Why had she avoided this before? This . . . this was *wonderful.* This was—

He pulled away. He held her face only an inch

or so from his and smiled at her. Marek was too stunned, too caught up in the moment to truly register the beauty in that smile, the warmth tinged with impish delight. But she did register his hands, still on both of her cheeks, holding her as gently as she'd ever been touched before. Her heart raced and blood thundered in her ears like a raging storm.

He spun her around and stepped to the side of her, hands falling to her shoulders as if to steady her. The movement broke the stillness and the shock of it like ice shattering over a frozen pond. Marek blinked and gasped, lips working slowly as if to make sure that what had just happened hadn't simply been something she'd imagined.

"What was that for?" Her voice came out far more breathless than she'd intended. Couldn't she at least hold it together? Apparently not.

Dagen walked away from her and didn't turn around when he replied. "I'm probably falling in love."

That made sense—

Wait, what?

She hurried after him, licking her lips. He didn't slow and Marek only caught up to him when he reached the mouth of the cave. That proximity forced any questions she might have had to be left unasked. For now, at least. Marek had no intention of simply letting the matter drop.

Dagen dropped down into the cave without any hesitation. Marek followed much more carefully. The cavern's mouth was wide—it had to be to allow an ogre in and out—but the ground was strewn with loose boulders the size of small houses intermixed with smaller, looser rocks. Marek picked her way down carefully, the ground sloping at an angle sharp enough that she marveled that her bad foot didn't cause her to slip and fall. Luckily, the brace held and she succeeded in picking her way carefully down the rocks. Dagen, naturally, seemed to almost dance from boulder to boulder, dropping so easily to the ground that Marek felt resentment well up within her before she could stop it.

A fire crackled about a score of paces from where the sloped, rocky entrance gave way to the sandy floor of the cave itself. Marek slid down onto the loose ground and moved up behind Dagen, who had unlimbered his bow and waited for her behind a large boulder.

"Who's out there?" a male voice called. "Is there someone there?"

Marek looked over at Dagen, unsure what to do. If the ogre was somewhere inside the cave and by some miracle hadn't heard the two of them entering, the shouting had just given them away. Dagen's face looked a bit pale, but he stood up and crept farther into the cave.

"Please," the voice called, sounding oddly hollow and muffled, even without the echoes. "Come in here and help me. Who's there?"

Marek swallowed and found her mouth dry. Dagen was right. This was impossible. Any second now the ogre was going to show up, find them, and kill them both where they stood. Seriously, how naïve could she have been to think this might actually work? Her hands gripped the sides of the rock she hid behind so tightly she wondered that it didn't break through her skin. Dagen crept forward, skirting the fire. Marek watched him with an intensity only fear could provide

"I'm trapped. I can't get out." Would that man ever stop talking? The longer he shouted, the greater the chance they'd get caught.

Dagen pulled one of the thick logs from the fire and used it as a torch, holding it high to cast light out as far as he could.

"Is there anyone there? I—I hear you."

Dagen moved toward the back of the cave. Marek narrowed her eyes, squinting to try and focus over the distance. Dagen's torchlight revealed bones scattered across the ground, skulls grinning at nothing, ribs and arm bones broken like sticks across the rocky floor.

"Is someone out there? Who's there?"

Marek chewed on her bottom lip, hoping Dagen

would be all right as she lost sight of him.

Dagen knelt next to a pile of stones which surmounted one massive boulder the size of a small horse.

"Who's there?" the idiot man yelled. "I'm in here. Here. I'm in here."

Dagen moved the torch closer to the ground and saw a small opening beneath the larger boulder. "Psst," he said. "Anybody home?"

A face appeared in the opening. Scraggy-haired and dirty, with the gaunt, haggard look of a man on the brink of starvation, the man shot a skeletal hand out of the opening, fingers curved into hooks as if he intended to claw his way to freedom. By the bloody scabs at his fingertips, Dagen wondered if the man had actually attempted just that at one point. Desperation made a man do strange things.

"Who are you? Just—just get me outta here." The man's voice shook with fear and a desperate need. A foul stench wafted up out of the opening and Dagen had to force himself not to gag. And he thought orcs had smelled bad.

"Shh, calm down, boy," Dagen said, glancing around to make sure the ogre wasn't about. He also took the liberty of reassessing his earlier view of the cavern's floor. Several other large boulders littered the ground near here. Were they prisons like this one? Perhaps Caeryn, Teela, and Thane were in one of them.

The man began to cry, his tears a soft weeping that bespoke an absolute loss of hope. Dagen recognized that sound from when he'd made it himself, many years ago.

"Is there anyone else down there with you? A beautiful yet tiresome priestess of Ana-Sett, perhaps?"

"No. I'm all alone. It's—it's just me."

Of course it is.

"All right. Just sit tight." Dagen picked up the torch and stood up, trying to decide which boulder to check first.

"Wait!" the man screamed. "You have to save me! Please! Please, get me out of here!"

Dagen did his best to shut out the screams. He felt a twinge of guilt well up in the hollow of his chest, but he swallowed it down before it could color his actions. If he stopped now and attempted to save the man, he might never find the others. No, if he played his hand right, he could save them all, but—Gods take it—the man had better shut up before he woke the fyking dead. The screaming didn't stop, it simply faded into the jagged wails of a broken man.

Torchlight revealed another opening a dozen feet deeper into the cave, this one a little larger, resting beneath a stone so large Dagen wondered how even an ogre could move it. He lifted the torch and peered into the darkness. Light glinted off a familiar looking pendant. Dagen felt a grin creep across his face.

"Knock, knock." Dagen wrapped his knuckles against the rocks surrounding the opening. Even in the middle of serious danger, the screams of the first man echoing behind him, he couldn't resist a little fanfare and showmanship.

A face, dirty yet more perfect than any Dagen had ever seen before, appeared in the small opening. The resemblance to Teela was unmistakable.

"Hello, beautiful," Dagen said, doing his best not to make his voice sound too much like a leer. "I'm Dagen. Your insane sister sent me here to rescue you."

"I'm not important," Caeryn said immediately. Her voice held a firm note of authority in it. She pushed a small leather pouch up through the opening. "Take this."

Dagen reached down and took the pouch from her, tugging it open. A small dark stone slid into his open palm as he upended the pouch. The stone seemed to shine with its own inner light, a purplish glow that gave off odd, spore-like sparks, though the stone itself remained cool to the touch.

"Take the stone," Caeryn said. "Bring it to the paladin at Sung Hill. They can protect it."

Just like that?

"Listen, sweetheart. We have gone through a lot of trouble to get you out of here."

The trapped man's screams picked up, echoing off the walls. "Please, please! You have to get me out of here."

Dagen picked up a small stone and chucked it at the other opening. "Shut it!"

"You fool!" Caeryn said, peering up at him through the opening, only her eyes showing in the narrow gap. "Escape with the stone. Nothing else matters."

Dagen snorted. "You remind me a lot of your sister." They were both stubborn fools. It was just one of the many reasons Dagen hated religious folk. Pious was just a polite way of saying pigheaded. He grabbed the torch and took a step back toward where he'd left Marek when a thunderous banging noise shook the ground.

CHAPTER 22

Kynall drew a long dirk from its sheath at his belt and began trimming his nails, watching the wizard pace back and forth along the length of the cave. The dirk looked small in Kynall's large hands, though it was long as a short sword would be in the hands of most men. Firelight played along its length as he worked it deftly over his fingers in precise, controlled, practiced motions. Jaffin was due to return from his scouting trip at any moment now, but Gojun was—as always—an anxious, impatient waiter.

Even back in his younger, hotheaded days with the Redthorns, Kynall's view on all issues had been relatively simple. Either things could be dealt with by bringing his axe to bear against them, or they couldn't. If they could, Kynall could take upon himself the burden of worry for the amount of time it took to rend the problem in twain with his blade. If he couldn't bring his axe to bear on the problem, it quite simply wasn't worth worrying over. Having children had complicated that view on life somewhat, but not terribly so.

"Peace, man," Kynall said, looking up from

his fingers long enough to roll his eyes in Gojun's general direction. "You'll wear a hole in the floor the size of Vitalia!"

Gojun grunted, but didn't slow or show any other signs of stopping. Kynall hadn't really expected him to.

He sighed, finished off his last nail, and sheathed the dirk. He groaned as he got to his feet, a dull ache smoldering along his lower back and down his legs. Age had been a gentle, kind mistress in his youth. She became a bitter, angry lover the older he got and punished his body mercilessly for his allowing time to pass, as if he had any control over it.

He moved over to the fire and pulled a long-handled spoon from a pack near the fire, sniffing the thick perfume from the stew bubbling in a pot over the flames. Kynall wished he had some sage, or perhaps a little more seasoning salt to add to the mix—Jaffin liked his food heavily spiced—but upon tasting it, found it good enough to eat, at least. He fished three wooden bowls from the same pack and filled them with stew. Steam wafted upward from the thick, heavy mess.

"Come on, wizard," Kynall said, laying one of the bowls on a rock to cool and holding another out toward Gojun. "Eat. Food does wonders for an overactive mind."

Gojun glanced sidelong at him, graying hair

splaying across his face and making a short curtain across his visage. The firelight played across his face, the shadows deepening the grooves in his face that marked his age. When had Gojun gotten so old?

"I'll give him until we finish the stew," Gojun said, stepping over and accepting the bowl from Kynall. "Then we go after him."

Kynall retrieved a couple of wooden spoons and tossed one to Gojun, who was holding the bowl close to his nose and sniffing at it. Gojun caught it and immediately began attacking the stew as if it were his last meal. Kynall couldn't help but chuckle. Some things never changed. Any good mercenary learned the value of good food and ate his fill as often as it was available. One never knew when a meal could be the last.

They ate in silence for several long moments until the scrape of a wooden spoon against a wooden bowl signaled that Gojun had reached the bottom of his portion.

"More?" Kynall asked, bending to retrieve the ladle.

"I don't think one more bowl is going to give him the time he needs," Gojun said.

Kynall grunted. He wouldn't have been much of a father if he hadn't tried. Despite not being easily riled, a small sliver of concern for his son had wormed into his gut and was working through his stomach toward his heart.

Gojun met his eyes, then looked down at the bowl in his hands. "I think there's room in my stomach for just one more bowl, though."

Kynall grunted. Grunts could convey so much without excessive effort on his part. It was a wonder mercenaries such as he didn't develop their own language. He hid a small smile and spooned more stew into Gojun's bowl.

"Save some of that stew for me, will you?"

Kynall's head snapped up and Gojun spun around, one hand immediately going for a glass vial at his belt. Jaffin stood in the cave's mouth looking weary and a bit wan, but otherwise unharmed. Kynall felt a wash of relief flood through him that was disproportionate to the amount of worry he thought he'd had. Becoming a parent certainly had changed him.

"You're late," Gojun said, hand lifting from his belt.

Jaffin walked forward without even glancing at the wizard, taking the bowl of stew Kynall had set aside for him and wolfing it down with two fingers without even waiting for a spoon.

"Well?" Gojun asked.

Kynall held up a placating hand and pushed another bowl of stew into Gojun's grip. Jaffin met his father's eye for a moment and Kynall saw fear there, and a darkness that hadn't been present before. Still, he knew his son well enough to wait for him to finish eating before prodding into what had taken place.

Gojun looked from one to the other of them, rolled his eyes, and then began eating his own bowl of stew. At least he had the sense not to press matters. Jaffin could be as stubborn as a young mule when he wanted to be.

At length, Jaffin finished his stew and wiped his fingers on his pants. Kynall offered him another bowl, but he shook his head.

Gojun paused with a spoonful of stew halfway to his lips. "Ready to talk, now?"

Jaffin scowled at the wizard, but nodded. "We've got problems aplenty, I think. Mekru's dead. Kishkumen killed him."

"The Darkspore?" Kynall asked.

Jaffin blew out a long breath. "They don't have it yet, but it's only a matter of time. Mekru lost it. He said something about a priestess and an ogre, though Kishkumen didn't seem to care. He had these archers with him, and a strange, hooded figure that felt like death incarnate. Kishkumen seemed to think it could track the Darkspore. He said they'd have all the shards soon enough."

Gojun swore.

Kynall glanced over at him. "What?"

"A decade or so back," Gojun said, "I heard rumors of creatures attuned to the dark magic of necromancy, creatures tainted and twisted by powers so vile they warp the souls they touch. The beings become almost wraithlike, neither living nor dead."

"They're not rumors," Jaffin whispered, voice distant and icy. "That's what the one I saw looked like."

"Sniffers," Gojun continued. "That's what they're called. Created to find necromancy. They can track the shards as easily as a hound tracks a criminal." Gojun tossed the wooden bowl to the ground. It struck stone and broke in half, the sound loud enough to make the horses whinny. Gojun blew out a long breath and then scowled.

"We'll chase it down and kill it," Kynall said. "That'll slow them at least."

Gojun shook his head. "No. You've done enough. If Szorlock gets his hands on even a single shard, war is inevitable. It'll cover all the lands in death and destruction." He ran a hand through his hair and met Kynall's eyes. "I'll hunt down Kishkumen and his ilk. You two should return home. Warn your people. Rally the defenses. They'll need you there far more than I."

"You'll get no argument from me," Jaffin said, shuddering visibly. "Get me as far from this place as possible. If I never see Deira again, it will be too soon."

Kynall got to his feet, body aching more than it had before. If what Gojun said was true about the war, Jaffin wasn't shuddering nearly enough. The death and destruction it would bring would make their lives as mercenaries seem a simple stroll through a wooded park. Kynall stuck out a meaty hand and Gojun took it, one eyebrow raised.

"There's been bad blood between us, wizard," Kynall said, finally laying down a stone he'd been carrying about on his shoulders for the last twenty years. "But no more. If there's anything me or mine can do for you in the days to come, send word through Orrin Tuck and we'll come."

Gojun nodded, but his face was grim, eyes cold and distant, living in memory. "Go with the Gods, old friend," Gojun said. "Keep your family safe."

Kynall nodded and released Gojun's hand. Some part of him knew he would never see the man again.

CHAPTER 23

Marek swallowed hard.

"It's coming!" The male voice rang out again, containing a fear so intense Marek swore she could feel it in the air.

Thuds rocked the cave walls in a steady rhythm. The ogre appeared out of the darkness at the far end of the cave, firelight making its gray-green skin look almost orange.

Dagen!

The ogre stopped before a large boulder, not even bothering to look around to see where the screams originated. Marek saw Dagen poke his head up from behind a rock and felt relief wash through her. Still, it was a momentary feeling. The ogre bent down and picked up the boulder, tossing it aside as easily as Marek would have a single brick. With a menacing growl, the ogre reached down into the hole and pulled out a struggling, screaming figure. The screams cut off abruptly as the ogre bit off the man's head with a sickening crunch. Without even putting the boulder back in place, it turned and thumped back the way it had come, idly gnawing on what was left of the headless man.

"Dagen, move!" Marek called, leaving her own hiding place. Her legs felt like sodden lumps of clay, but she forced them into action anyway. Dagen shook his head and got up, retrieving his impromptu torch. His face looked pale, but he didn't wait for Marek to catch up to him before moving on toward another of the boulder-prisons. Marek felt a flush of irritation at that, but let it slide. In the face of what they'd just witnessed, it was a trivial frustration at best.

"Did you two want to quit lying around and give me a hand?" Dagen asked.

Marek's heart skipped a beat. She reached Dagen's side just as Thane and Teela looked up at them through the gap in the rocks. Marek felt tears of joy well up in her eyes, but she blinked them away. Thane's face was dark with dirt and fatigue, and Teela's pale skin was still remarkably clean, but her hair—what Marek could see of it at least—was matted and tousled. They both squinted up at them against the light.

"Dagen." Thane's voice was rough, even for a whisper. "By the Gods, I never thought I'd be happy to see you again."

"Yeah, well, I was missing Teela's sunny demeanor."

"Where's Marek?"

"She's here," Dagen said, shifting slightly so

Marek could move forward.

Marek smiled down at them, hoping her joy at finding them alive came across in her expression. "We're going to get you out of here."

Thane and Teela nodded.

At an unspoken command, both she and Dagen started pushing on the boulder that covered the pit in which Thane and Teela were trapped. Grunts from below announced Thane and Teela doing the same from the other side.

"Ready, push!" Dagen grunted.

Marek heaved with all her strength. The boulder didn't even so much as shift half an inch. After a long moment, Marek slumped to the ground. Dagen knelt down beside her. Any minute now, the ogre could be back. A small note of panic began playing in the back of Marek's mind. She looked down at Thane and Teela's anxious faces peering up at her, then turned to Dagen.

"Okay, um . . ." Dagen began.

"Maybe—maybe we could get the ogre to—"

"He doesn't take them out to play with them," Dagen said in an exasperated tone. "He takes them out to eat them."

Right.

Dagen gave her a level look. The expression seemed to say it was her turn to think of something.

Fine.

"I have an idea." Marek leaned down toward the opening. "Teela, remember that spell in the hideout?"

Teela's eyes widened. "The one you were practicing on the kettle?"

Gojun's word of warning sounded in her mind alongside the image of a kettle sticking out of a stone wall.

"Yes," Marek said with a small nod.

"Ana-Sett be merciful," Teela whispered.

What happened to faith?

"Hang on to each other. Tightly."

Marek stood up and took a step back from the opening. She planted her feet and took several long, steadying breaths through her nose.

"Ready?" Marek didn't hear a response, but took that as an affirmative.

She closed her eyes, calming her mind to focus on the spell. She'd memorized the words to the incantation, burning them into her mind's eye so she wouldn't have to speak them aloud. Instead, she began speaking them mentally and moved her hands in a long sweeping arc as if gathering something out of the air.

Marek felt the power build within her almost immediately. It swelled in response to the mental incantation, flowing from the pit of her stomach, up through her chest, and out through the tips of her fingers. Energy crackled there. She didn't have to see it to know it shone a deep, violent blue, snapping with power. Marek heard Thane whisper something to Teela as if from a great distance away.

The power flowed through her. She felt it working, beginning to pull on the pair trapped down in the pit. Her blood sang with it—

The energy died.

Marek felt it slip away and grasped at the fleeting tendrils of power that danced out of her reach.

No!

She gasped and fell forward, catching herself at the last minute. What had gone wrong?

No!

A hunger clawed up from the pit of her stomach, a dark, deep, ravenous need. Marek recognized it from when she'd nearly killed Vagamal. She caught a glimpse of herself in her mind's eye, face a vibrant, glowing green, eyes as black as midnight without a trace of white. An ebony tear dripped down her cheek. Power raged through her, seeking a source, seeking life. Her jaw locked, lips curled up into a snarl, her back straightened, and her arms shot out and burst into white-green flame. A small voice inside her mind cried out in muted agony.

Power poured into Marek. She registered Dagen gagging and gasping for breath at her feet, and realized she was feeding off his life force. She was using him to draw power, but the force of it pushed her onward unchecked.

Marek focused on Thane and Teela down in the pit, picturing them in her mind. She felt them vanish, sensed the magic taking hold, stealing even more life force from Dagen with each second that passed. She reveled in it. Her heart beat within her chest, sounding like the pounding of a drum.

Beat.

Beat.

Beat.

Thane and Teela reappeared in a cloud of cascading blue sparks that vanished in an instant. They both gasped and looked around, though they clung to one another long after the sparks went away.

Marek drew in more power, her body, no, her soul, feasting upon it as if there would never be enough. Images flashed through her mind in rapid succession. Dagen gasped and gagged at her feet, his face turning an ashen, pallid gray. More images. Dagen kissing her, holding her face. A blackened tear dripping down an ash gray face. Death.

No!

She forced it away. The effort was as if she were pushing back against a river that had suddenly decided to flow freely again. The force of the severance hurled her from her feet, sending her through the air as if struck by a giant's hand. She landed in Dagen's lap, her stomach hitting his knees. They both lay there for a long moment, gasping. Marek felt bile well up in the back of her throat, nausea threating to force the contents of her stomach back out again.

What did I do?

More coughs came from behind them. Thane and Teela. Dagen stumbled to his feet, hand against his knee. The salty tang of utter terror clung to the air.

"What was that?" The whites of Dagen's eyes shone bright, pupils contracted within the deep green of his inner iris.

"Sorry," Marek said between coughs. "I'm sorry. It—it was the only way. I didn't mean to . . ."

Dagen waved a hand. "Yeah, well, let's never do it again, okay?"

Marek gave him a minute nod. She didn't really know how she'd done it to begin with, but the feeling it left within her—like her insides were coated in rancid oil that had worked its way down her throat to pool in the pit of her stomach—*that* she never wanted to feel again.

But the power, a small voice whispered in the back of Marek's mind. She pushed it away.

"Did you find Caeryn?" Teela asked.

Dagen gestured to a nearby boulder.

Teela dashed over to it, dropping to her knees beside the opening. "Caeryn!" she called, reaching out a hand to grasp the fingers stretching out from beneath the rock.

Thane surveyed the boulder and then gave it a small, exploratory shove. He gestured for Dagen and Marek to join him.

"Here, together we might be able to move it," Thane said.

Marek moved woodenly, trying to force the nausea out of her stomach and focus her mind on the moment. Dagen, on the other hand, gracefully, eagerly, whipped off his bow and quiver and took a spot next to Thane against the boulder.

"All right, push!"

The two men groaned with the effort, but heaved against the stone. The boulder shifted. Thane let out a muted shout. The opening widened enough for Caeryn to get her head and shoulders through the gap.

"She's almost through!" Teela said, yanking on one of her sister's arms. Marek rushed forward and grasped the other one, pulling her all the way out.

"Sister!" Teela cried, wrapping her arms around her sister's slight frame.

"She's out, she's out!" Dagen grunted.

They dropped the boulder with a roar of effort, letting it thud back into place. The shock of it reverberated through the ground. Marek felt it through the soles of her boots.

A roar echoed down the cavern.

Everyone leaped into action. Thane spun on his heel, armor clinking, and dashed for a nearby pile of bodies.

"I need something sharp!" he shouted.

Dagen grabbed his bow and threw his quiver back over one shoulder. Marek grabbed Teela and Caeryn and began herding them in the direction of the cave's mouth. Dagen stayed where he was, waiting for the three women to pass him, gaze fixed intently on the source of the noise. After a moment, he fell in behind them. Adrenaline and fear burned away the vestiges of Marek's earlier sluggishness.

The ogre thundered into the cave with a cacophonous roar. The ground shook with each weighty impact of his feet. Dust filtered down from the air. Marek tried to force her mind to work, to come up with something she should do, but all she managed to do while running around the fire with Teela and Caeryn was watch Thane rush over to a pile of bodies and wrench free a long spear. Marek skidded to a stop just as the ogre noticed Thane and let out a roar that sounded like the grumbling gurgle of a rockslide. Thane's answering roar as he hurled the spear seemed somehow diminished in its wake.

The spear hissed through the air, flying true, and buried a foot of steel in the ogre's left breast. Marek let out a mental cry of exaltation as the ogre bellowed in pain and clutched at the spear sticking out of its chest. It had been a near-perfect throw. Marek marveled at Thane's skill as a warrior, glad she'd met the man when she did, despite the circumstances of that meeting.

The ogre stumbled back, pulling at the shaft.

"This way!" Caeryn shouted.

The thin priestess hiked up her skirts and darted toward a smaller opening that Marek hoped marked a side passage. They all raced after her as Thane dashed around the staggering ogre, taking up the rear. Marek glanced back over her shoulder as she ran, making sure Thane was all right. He was there, face screwed up in concentration as he ran, armor clinking. Marek started to smile, but it died on her lips as she noticed the ogre pull the spear out of its chest and toss it aside. She didn't even have a chance to call out a warning as the monster picked up a nearby boulder and hurled it in their direction.

The rock struck Thane squarely in the back with a crunch of bending metal and snapping bone. Thane cried out, mouth forming a small O of surprise even as he fell. He hit the ground with a crash and a grunt of purest agony.

"Dagen, shoot him!" Marek cried, rushing back to Thane's side.

Dagen had an arrow to the string of his bow in a second, sending the shaft straight into the ogre's eye in the next breath. The ogre roared and clutched at its eye, once again stumbling back away from them. Marek pulled on Thane's arm, trying to get the large man to his feet. His back was a mangled mess, the armor bent and dented. Marek tried not to focus on it.

Dagen dropped to his knees on Thane's side and grabbed his other arm. "Come on," Dagen said, grunting with the effort of lifting Thane. "Get on up."

Between them, Dagen and Marek got Thane up and supported his weight between them. Thane moaned in pain, but Marek couldn't spare him any attention. It took all her effort to stay upright and supporting him as they staggered toward the side passage where Teela and Caeryn waited.

CHAPTER 24

The side passage sloped downward, the ceiling so close to their heads that even Marek, the shortest by far, felt like it was uncomfortably close. Caeryn led the way with a flaming brand she'd taken from the fire on her way toward the tunnel, though she and the others all kept glancing back over their shoulders at the ogre's angry roars.

Marek and Dagen supported Thane, slipping and sliding down the narrow slope. Thane screamed with each bouncing step. Marek winced each time, both in response to his screams and the pain jolting through her own foot. Even with the brace, the slopes and angles pulled at her muscles and left her in agony. Marek didn't dare look back again as she slipped down the rocks, though she hoped the passage was too small for the ogre to pass through.

"I feel fresh air moving," Marek said through her clenched teeth. "This must be another way out."

Cobwebs brushed her face but she didn't have a free hand to wipe them away. More appeared on the walls, looking like the translucent threads of ancient dying tapestries in the flickering light of Caeryn's torch, though much larger. She felt her skin crawl and she suppressed a shudder at the thought of what could possibly have made such large webs.

"I see light this way!" Caeryn called.

The ogre growled from behind them, the sound echoing off the passage walls and making it seem as if he were right behind them. Marek glanced back over her shoulder again, seeing the ogre's massive arm snake through the opening after them.

"Go, go!" Dagen cried.

Marek hurried down the rest of the slope, momentum—or Dagen's pushing—helping them slide down and onto the ground. Thane groaned and swore under his breath. They reached the bottom of the slope where the ground leveled out. Marek glanced ahead of them, ignoring the sounds of the ogre's hand scratching at the walls and pulling away chunks of stone in an obvious effort to enlarge the opening enough to come after them. Its angry, frustrated roars deafened her in the narrow confines, and Marek felt her fear rising, despite the distance between them. If there wasn't another opening down here, they'd effectively just left themselves entirely at the ogre's mercy. She wasn't sure which would be worse, being eaten by the ogre or starving to death trapped down in the side passage.

A small pillar of pure sunlight illuminated a

small chamber at the end of the passage, littered with cobwebs and shrouded in dust. She and Dagen eased Thane to the ground in the center of the room. Marek tried not to groan with relief, but the sudden release of his weight from her shoulders was almost as exhilarating as her joy had been at momentarily escaping the ogre's clutches. Her foot throbbed. Teela and Caeryn rushed over to Thane and Marek and Dagen shifted out of the way.

Marek looked up at the narrow opening in the ceiling from which the light entered the room. Webs splayed across it, appearing like the tattered shrouds of the dead. Marek felt the hair on the back of her neck rise even as she considered the opening.

"Think you can make it?" she asked Dagen. It looked large enough to let him through, if he could get up to it.

"Probably," Dagen said, voice pensive, "but how am I going to get the rest of you out?"

Marek blew out a long breath. A good question. She, Teela, and Caeryn would all easily fit through the opening, but Thane, even if he hadn't been wounded and barely able to move, would never fit. She looked over at the large warrior, mind racing in an attempt to come up with some sort of a plan. The ogre's bellows rumbled down from the top of the slope and Marek had to force herself not to look in that direction.

One problem at a time.

"Help him!" Teela said, leaning over Thane and fixing her sister with an intent stare.

Caeryn clutched her amulet in one hand and placed her other over Thane's chest. Teela cupped Thane's head in her hands, stroking the side of his face with as tender a touch as any Marek had ever seen. Caeryn closed her eyes and the hand on Thane's chest began to glow with a powerful golden light.

Thane screamed.

Marek looked away, unable to bear the sight of Thane's thrashing form.

"What is that?" Dagen whispered, eyes fixed on the narrow opening above them.

Marek looked up in time to see a long, segmented leg covered in hair poke through the opening. A sound like tiny voices, or the rasp of dozens of arachnoid legs against stone and web, filled the cavern. Marek felt a shiver creep down her spine, filling her with a cold dread.

Spider.

"I've got a bad feeling about all this," Dagen said.

Something moved in the opening. The spiders blocked out the light for half a moment before moving on. The light flickered as more of the many-legged creatures passed in front of the light, casting shadows against the wall. Marek shuddered and felt her throat constrict with sudden dryness.

Thane's screams faded. Marek looked back over at the small group on the ground behind her. The two priestesses scooted back as Thane sat up, his face incredulous and awed. Teela got to her feet and retrieved her staff, rushing over to the opening above Dagen as Marek went to Thane's side. He didn't have time to marvel over the miracle of his healing right now.

Marek helped Thane to his feet and then started back towards the entrance, not looking back to see if anyone followed.

"If you want to eat us," Marek said, voice echoing in the small space as she called out to the ogre defiantly, "you'll have to crawl in after us. We're not coming out."

"I'm not so sure about that," Dagen called back to her.

Marek didn't turn around, but the pale white light from the opening flickered even more rapidly and then vanished almost completely. They were coming in after them.

"Here come the spiders," Dagen hissed.

Marek reached the end of the short passage and pulled to a stop. The ogre's arm still filled the only exit, long fingers grasping at stone. Behind them, Dagen's bow sang as he launched arrows back down the cavern toward the approaching spiders. Thane charged past Marek, drawing his sword with a steely rasp of metal and leather, roaring his defiance as he ran toward the ogre's arm. Marek looked over her shoulder and saw dozens of glowing eyes in the darkness, pouring from the walls, the floor, even the ceiling.

Thane cried out.

Marek spun back in that direction. The ogre had managed to pin Thane against a wall, thick muscles bulging as it shoved him back against the stone repeatedly. Thane's head flopped on his shoulders like a rag doll as he was tossed back, then brought forward again, armor scraping against the stone.

Not again!

Marek drew her dagger, feeling utterly useless. The blade would do almost nothing to the ogre, and she'd have to get entirely too close to the spiders to do any harm. She nearly laughed at the insanity of it. Behind her, Dagen's bowstring hummed, and a moment later a sickening squelching sound announced that the arrow had found home in arachnid flesh. Marek reached into her pockets, searching for anything that could help them, anything at all. Her fingers closed over a small pouch.

She pulled it free and used her teeth to pull it open. Marek recognized the red powder and nearly cried with relief. She'd thought she'd been out of spell components, but . . . Pushing all thought aside, she dumped a small portion of the powder over the dagger and then stashed the pouch back into a pocket. Thane fell to the ground ahead of her, his limp form barely outside the ogre's reach.

"I'm out of arrows!" Dagen yelled, running up behind her, his breathing heavy and belabored.

Marek glanced back at him and saw Teela rush toward the oncoming horde of spiders, an old lantern in one hand, torch in the other. The priestess smashed the lantern onto the ground just in front of the spiders and hurled the torch on top of it. Flames leapt up from the oil, racing into the sky. Marek felt the heat of it from over a dozen feet away.

Marek shut them all out. She closed her eyes and focused on the dagger, muttering an incantation under her breath. She ran her free hand across the length of the short blade and where her fingers passed, blue-green flames leapt to life, smoldering and crackling as if hungering for fuel. Marek's eyes snapped open. In one smooth motion, she turned and hurled the dagger across the tunnel.

It spun through the air, flames swelling into a fireball. The blade struck the ogre's arm and buried itself deep into the flesh. The flames burst upward and out, appearing more like a liquid geyser than flame for half a moment before they began to race up the ogre's arm. A bellowing cry of pain rang out and the arm pulled back out of the cavern. Marek turned back to the others.

"Quickly! Before he recovers!"

Caeryn raced by her immediately and attended to Thane, waking him with a quick jolt of that strange golden light. He seemed disoriented for a moment, but then rolled to his feet and dashed up the slope, Teela only a few steps behind him.

Marek waited for half a moment, noticing Dagen pulling the corpse of one of the spiders along behind him by the arrow embedded in its face.

"Up, come on," he grunted, bent almost double as he dragged the thing along. "You stupid fykin' spider."

Marek only allowed herself a moment to wonder what Dagen was about before she raced back up the steep slope toward the main cavern. She managed to clamber up past Thane and come out into the main passage where the prisoner pits were kept at the same time as Teela and Caeryn. Light streamed in from the entrance to the cave. The ogre was nowhere in sight.

"There's the entrance!" Marek called. "We can make it if we run!"

She felt a flush of victory and pride run through her as she ran toward the entrance, the others close on her heels. They'd done it. *She'd* done it. In the end, it had been her blow which had driven the ogre back and given them this chance to escape. She—

The ogre stumbled out of a side passage, roaring with rage and pain as it slapped at the flames running up and down its arm. It passed only a few feet in front of Marek, cutting off their escape. Marek felt her heart drop into the bottom of her stomach as the ogre beat out the flames before her eyes and knocked the dagger free. It turned on her, fixing her with a gaze that was as full of murder and hatred as any Marek had ever seen.

Thane appeared in the corner of Marek's vision, sword already swinging in vicious swipes. The warrior roared as he charged, his blade a blur as it spun through the air. The ogre batted Thane aside without even turning. Thane flew backward, knocked aside as if he were little more than a pile of straw. He crashed to the ground with a clatter of metal and rock and then lay there, unmoving. The ogre leered, his pig-like eyes narrowing.

Teela shouted and darted between Thane and the ogre before Marek could react. Teela raised her staff before her in both hands, holding it parallel to the ground but above her head as if to fend off a descending blow from an enemy. The ogre sent her flying back as well with a single swipe. Her limp form landed not far from Thane's. The ogre, apparently tiring of the game, backhanded Caeryn for good measure. The priestess crumpled to the ground beside her sister.

Marek felt her mouth grow dry. Her mind screamed at her to move, to run, to find some measure of safety somewhere, but her body simply wouldn't respond. Her eyes darted this way and that, taking in every detail. Marek had heard soldiers passing through the apothecary talk about how, in the midst of battle, their focus narrowed, becoming so dogged and pointed they missed everything else going on around them and were only able to see the one enemy before them. For Marek, the opposite was true. She saw it all, and it left her dazed.

Then she noticed the dagger. Light glinted off the short blade. If she could get to it . . .

Suddenly, Marek's legs and body were able to move again. She leapt forward and dove into a roll as the ogre lunged for her. The ogre's hands passed within inches of her—she felt the push of air against her head as she passed—but she managed to escape it. Completing the roll, Marek came up with the dagger in her hand, the blade still ringing softly from where it had scraped across the ground as she'd snatched it up. She stood, but remained half-crouched, dagger at the ready.

Between the ogre's legs, Marek could see Dagen now, still standing in the entrance to the spider passage. The spider he'd been dragging along with him lay abandoned among the rocks. Dagen spared her a small glance, then drew his long knives and charged. The ogre grunted out what could have been a laugh and knocked Dagen to the ground as easily as it had the others. Dagen's knives spun through the air and landed in the dirt with a clatter.

Marek rushed in while the ogre was still focused on Dagen's fallen form. Fear coursed through her, but instead of slowing her, it gave her focus and strength. She used it to fuel her arm as she dragged the dagger across the ogre's calf and then spun out on the other side of it. She nearly stumbled halfway through the spin, the weight on her bad foot almost proving too much for it to bear, but she managed to keep her feet and place herself between the ogre and her companions. It was just her now, alone against the monstrous beast before her. She was well aware that the only thing standing between her companions and a brutal, painful death was the tiny dagger in her hand.

The ogre roared and reared back from the pain of the dagger's shallow cut across its leg, then swung a ponderous arm at Marek, clearly intending to swat her aside like it had her companions. Marek ducked under the blow and swung her dagger. It bit into flesh, but dug barely deep enough for the ogre to even notice. The ogre pulled his arm back for another blow. Marek scrambled backward, trying to put some distance between her and the ogre's enormous reach. As she did so, her bad foot suddenly twisted beneath her and she fell, landing hard enough to knock the air completely from her lungs. She sucked in a breath and then cried out as her foot erupted in pure, unadulterated agony. The ogre had taken a step forward and dug its heel into Marek's bad foot.

Marek screamed and tried to pull herself free. She heard more than felt her bones crunch and give way, though her vision darkened noticeably. She gritted her teeth, trying to clear her mind. Fear clouded her every thought. All the ogre had to do was step on her with the rest of his foot or simply squash her with a rock while he had her pinned like this. She was trapped, completely and totally, and the ogre knew it. It laughed, a deep, throaty sound that made Marek shiver despite the pain.

The ogre leaned toward her, putting more weight on her foot. Marek bit her bottom lip and turned away, unable to take the sight of her leg being crushed under the ogre's foot any longer. Dagen's spider rested on the ground only a few inches from her face, arrow still sticking from its bulbous form. Poison dripped from its lifeless fangs in long, green tendrils. The fragments of an idea formed in Marek's mind, cutting through the pain.

Her hand darted to her waist and into her pocket, coming out with the pouch of red powder she'd used on the dagger earlier. Powdered basilisk blood. Her hands moved of their own accord, tugging open the pouch and pouring the powder into her hand before tossing the pouch aside. Marek looked up into the ogre's face, seeing the malice and evil there. It leered down at her, showing blackened, stained teeth speckled with fresh dots of red. A bit of pure white bone stuck out from between a pair of teeth. The ogre lifted his foot and reached for her.

Marek twisted away and hurled the powder up into the ogre's face. *"Domah noesthis kaspil!"* she shouted, continuing her twist into a roll.

The powder burst into a raging fireball an inch from the ogre's face. It roared and clawed at its eyes, staggering back. A blast of heat washed over Marek, singeing her face, but she pushed away the pain. It was trivial compared to the agony of her leg, and even that got pushed aside.

She scrambled over to the spider on hands and knees, silently praying to whatever God may be listening that the ogre would remain occupied long enough for her desperate gamble to have a chance at working. She didn't really expect any of them to listen, if they were even real, but she'd take whatever help—divine or otherwise—that she could get.

Holding herself up with one arm, she pulled the

arrow out of the spider's abdomen with a sickening squelch. Dagen's efforts earlier must have loosened it because it came free much more easily than she'd thought it would. She shifted her weight again and dipped the point of the arrow into the globs of poison dribbling from the spider's fangs. The metal tip of the arrow dripped with it when Marek pulled it free.

She heard the ogre moving toward her, felt the beating of her own heart thundering in her ears and pounding against her ribs with enough force that she thought they might burst asunder. Time seemed to slow, then speed back up again past the point of normalcy. The ogre lunged for her, bending down to grasp at her with both hands. Marek twisted onto her back, leaped to her feet, and jabbed upward with the poison-coated arrow in a single fluid motion, aiming for the creature's face. The ogre's eyes widened and a moment later, Marek's arrow pierced its left eyeball, sliding into the soft fleshy *something* until it struck bone.

The ogre jerked back, tearing the arrow from Marek's grip. She swayed to one side, favoring her injured foot, but kept her eyes locked on the ogre as it thrashed back and forth. One hand managed to yank the arrow free, but the other hand opened and closed repeatedly in midair, as if it were attempting to grasp at something that simply wasn't there. The ogre staggered to one side, roars turning to gurgles. It fell backward, arms flailing for a moment, then it landed on the ground with a thud that sent tremors through the ground and dust and loose rocks toppling from the ceiling. The ogre didn't stir.

Marek stared at the ogre's still form for a long moment, not fully registering what had happened. She'd done it. She killed the ogre . . . and on her own at that. Maybe Thane and the others hadn't been too crazy to put their trust in her to begin with.

Right. The others!

Marek limped over to Dagen's still form, putting a hand on the side of his face. He still breathed, and Marek felt a flood of relief so deep she felt tears well up in her eyes. He stirred at her touch, head jerking slightly to one side and then back again. His eyes fluttered open and one corner of his lip tugged up into a pale imitation of a smile.

"Well done, wizard," he whispered.

Marek smiled through her tears and laughed.

CHAPTER 25

Caeryn and Teela managed to heal much of the damage done by the ogre on Marek's leg. Granted, the muscles in her foot still lay twisted in knots and she was no closer to the original healing she so desperately wanted, but the sheer joy of her recent victory only slightly paled at the thought. By the time Caeryn and Teela had revived Thane and healed what injuries their arts could touch, they both appeared quite tired. Teela's face, however, still retained a hint of her smile in the set of her jaw, the light dancing in her eyes, and the easy way in which she moved. Marek hadn't fully grasped how rigidly formal Teela had been until she saw her current state of relaxed happiness.

"Where is the stone?" Caeryn asked, taking a seat on a rock and turning her back on the ogre's corpse. Thane had removed both of the ogre's ears with a few deft slices of his belt knife. Both now rested in a pouch inside Marek's own pack.

Teela looked over at her sister and frowned, an expression that mirrored Marek's own curiosity. "What stone?" Teela gestured around the cave. "There are lots of stones here, sister. To which are you referring?"

Caeryn spun and fixed her eyes on Dagen so quickly it made Marek dizzy just looking at it. Dagen, who was busy poking through the various corners of the cave, presumably looking for valuables or other items of like nature, didn't notice.

"I gave it to the elf." A note of panic soured Caeryn's otherwise melodic voice.

"Half elf," Dagen corrected, turning to face them all.

He dug in a pocket for a moment and then produced a small pouch. He held it up in one hand so everyone could see it. Thane, standing on Teela's other side, grunted. Marek frowned. Though the pouch looked rather small and innocent, Marek swore she could sense something coming from it, a hunger of some kind, a, well, a *darkness.* She shook her head and pushed the thought aside.

"Don't get your clothes twisted in a knot," Dagen continued, tossing the pouch to Caeryn with a quick flick of his wrist. "I wouldn't take your glowing little rock."

Caeryn snatched the pouch out of the air before it could fall and stashed it inside her dirt-stained robes. Marek frowned.

What's all that about?

"There's no treasure," Dagen said, breaking the strange, heavy silence.

"Seriously?" Marek asked. She ran a hand through her matted hair, feeling a small seed of cold disappointment plant itself in the bed of pride still smoldering in her stomach. This whole quest hadn't been about treasure. It had been about saving Caeryn, and they'd accomplished that. Finding a bit of gold along the way wouldn't have been bad though, either.

"I'm not kidding." Dagen walked over to the pile of bones and armor from which Thane had pulled the spear he'd used on the ogre and kicked it, sending bones and useless bits of metal flying through the air. "I have always heard that ogres amass hoards and hoards of treasure."

Dagen bent down and started picking things up as Marek and the others walked over to him. He tossed items over his shoulder as he examined them, cursing beneath his breath. Thane had to grab one of the thrown items out of the air to keep it from hitting him in the face. It was a small wooden carving of an owl, perhaps only a foot tall.

"That belongs to the temple," Teela said, sounding affronted. Marek couldn't tell if the offense came from the simple idea of it being here among the ogre's hoard or from Dagen's lack of respect for an object she considered holy. Thane handed it over to her with a shrug. Teela examined it, then passed it over to Caeryn, who stowed it in a satchel she then slung over one shoulder.

"So, Marek," Thane said, ignoring Dagen's continued barrage of discarded items flying through the air. "You're an ogre slayer now, a real hero. How does it feel? Is it everything you hoped it would be?"

Marek looked over at the warrior and shrugged, unable to articulate her thoughts and emotions. What they'd managed to do and what she'd personally been able to accomplish on this quest was worthy of pride. But she also couldn't help but feel that something was amiss. It was probably just her own insecurities at work again.

"The sun is setting," Caeryn said, pointedly rising and striding toward the cavern's main entrance. "We must hurry. This country is unsafe at night."

"Night?" Dagen said. "This country is unsafe at night? I can hardly imagine anything worse than this country during the day."

Marek suppressed a chuckle and followed her friends toward the mouth of the cave. At the thought she gave a small, wry laugh, a silent thing, almost to herself. She'd never had friends before.

Marek wished a painter or artist of some sort had been present to capture the look on Hammerhead's face when she slapped the ogre's ears down on his wooden counter. Dagen and Thane flanked Marek on either side. The ancient-looking orc scrubbed at the floor a few feet away and a half dozen late-night patrons nursed drinks at a nearby table. Every eye was on the trio at the bar.

"How much for an ogre's ear?" Marek asked, giving the dwarf as wide a smile as she could muster. He had thought she couldn't do this task. He'd turned both her and Teela away. What would he say now?

The dwarf pursed his lips, bushy beard and mustache quivering as he appeared to mull over the question. Marek watched him intently, but he didn't betray any signs on his face of what was going on inside his head. A deathly silence hung over the common room, not a sound breaking the stillness.

"An ogre's ear, ya say?" Hammerhead said. "I'd say that's worth a free drink and a smidgen of respect." He passed a large clay tankard of ale across the bar toward her. Dagen and Thane both groaned, though Thane's at least sounded like he was trying to hold it back.

"Done!" Marek said.

Hammerhead flashed a brief smile and nodded at her. Marek picked up the tankard, ignoring Dagen's mutterings about nearly dying for absolutely nothing at all, and took a deep, long drink. Never before had anything tasted so sweet.

—·—

Teela wrung her hands and studied her sister carefully, attempting to memorize every last detail of her features. The pair stood just outside Hammerhead's Inn, Teela having come to bid Caeryn farewell. Laughter billowed out from the inn's open door behind them.

"I won't stop until I reach the monastery," Caeryn said. "The paladin will send the team their silver."

Teela nodded, biting back her emotions and the fear that welled up within her. Whatever it was Caeryn carried—and her sister had insisted she knew not what it was called—had already caused so much death and pain. Orcs had raided the temple for it. Temple elders, patrons, and innocents alike had all been brutally murdered over that little stone.

"I'm afraid for you," Teela said. "Why must you travel alone?"

Caeryn shook her head. "My path is sure. I have no fear and the Goddess says you are to stay here for the time being. I must take the stone to the Paladin. Farewell, my sister."

Teela swallowed hard, but welcomed Caeryn's hug, pulling her in tightly for a brief, but powerful moment. The last time they'd been apart, Teela hadn't known if she'd ever see Caeryn again. At least this time, they'd been able to say goodbye first.

"Now go," Caeryn said, her face devoid of even the smallest measure of sadness. "Be with your friends."

Caeryn pulled her hood up over her head and smiled at Teela before turning away without another word and vanishing through the door into the night. Teela turned back to the common room and searched through the crowd, finally finding her friends at a table close to the bar. She heard a piece of a story Thane seemed to be telling Marek and Dagen, his rough, manly hands making wild gestures in the air before him. Marek and Dagen both chuckled at whatever he'd said. Teela smiled and decided she was glad the Goddess had decided she should stay here. There was no place else she wanted to be but beside her friends.

EPILOGUE

Caeryn breathed out a long, low breath and watched it puff into a thick white mist before her. Lamplight streamed outward from the sides of Hammerhead's Inn and the braziers on either side of the door offered some measure of warmth. Still, she couldn't help but suppress a shiver both from the cold and the level of debauchery present within the inn's common room even at this late hour. She worried over Teela's remaining here, especially with the way that brute, Thane, looked at her, but the Goddess's will was clear. Caeryn blew out another long, low breath, and then started forward, step sure and firm upon the frozen ground.

Only a few steps from the inn, the light from the braziers gave way to darkness. Caeryn blinked a few times to allow her eyes to adjust to the gloom, but did not slow her pace. The stone she carried was too precious for any further delays. Even wrapped as it was within the leather pouch and then again in cloth trappings, she felt its malevolence, the burning hunger within it just longing to burst free. Had the Goddess not willed it, Caeryn would never have gone near the thing. As it were, she wanted this over as quickly as possible.

Something moved in the darkness.

For half a moment, Caeryn thought it merely a trick of the light, but then she turned her head and a figure resolved in her vision, a figure with glowing golden eyes. Something inside her screamed a warning, but before she could even move, the figure leaped forward, arm raised. She caught a glimpse of darkness around the man's eyes, a bald head, and a slightly too-large nose, before pain lanced through her body. Memories flashed through her mind even as pain made her muscles go limp and she collapsed to the ground. Blue-white light poured from her, clouding her vision.

Teela.

Caeryn focused on the image of her sister in her mind's eye, even as she felt herself dying. She couldn't move, couldn't think, couldn't *feel.*

The Goddess. Where is the Goddess?

Caeryn's vision darkened, slipping toward absolute blackness.

Teela.

Inside the inn, Teela felt a stab of pain lance through her chest, as sharp as anything she'd ever felt. She clutched a hand to her chest, missing the end of Thane's rather brazen joke. The pain had been a fleeting, sudden thing, gone in an instant, but half a breath later, dread spread through her and replaced the void with a fear far more profound. An image of Caeryn sprawled on the frozen ground danced through her mind. In the far distance, perhaps even in her mind alone, she heard a distant owl's hooting.

"Something is not right," she said, leaping to her feet with enough force to knock the table a few inches away. The wooden legs scraped across the floor.

Teela ran toward the door. Her feet caught on the edges of her white robes, so she gathered them up in one hand and pulled them high, not caring that it showed an improper amount of leg. The cold air bit at her as she burst into the night, but ice formed in her heart as her eyes fell on Caeryn's still form only a dozen paces away.

Thoughts, emotions, images, and pain all flitted through Teela's mind. The look on Caeryn's face when Teela had fled their father's estate to join the order, the joy at having her little sister with her, was most prominent among the memories. Her sister lay still and unmoving, face as white as the snow around them, lips a deep blue. Teela stretched out a trembling hand, lips moving, though no sound came out. Her mind refused to work, to think, to do anything but look down at her sister's prone form.

"Oh dear Goddess," Teela prayed, finding some

measure of thought in the jumble of her mind. "Save her. Save your daughter!"

Marek and the others moved in around her. Teela couldn't remember them arriving.

" . . . The stone . . . "

It took Teela a long moment to realize Caeryn was speaking. Hope flared up within her chest like the roaring flames of a burning building.

"Caeryn?" Teela grasped her sister's shoulder and rolled Caeryn to face her. Her eyes stared blankly up, not seeing anything.

" . . . He took the stone . . . paladin . . . Sung Hill . . . he took the stone . . . "

The words trailed off. Teela knew they'd never return. She'd felt the moment Caeryn's soul had gone to be with the Goddess.

"No!"

Hot tears spilled down Teela's cheeks. An arm fell across her shoulders.

"We'll find whoever did this and make them pay," Thane promised. Death danced in his voice.

Teela looked up and met his cool, dark eyes, not letting go of her sister's still form. Anger burned through the despair, a rage so fierce it steadied her trembling hands and stilled the torrent of tears.

Her voice mirrored the dancing promise of Thane's earlier words. "That is just the beginning."

ACKNOWLEDGEMENTS

Outside of those mentioned previously, I would be remiss not to mention and thank a few other individuals who were all instrumental in making sure this book came to fruition. Jason Faller and Kynan Griffin over at Arrowstorm were amazing to work with and are the original minds behind this work in any and all formats. After speaking with both, I was able to return some of the original intentions of the first drafts of the screenplay to this manuscript.

My publishing house should also be thanked for their part in making the initial overtures. On the writing side, I must thank Melissa Meibos (aka Lysandra James) for her invaluable insight and beta reading countless drafts despite a lack of time on her part. Alyson Peterson provided incalculable assistance and motivation. Nathan Hoffman and Jeremy Cole also were kind enough to read various drafts of the manuscript and provide feedback.

My writing group—Luke Peterson, Beth Fewkes, Amy Sandbak, Beau Peterson, and Jessica Allen Winn—was also quite instrumental in reviewing and providing feedback on the prologue. Time was simply insufficient to get their input on any other section of the novel.

In addition, I'd like to thank the many Kickstarter backers who also helped see the printing of this book through, including Alexis Arenas Alicea, Brian "Nitehood" Johnson, Brian & Glenda Cartwright, Camm, Cara Crane, Charlie Berglund, Chris Ng, Christian Meyer, Christian R. Meyer, Chuck "Realmwright" Workman, Clato Pictures Filmstudio, Craig Johnson, D. W. Vogel, D. J. Cole, Daniel Satchwell, Dawn Diana Hathcock, Derek Morgan, Diego & Ana Isabel Feliu, Franklin E. Powers, Jr., Frostholm Søe-Larsen, Gail L. Rancourt, Gary Fewkes, Gary Phillips, Gerald P. McDaniel, Gerard Wilcox, Giancarlo

Tambone, Heather Bond, Ian Hopkins, Jack Hepburn Raine, Jacqui Dennett, James D. & Mary Nielsen, James Rowland, Janice O'Connor, Jennifer L. Pierce, Jim Longley, John R. Osborne, John Truong, John Unverferth, Jon Erik Johnson, Jon Newlands, Jonathan Mitchell, Juliana Anjos, Justin A. Clutter, Karamu Phoenix, Kev "CpT GoThMcLaD" Foster, Kevin & Valerie Whitcomb, Kim Haas, Kim Korshavn Kjeldsen, Lady Lyndsay Omond, Lark Cunningham, Lars Juul, Louis Meyer, Louise Lowenspets, Lutz Pape, LynnMarie Panzarino, M. Scott Reynolds, Melissa Showers, Michael Darling, Michael Ghek Still Lives Morrow, Monika Pollwein, Paul Schleicher, Ray Pond, Revek, Richard Chang, Richard J. Ohnemus, Ron & Elizabeth Howard, Simon Etwell, The Bryson Family, The Das Family, Tim Flemmer, Tony Arquette, Wendy Woodwell, William Liggett, and William M. Weist.

To all else who I may have forgotten, I thank you as well. Until we meet again on the pages of another book, read on!

ABOUT THE AUTHOR

Kevin L. Nielsen's journey into writing began in the 6th grade when an oft-frustrated librarian told him there simply wasn't enough money in the budget to buy any more books. She politely suggested he write his own since there were no more unread books left in the entire library. His teacher at the time also challenged him to read the Iliad by the end of the year (which he did). Kevin has been writing ever since (and invading libraries and bookstores everywhere).

Kevin currently resides in Utah with his amazing wife and two wonderful children. He's still writing and continuing a lifelong quest to become a dragon rider. He also has a thing for purple shirts.

Connect with Kevin:
Blog: http://kevinlnielsen.com/
Twitter: www.twitter.com/kevinlnielsen

Made in the USA
San Bernardino, CA
16 March 2017